CRITICS PRAISE JANEEN O'KERRY!

MAIDEN OF THE WINDS

"A delightful romantic fantasy.... Fans of the series will enjoy the latest entry."

—Harriet Klausner

KEEPER OF THE LIGHT

"O'Kerry's world and characters are likeable. If you are a fan of [this author] you will enjoy *Keeper of the Light*."

—*Romantic Times*

"This enjoyable paranormal historical romance acts like a roller coaster.... Fans of Janeen O'Kerry or the sub-genre will rate highly *Keeper of the Light*."

—Harriet Klausner

SPIRIT OF THE MIST

"Janeen O'Kerry breathes the misty atmosphere of ancient Celtic Ireland into a tale that mixes warriors, magic, legend, and a love that will not be denied into a romance that satisfies."

—*Romantic Times*

"An exciting magical historical romance that makes Druid Ireland seem vividly alive."

—*Midwest Book Review*

THE DAUGHTER'S CHALLENGE

"Here is what I will do," Niamh said, as though he had not spoken. "I will tell you that there are three things that every woman wants from the man in her life. Perhaps you could take it as yet another contest—another challenge—to see if, by the end of the fourteen nights of the Fair, you can learn what those three things are."

"I do accept your offer. I never turn down a challenge!" Then the warrior paused, looking closely at her with a bright gleam in his eye. "Yet what is a contest without a prize? What have I earned, if I succeed at this challenge of yours?"

Niamh knew what he wanted. He wanted *her*.

Daughter of Gold

Janeen O'Kerry

LOVE SPELL NEW YORK CITY

For every lady who knows
that a true man is worth the wait.

LOVE SPELL®

October 2004

Published by

Dorchester Publishing Co., Inc.
200 Madison Avenue
New York, NY 10016

ISBN 0-505-52584-4

The name "Love Spell" and its logo are trademarks of Dorchester Publishing Co., Inc.

Printed in the United States of America.

Visit us on the web at www.dorchesterpub.com.

PRONUNCIATION GUIDE

Aine—AH-neh
Ardal—AR-dahl
Beltaine—BEL-tin
Cahir Cullen—KYE-er KULL-en
coibche—KAH-ib-keh
Criostal—CRYST-al
Eire—AIR-eh
Fianna—FEE-ah-nah
Geal—gyall
Leary—LEER-ee
Luath—LOOH-ah
Lugh—LOOH
Lughnasa—LOOH-nah-sah
Niamh—NEEV or NEE-ahv
puca—POOH-kah
Rua—ROOH-ah
Samhain—SOW-when
Tailte—TEL-sheh

Chapter One

"Stop him! You cannot gallop a horse on the rocks of the riverbank! Stop him, Ardal! Turn him away from there!"

Bryan shouted at his cousin in the deepening late-summer twilight, even as his own stallion raced down the soft dirt road. But he could only watch as Ardal's horse, forced over the rocks and toward the river by his laughing, drunken rider, stumbled and tripped and then went end-over-end into the dark water. Ardal vaulted away and managed to land on his feet in the grass, taking only a few running, staggering steps to keep his balance.

Bryan pulled his horse to a stop and quickly swung down, just as his brother Leary finally caught up to them on his own exhausted animal. "Ardal!" Bryan shouted again, throwing the reins to Leary. He raced over to his cousin just as the tall man dropped to the ground, shaking all over.

"Are you all right? Are you hurt?" Bryan grabbed his arm to look into his face—and was shocked to see that Ardal was laughing.

"I won! You thought I'd never beat you and Luath on

this road, but I won! Anfa has beaten Luath, and he will beat him again at the last race of the Lughnasa Fair!"

Bryan turned away in disgust from his handsome blond cousin's wine-laden breath. "You won only because you cheated. Because you forced your horse to take a treacherous path over rocks instead of the longer way on the road. Is this how a man of the Fianna and the leader of the king's own patrol treats his animal? Do you care nothing for what might have happened to him?"

Ardal shrugged. "He won. That is all that matters."

Bryan glared down at his cousin, and then pushed him away. "Anfa," he whispered, and then turned and ran for the river.

There was a great splashing as the young bay stallion tried his best to lunge out of the rushing water and up onto the bank. His eyes glittered with fright and pain as he struggled to find a purchase on the steep, slippery rock bank, but it crumbled beneath his hooves every time he tried to climb out.

Speaking softly to the frightened animal, Bryan waded knee-deep into the cold river and managed to grab hold of the trailing bridle reins where they floated in the water. Slowly, with the horse moving one awkward, lunging step at a time, he got Anfa positioned at a lower section of the bank so that the horse could clamber out and stand soaked and trembling on the grass.

"Is he all right?"

Bryan glanced at Leary, who had dismounted and now held both his own horse and Luath, and led Anfa forward a few cautious steps. The stallion was very unwilling to move and would hardly bear any weight at all on his left front leg, throwing his head up each time it touched the ground in an effort to keep his bulk off of it.

"He won't be racing at the Fair. If he simply rests for

the entire fortnight, he may be able to walk well enough by the time of the final race, but he will be in no condition to run it."

Ardal swaggered over to them. Bryan thought it was to see to the horse, but his cousin only untied the wineskin from the wooden frame of the saddle and raised it to his mouth.

Bryan knocked it angrily away. "Don't you think you've had enough of that?" he asked, glaring at his cousin. "I'm sure your horse thinks you have. Do you see what you've done to him?"

Ardal just laughed, and took another drink from the skin. "It was only an accident. How was I to know there was a hole there along the riverbank? The high grass obscured it."

"You should never have forced Anfa to gallop in such a treacherous spot. If you'd not begun drinking so early, you would have had sense enough to remember such things."

"Well, I was only trying to get ready for the Lughnasa Fair."

"How? By laming another young steed?"

"By doing two of the things that I plan to do as often as possible at the fair—drinking good bilberry wine and racing my horse!"

"You will be doing no racing with Anfa," Bryan growled, his voice low with barely concealed disgust. "Look at him. The tendon grows more swollen with every step."

"Ha! He'll recover. It's not the first time a horse of mine has gone lame. They get over it."

Bryan gently ran his hand along the animal's shoulder, and then crouched down to look closely at his left front leg. "Do you see this? Instead of running tight and firm up to the knee, the tendon sags. The lower leg fills with heat and pain. You've ruined him for good this time."

Leary looked up at Bryan, his eyes a little unfocused like Ardal's, and grinned. "Once we get back to the Fianna's camp, I'll have him stand in a stream for a time. Cold water will cure an injured leg."

"And if it doesn't?"

Ardal shrugged. "If it doesn't, then I'll get another horse at the Fair. That's what it's for, isn't it? The best animals in Eire will be there, all available for trade. I've got nothing to worry about."

"So if you ruin one, you simply barter for another, the way you might trade an old ripped tunic for a new one?" Bryan shook his head. "A shame it is that you care so little for the horse that carries you and all but gives his life for you. I wonder what it would take to teach you a lesson?"

Ardal's only answer was to take another long drink of wine. "I don't need a lesson—and certainly not from you, my young cousin. All I require of you is your horse."

Bryan stood up and dropped Anfa's reins. "You will never take Luath. Do you think I would let you ride off on him and cripple him, too, the way you crippled first Mil and now Anfa?"

Ardal tossed aside his wineskin. "You will give me whatever I require. I am your better in every way—a better fighter, a better rider, a better man to be the leader of the Fianna, and a better choice to be the next king of Cahir Cullen once King Nessan departs for the Otherworld. I have proven many times over that I am all of those things, and no one is going to say otherwise—certainly not my overprotective young cousin who cares more for horses than he does for men." Ardal grinned. "Or for women."

Instantly Bryan flew at his tall blond cousin and knocked him hard to the grass. "You will never be any of those things," he snarled, struggling to force Ardal's shoulders to the earth. "You've proven only that you are arrogant to your men and cruel to your mounts. You'll never have Luath!"

"Then I will take Anfa," Ardal said, grappling with Bryan. "I will ride him until he is finished. That is his purpose—to serve me to the last of his strength—and you are as weak and teary-eyed as any twelve-year-old girl over a newborn pup if you believe otherwise."

Bryan swung his fist at Ardal's taunting face, but his cousin managed to roll out of the way at the last instant. The two of them wrestled and struggled on the wet grass until Bryan felt a frantic tugging on his shoulder.

"Bryan. Bryan! Get up! He can have my horse! I'll give him mine. He doesn't really want Anfa. Just get off of him, please, before you kill each other."

Bryan glared down at Ardal, then got up in disgust when his cousin only laughed at him again. He said to his brother, "Give him your horse, then, Leary. Let him ride back alone to the Fianna's camp and continue his bragging to the rest of the king's men. You and I will stay here and take care of what he has ruined."

"Why, thank you, Leary," Ardal said, getting to his feet and picking up his wineskin again. Taking one last long drink from it, he tossed the half-empty skin to Leary. "Keep it, boy. You're not a half-bad drinking companion, though you've still got a long way to go." He went straight to Leary's horse, swung himself up into the saddle with only a little difficulty, yanked the animal's head around and kicked him into a gallop down the road. He headed back the way they had come, back toward the camp of the Fianna, and never so much as glanced over his shoulder.

"I should never have taken him up on his challenge to race," Bryan said through clenched teeth.

Leary grinned. "But everyone knows you never turn down a challenge." He took another drink of wine and added, "Especially from Ardal."

Bryan grabbed the wineskin away from his brother and threw it hard into the river. "Do you want to be just like him? Arrogant, drunk, and caring for nothing and nobody but yourself? I like my wine as much as any man does, but not when I am supposed to be riding with King Nessan's Fianna, and not when I am racing my horses!"

Leary shrugged. "Ardal is the leader of the Fianna. Men are drawn to him the moment he begins to speak—I never heard anyone so good with words. And I never saw anyone so confident and sure of himself. They find it easy to follow him." He looked intently at his older brother. "If I'm to be anything more than a serving-man among them, I've got to get on his good side."

"Stay on your own good side, Leary," Bryan advised, walking to Anfa and taking hold of his trailing reins. "That will serve you far better."

Slowly, painfully, he began leading Anfa back toward the road. Leary followed with Luath. Night was fast approaching and twilight should have been steadily descending, but as the two men approached the road, they quickly raised their hands and shielded their eyes from the sudden bright light of the sun. It had slipped below the heavy clouds but now suddenly appeared bright and glaring just above the horizon. And before the men even had time to pull their large rectangular cloaks up over their heads, the clouds above them let go the rain they held and began a summer downpour.

"Strange, this," Bryan muttered, wiping the big splashing drops from his face. "Rain pours down on us, but still the sun shines in our eyes. Have you ever seen such a thing?"

"In Eire? This place is naught but clouds and rain, rain and clouds. Now and then the sun pokes through." Leary laughed. "I think you are the only one who would be surprised by such a sight."

"Never mind, then. Come here and look at Anfa." Bryan's anger grew at the sight of the horse's pain and trembling after moving only the short distance from the river to the road. "Do you see this? He'll never make it back to camp. You go back there yourself and get what we need to stay here for tonight."

"All right, then." Leary reached for Luath's reins, but Bryan grabbed them away from him. "Do you think I would let you take Luath? You are nearly as drunk as your hero Ardal, and he took your horse—remember? That leaves nothing but your own two feet to get you back to the Fianna's camp and bring back what we need to stay here. I'll not have Anfa forced to hobble all the way back there tonight, newly injured as he is. Maybe you'll have a clear head by the time you return."

Leary looked as though he were about to speak, but then thought better of it. "I'll hurry," he said, and started toward the road, leaving his brother and the two horses standing in the grass in the rain.

It was a long way, and as Leary walked the sun slid below the horizon and the rain began to ease, leaving the world in soft grey shadow. He traveled down the road the way they had come, back toward the place where the rest of the Fianna had stopped to make their camp.

When Ardal had challenged Bryan to a race, Leary

had followed them, hoping to prove to Ardal that he, too, could keep up with the two top men of the king's patrol—but it had certainly not ended in the way he would have liked. The good stallion Anfa was now so lame he could not make his way back to camp, Bryan was furious, and Ardal had taken Leary's mount for himself— leaving Leary with a long walk to the camp and plenty of time to think about the heavy burden of food and equipment he would have to carry back.

He knew none of the other men would help him, even if they were around. They would only laugh at him for trying to keep up with Bryan and Ardal and tell him that such extra work was nothing more than he deserved. Leary sighed heavily, wishing he still had Ardal's wineskin, and kept walking.

Not long after he rounded the first corner in the road, a movement at the edge of the forest caught his eye. Leary blinked, not sure of what he was seeing, but when he looked again, it was still there. A shaggy black pony, invisible a moment before in the dark shadows beneath the trees, swished its tail and swung its heavy head in his direction.

Leary glanced all around him, peering into the deepening shadows, but did not see any other horses around. He caught his balance as the wine swam through his head once again, and then he grinned.

"Are you all alone, then?" he called to the pony. "No herd, no rider? How did you come to be out here like this? Are you going to the Lughnasa Fair too, just like me?"

As though in answer, the pony turned toward Leary and began plodding toward him and the road. Its steps were slow and it carried its head very low, as though it were greatly aged or terribly weary. Or perhaps both. And

8

Leary noticed that the creature wore an old flax-rope halter twisted around its big head, with the frayed ends of the rope dragging alongside in the grass.

"Well, now. You're someone's stray, aren't you?" Leary said with a laugh, as the old black pony continued to approach. "And just what I need right now. Old as you are, you look strong enough to me, and all I need is for you to make it as far as the camp."

The pony stopped just a few steps away, its head down and its sleepy eyes nearly closed. Leary reached out and caught the trailing rope. The creature never moved. "I'll bet we can find your owner at the Fair," Leary said. "And I'm sure he would have no objection if I rode the rest of the way there, after I so kindly rescued you!"

Gathering up the rope, Leary placed both hands on the animal's neck and went to swing up—and found himself lying flat on his back in the soft thick grass beside the road.

Leary looked up at the dark night sky, blinking. "Now then, stray fellow!" he said, struggling to find his way back to an upright position. "This is no way to treat one who only hopes to get you back to your owner. Where are you? How did you move so fast? You could not have got far, not an old piece of wolf-bait like—"

Leary staggered to his feet, searching all around for the wayward pony, and nearly jumped out of his skin at finding the creature standing exactly where he'd left it.

The pony gave a heavy sigh.

Leary burst out laughing, and with only a little difficulty reached down and caught up the rope once again. "One more try, and then it's off to the Lughnasa Fair we go!" This time he used all his strength, and this time he found himself sitting securely on the old pony's broad black back.

9

"There's a good fellow," he said with a grin. "Won't my brother be surprised to see me riding, when last he saw me I was walking! Come on then, old Wolf-Bait, let's be on our way."

He gave a good hard tug on the rope to get the beast's attention, and kicked it hard in the sides to get it going. The pony grunted at the kick but did not move. Leary yanked hard on the rope once again.

This time, the creature raised its big head and looked back over its shoulder at him—and Leary saw that its eyes were a bright glaring red-yellow, bright as flame. Its ears were pinned flat and its lip was curled and its teeth bared in a snarl of pure malevolence.

"What is this?" Leary gasped. He tried to swing down, but found that he could not. His hands were locked securely in the roots of the long thick mane and his legs were clamped firmly to the creature's sides. He could not move at all—he could do nothing but cry out as the pony tore away into the darkness, and listen to the sound of pounding hoofbeats and rasping, evil laughter as the monstrous creature bore him away.

Back down the road, the horses Bryan held threw their heads up and looked into the darkness in the direction Leary had gone. And then Bryan heard the sound of fast galloping hoofbeats and his brother's terrified shouting.

"Stop! Stop! Let me go—let me off! *Stop!*"

And down the road, all but invisible in the cloud-covered night, charged a powerful black pony with Leary clinging to its back. Yet Bryan could see in an instant that this was no natural animal. It wore an old rope halter with a trailing lead, but its eyes blazed a furious orange. By their light Bryan could see the creature's bared teeth and flattened ears.

10

"Leary! What are you doing? Get off of that beast. Get away from it!"

"I *can't!*"

And to Bryan's horror, the malevolent black pony slid to a stop right in front of him and the two horses he held.

Bryan held tight to the reins, certain the horses would be terrified of such a monstrous beast. His own heart beat wildly and he wanted nothing more than to turn and run away, where he might at least have a chance to draw his sword.

But to his amazement, the two horses he held did not move at all. And the black pony ignored him entirely. Instead, it reached out its heavy head to touch noses with Anfa, who calmly returned the gesture. All the while Leary clung desperately to its mane, his face white with terror.

"Leary, get down. Get down!" Bryan whispered.

"I can't." Leary's voice shook with fear. "I cannot move!" And Bryan could see that his brother's fingers were locked to the creature's neck, entangled in its wild thick mane, and that his trembling legs were clamped tight to the shaggy sides as though lashed there with rope.

Then Leary cried out as the beast whirled around and bolted down the road again, snapping its terrified rider's head back and leaving Bryan and the horses standing alone in the grass. Anfa nickered softly, and both he and Luath peered into the darkness where the strange creature had disappeared.

Bryan dropped Anfa's reins and in one swift move vaulted onto Luath's back. "Leary!" he shouted, and sent the stallion racing down the road. "Leary! I'm coming! Keep trying to get away from it!"

Far ahead of him in the darkness, Bryan could see the glowing yellow eyes of the beast as it continued to gallop and could hear the pounding of its heavy hooves on the road. He urged Luath on faster, determined to catch up, but it seemed the creature would allow him to close in and then draw away whenever it pleased. It raced at speeds no natural horse could ever have attained.

Bryan could do nothing but grit his teeth and keep following, urging Luath on and straining to keep those hideous yellow eyes in sight. Leary had been right when he'd said that Bryan could never turn down a challenge—he hated to lose at anything, and was even more determined to win this particular race as his brother's terrified cries floated back to him on the night wind.

Suddenly the animal swung off the road and headed straight for the river. The water was dark and glistening by the faint light of the cloud-veiled stars. Bryan heard Leary cry out again as his wild mount took him for a gallop right along the riverbank, right down the treacherous path where the water met the earth and where high grass hid the holes and mud and rocks that might well cripple any racing horse and send its rider flying headlong into the shallow, rock-strewn riverbed.

Leary's terrified screams filled the night.

At last the treacherous pony swerved away from the riverbank and raced down the road again with Bryan and Luath still giving chase. It tore down the path for a time—for what seemed to Bryan to be forever—until it turned toward the river again, dashed between the trees separating the water from the road, and ran straight toward a campsite—a campsite where a small fire burned and where a family and their wagons and cattle had settled for the night.

As it galloped in a wide circle around the small encampment, the black pony threw up its head and neighed—though it sounded like deep raucous laughter instead of the natural call of a horse. Leary added his own terrified cries to the awful sound.

The little group of people around the fire instantly leaped to their feet and stood huddled together near the flames. A glance showed Bryan that they were an older man, an older woman, a couple of younger men and a younger girl—and then, there, walking out toward the monstrous black pony that had invaded their camp, was a tall young woman with flowing hair and a simple gown and the glint of a bright gold comb just above her forehead.

The beast went on tearing around the clearing in a wide circle, the light from its yellow eyes blending with the glare of the fire. Bryan pulled Luath to a stop near the big wooden wagon. "Stay away from it!" he cried to the young woman. "It is no natural horse! It is a monster! Stay away!"

But she continued to walk, looking the beast straight in its terrible yellow eyes and moving as though she intended to step directly into its path.

Chapter Two

"S*top!*" Bryan shouted again, as the animal bore down upon the tall young woman. To his amazement the woman did stop—and so did the hideous pony, jolting to a halt right in front of her and tearing up the grass with its hooves.

Leary continued to cling to the creature's neck. His face shone white with fear and he was nearly sobbing with terror.

The woman walked close to the beast. Though Bryan's heart leaped and he reached for his sword, the black pony's ears came forward as it regarded her. Its awful eyes softened somewhat. The woman halted a few steps away, looked steadily into the monster's glowing eyes, and calmly folded her hands in front of her.

"What is this?" she asked in a soft, gentle voice. "What has happened here?"

The pony snorted. And then Bryan heard a deep, raspy voice say a single word: "*Revenge.*"

At first he thought that Leary must have spoken, but one look at his brother's terrified face told him this could not have been the case. Leary was too frightened to squeak out a sob, much less speak with such a deep voice.

"*Revenge,*" the voice said again, and this time Bryan saw that the creature's lips twitched and its mouth moved. For an instant he felt as terrified as Leary. Not only did the monster steal men for horrific rides and have eyes that glowed like burning flames in its head, it could speak, too!

"Why do you speak of revenge?" the woman asked. "Please—let your rider go. I will listen to you. You can tell me why you seek revenge and I will help you if I can. But first, please, let this man step back down to earth where he belongs."

In answer, the pony raised its head and snorted once more. Its ears went flat and its eyes burned bright as it swung around and tore off again, with Leary's screams filling the clearing. The beast made another wild run along the riverbank, right along the worst of the rocky uneven ground—and then stopped dead, lowered its head, and sent Leary flying into the river with a huge splash.

Apparently satisfied, the creature trotted over to stand beneath a tree and watch Leary flounder in the waist-deep water, struggling to breathe while overwhelmed with terror and pain and cold river water.

"Leary!" Bryan jumped down from Luath and raced to the riverbank, reaching out to pull his brother the rest of the way to the shore. Together they collapsed on the damp grass.

"Where is it? Has it gone? I've got to get away from it!" Panic took hold as Leary struggled to get his shaking legs under him and run away—but he only stumbled and fell again. "I've got to get away!"

Bryan grabbed hold of his brother's arm and held him still. "Wait. Wait! Look. It's way over there, beneath that tree. Do you see? Right there—"

But there was nothing under the tree except grass.

Sheer terror overwhelmed Leary again as his eyes darted around the firelit clearing. "Where . . . where is it? It will catch me again! It will come back, I know it!"

"Please do not fear, Leary. It has gone. We will not see it again tonight, I think."

The voice was soft and gentle and feminine. Bryan looked up and saw the same tall young woman who had so boldly walked out to face the terrifying beast that had captured his brother.

Bryan got to his feet, leaving Leary to curl up in a ball in the wet grass and cover his eyes to shut out the sight of the monster he was sure would return.

"We thank you for your help, my lady," Bryan said, walking toward her. "Are all of you and your family safe?"

The woman nodded at her relatives, who stood close together by the fire. "We are," she said.

Her long hair, dark and gold like the oak leaves in autumn, hung freely to her slender hips and rippled in the fire's light. Her face glowed, outlining her fine features. Her eyes shone almost like pale gold, so light a shade of hazel were they; her nose was straight and delicate, and her lips slender and gentle. She wore a simple gown of pale undyed linen and a rectangular cloak of lightweight dark brown wool, the same color it had been when the sheep had worn it before shearing. A worn copper brooch fastened the cloak at her shoulder.

"Those are my parents and my sister, and the two working men who travel with us to the Fair. All are safe— though a bit shaken, I will admit. What sort of creature was that?"

Bryan shook his head. "I was hoping you might know. I have never seen its like before. And I don't think my brother will ever forget it."

17

They both looked over at Leary, who had managed to get to his hands and knees but still could not bring himself to look up. The tall young woman walked over to him, and Bryan found himself captivated by the way her rippling dark-gold hair cascaded across her back as she bent down to his brother.

"Come, now. Come, now! The creature is gone. You are safe here." She placed her slender hands on his shoulders and gently lifted him up, and to Bryan's surprise his brother got slowly to his feet. The woman began to steer him toward the fire. "Stay here with my family for a time. You will be safe there with them, safe by the fire." She walked with him until her parents took him by the arms, and then turned and walked back to Bryan.

"Again I thank you, my lady. I don't know how I ever would have got him up from the ground, much less back to our camp."

He saw her eyes flick over him, taking in his good wool tunic and new brown leather trews and his wide green-and-gold plaid cloak. She did not fail to notice the heavy gold brooch that held the rectangular cloak at his shoulder, nor the good iron sword in its oaken scabbard, its hilt set with softly glowing amber. He knew he was quite a contrast to her and her simply dressed farm family. Most likely she did not often see the king's warriors or other such nobles from the great fortresses.

"I did not know anyone else was camped nearby," she said.

"Oh, you are right. We are not nearby. We are all camped far back up the road—"

"We?" She cocked her head with a faint smile. The gold comb gleamed in her hair. "How many of 'we' are there?"

"Well . . . I am sorry, I . . . that is, we . . ." Bryan stopped, and made himself start over. He did not know which had unsettled him more, the monster that had terrorized his brother or this cool golden beauty who seemed shaken by nothing.

He drew a deep breath and looked directly into her pale gold-hazel eyes. "My name is Bryan, and this is my younger brother Leary. We are from Cahir Cullen, a kingdom to the north of here, and we are riding with King Nessan's Fianna to the Lughnasa Fair."

"We, too, are going to the Fair," she said. "We live not far from here, within these borders of Dun Solas where King Conaire rules. But King Nessan's patrolling warriors must be a small group indeed to consist only of you and your brother—and one very strange mount."

"Oh—but there are many more than just Leary and I! There are thirty-one warriors who ride the borders and guard the roads and fords of Cahir Cullen, and all of us will be at the Fair with our king."

"As will the folk of four other kingdoms. It will be quite a gathering, as always." The lady flicked her eyes first left and then right, and then cocked her head at Bryan. Her long locks rippled in the firelight behind her. Clearly she wished to know where these twenty-nine other warriors were hiding.

"Well . . . you see . . . you have not seen us because we have not yet come this far. The Fianna's camp for the night is far back along the road. My brother and I are out alone because he was forced to give up his horse to another man of the Fianna, who injured his own mount in a foolish race. I felt that I should stay with Leary."

"Because you wished to see to the injured horse? Or because your brother is very drunk this night?" Her eyes were penetrating.

Bryan looked away for a moment. "Both reasons, I must confess." He glanced toward the fire again and saw Leary sitting as close to the flames as he could get. One of the women there, no doubt the mother of the family, handed him a cup, which he quickly accepted.

"But we have troubled you long enough," Bryan said. "I will get my brother and go. I thank you, and your family, for your hospitality."

The young woman took a step toward him, and her slender lips curved into a smile. "It is no trouble, Bryan of Cahir Cullen. Perhaps you would like to go and get your poor injured horse and make your camp here, so that the animal will not have to struggle all the way back to the Fianna's encampment. The night is a strange one indeed, with all manner of creatures roaming about."

Bryan smiled back at her. "All manner of creatures, indeed. I thank you, my lady. My brother and I will make your camp with you and your family tonight."

He glanced out into the darkness again. "I do not brag when I say I have crossed swords and won against every sort of opponent, and never known a moment's fear—but the beast that appeared tonight is like nothing I have ever seen before. How is it that you approached it unafraid?"

She laughed a little. "Not entirely unafraid—but though its behavior was clearly that of some fey creature and not of any normal horse, it looked directly at me and seemed to have some purpose. I felt certain that trying to destroy it would only make it more angry—more dangerous. And it did respond and it let Leary go, rough though its treatment of him was. I am sure that it must not be harmed. That would only lead to worse destruction from this fearsome creature."

She paused, then shook her head. "I have never seen such a thing, never heard of any such beast—not even in the oldest tales." She looked up and met his gaze, her expression serious. "I saw a monstrous creature that should have been a horse, but instead had eyes of fire and a rider trapped on its back—and it spoke in a most unnatural voice."

"And I saw, and heard, the same." Even now, the sound of that awful rasping voice saying *Revenge* was enough to send a chill up his spine. "Your senses did not mislead you. It also ran at speeds that even Luath could not match, and Luath has never been bested by any horse in Eire—not by any natural horse."

The lady also drew a breath, and her eyes flicked to the deep black forest. "Please, go and get your brother's horse, and stay with us tonight. I am one who has always lived among the creatures of the forests and fields, and never have I seen such a beast. We would all be glad to have you."

"I thank you. I will go and fetch Anfa."

"He must be quite unnerved at being left alone in this forest in the dark, especially with such a creature about."

"One would think so—but in this night filled with strange happenings, I can add one more. Neither Luath nor Anfa showed the slightest fear of this creature. They actually stepped up to greet it when it approached them."

The woman's fine features drew together in a frown. "This bears watching," she said. "I am certain we have not seen the last of it—the last of this *puca*."

"This . . . what?"

She smiled. "*Puca*. An angry spirit. It was clearly driven by rage as it uttered only one word: *revenge*. A more furious beast I never hope to see."

Suddenly both of them tensed and looked toward the road. There was a sound of hoofbeats coming through

21

the line of trees between the campsite and the road. The woman caught her breath and Bryan reached for his sword—but then the young woman picked up her skirts and hurried straight toward the sound. She disappeared into the night.

"Wait. Wait!" Bryan ran after her, his heart beginning to pound as he searched the darkness for the glare of flame-yellow eyes.

"You were quite right. This creature is very lame indeed." And as Bryan skidded to a halt, the woman emerged from a grove of trees with Anfa following close after her. "We will care for him, too."

"My lady!" Bryan said, feeling a great wave of relief.

She stopped the horse and turned to look at him.

Bryan said, "Again we thank you for your hospitality. But there is one thing I wish for more than anything right now."

"And what would that be?"

"Your name, beautiful lady. I wish to know your name."

She smiled. "Niamh," she said, and walked ahead with Anfa once again. "My name is Niamh."

"Niamh," Bryan breathed. *Bright and beautiful.* "Well, then," he said, walking after her, "if the strange beast that took my brother for such a wild ride has also led me to you, it may well have been worth the trouble."

She glanced over her shoulder again with that small and mysterious smile, and the golden comb in her hair glinted in the firelight.

Chapter Three

A sense of calm began to return to the evening, though it was clear that everyone had been shaken by the appearance of the strange beast that Niamh called a *puca*. Even Bryan had to admit that he was glad enough to camp in the company of others, instead of alone with Leary in this very dark and entirely unfamiliar forest.

Not that Leary would have been much help to him anyway. His brother stayed sitting on the ground near the large bright fire, huddled under his rectangular cloak, and his eyes constantly searched the darkness that surrounded them. He seemed to calm down a bit when Niamh's younger sister brought him a plate of food and sat down beside him.

"Aine can soothe any frightened creature," Niamh said, as she ran her hands over Anfa and examined him thoroughly. "She will calm your brother and see to his wounds. He did get quite scraped on the rocks, though I do not think it is anything serious."

"I have never seen any man so thoroughly frightened,"

Bryan said. "I fear it will stay with him for a good long time."

"Perhaps so," she said. "But perhaps if we can solve the mystery of this strange beast, Leary will come to know that he is safe. It is all we can do."

Niamh's parents stayed close to the fire and to their belongings, and kept a calm but steady watch on the forest and on the two men of another king's Fianna who had come to stay with them. They didn't necessarily trust Bryan or Leary. The two working men kept watch on the two pairs of oxen and on whatever was loaded in the wagons, which were both covered with sheets of cowhide securely tied down with ropes.

Once Leary had eaten a little, and Aine sat beside him with a cloth and a cup of water gently cleaning his cuts and scrapes, Niamh took Anfa's reins and led the crippled animal slowly to the river. Bryan took Luath and led him alongside, and once they reached the water they let both animals drink. Bryan found himself watching the darkness closely for a glare of yellow and listening for the sound of ominous hoofbeats, but then he forgot all thoughts of strange wild spirits and malevolent ponies at the sight of Niamh slipping her feet out of her folded leather boots and catching the ends of her long cream-colored skirts, raising them above her knees and throwing the hems over her arm.

Her legs, strong and slender and impossibly long, glowed in the soft light of the distant fire. When Anfa finished drinking, she led him out a few steps into the cold rushing water, and turned him around to face the shore. The horse stepped high as he made his way through the river, and then stood quietly with his soft nose touching Niamh's arm.

Bryan stayed on the grassy bank with Luath reaching out his head to drink. "You will grow cold standing in that water," he warned.

Niamh stroked Anfa's face, and the exhausted horse closed his eyes. "He will not need to stay here long. No doubt he would like to graze and rest, as would Luath. But a little time in the cold water will help draw the heat and swelling from his leg."

Bryan felt silly. "Even Leary said as much. I thank you for caring for him, Lady Niamh of Dun Solas."

"You are both welcome. But you need not call me 'lady.' Though I live on King Conaire's lands, I do not reside in his great walled fortress. I am only Niamh, born in the countryside in my parents' simple *rath*, and living all my life in that small earth-ringed home with the forest creatures for companions.

"Neither I nor any of my family are among the highborn. We are all farmers, herders and servants. I do not wear the brightly colored gowns and cloaks that only noblewomen are permitted to wear, living as they do in the great stone-ringed *duns* among hundreds of other folk. My colors are in the yellow primroses and in the blue and pink and purple violets that bloom in the spring and summer, and in the leaves that turn to russet and gold in the autumn.

"I have no talent for delicate embroideries that take months or years to complete. Those are of use only to decorate a richly made and brightly colored gown never worn anywhere but the safe and protected king's hall with its fastidious covering of clean straw. My skill lies in growing the fields of flax, and in caring for the herds of sheep that provide good strong linen and wool for the sturdy clothes working folk must wear.

"And I cannot adorn myself with gold the way the fine royal ladies of the great *duns* can do. My father is only a farmer and a herdsman, not a learned druid or accomplished warrior living with the king in his fortress. He has no store of beautiful golden treasures for his daughters to wear. Our gold lies in the wagons you see near the fire: new-cut wheat as bright as any other gold that one might coax from the earth."

She nodded toward the camp, her shining hair once again rippling and falling across her shoulder as she did so and nearly touching the surface of the water. Bryan found it impossible to look away.

"Yet you do wear *some* gold," he said. "There is a lovely golden comb in your hair."

She reached up to touch it. "A small one, but you are right—it is indeed gold. The only true gold my family possesses."

"And they choose you to wear it. They want the most beautiful lady in the family to wear their gold, and so it was given to you."

She smiled. The horse she held shifted his weight, trying to stand comfortably in the cold rushing water. "Not the most beautiful. I am merely the oldest daughter. My mother wore this comb before she was married, and her mother as well."

"And if I might ask—how did your family come to have such a custom?"

"I think you are really asking how a family such as mine—simple farmers with no fine things of their own—could have a piece of gold like this. But no matter. I will tell you."

Niamh threw her hair back over her shoulder and reached up to touch the golden comb firmly anchored in her hair. Bryan could see that the top of it was in the

26

shape of a gracefully curving stalk of wheat, with the full-ripened grains most carefully worked at one end.

"It has been in my mother's family for so long that no one is certain just where it came from," she said. "The story is told that a father, long ago, so loved his only daughter that he traded all he had of value to have this made for her, to remind her that she, a child of forest and field, was still as precious as any high-born lady might be. It has remained in our family ever since, always handed down to the oldest daughter of marriageable age. When I am married, it will go to my sister, Aine."

"And what if she should find someone to marry before you? Will you keep your beautiful golden comb?"

She rested one hand on Anfa's shoulder, still holding her skirts up out of the rushing waters with the other. "I do not think that is likely. I am twenty-two years of age and Aine has just turned seventeen. She will take a bit of time before she is ready for a husband, I think, while I would be quite happy to have a home and family of my own . . . and just as happy to give Aine my golden comb."

Niamh began to step forward through the cold water. Anfa followed, stepping up onto the bank to stand quietly beside her. "He does look a bit better," Niamh said, running her slender fingers down the horse's still-swollen leg. "Help me take this saddle and bridle off of him, and we'll set him loose to graze. I think he will be glad to stay close to camp tonight."

Bryan and Niamh worked together to quickly remove the equipment from both horses, and in a moment Anfa and Luath grazed in contentment side by side. Bryan took the saddles and bridles and set them down against one of the trees by the riverbank. Niamh sat down nearby and pulled on her fleece-lined folded leather boots, vigorously rubbing her wet legs with the coarse linen of her gowns.

"Oh, you were right! My legs are very cold. But it was worth it to see Anfa move a bit easier."

"He is grateful to you, my lady," Bryan murmured, unable to take his eyes from the glowing, reddened skin of her legs. "As am I."

She glanced at him and quickly pulled her skirts down to her ankles, then folded her hands over her knees. "So, you and your cousin were racing your horses when Anfa fell and took your cousin down with him. Was your cousin hurt as well?"

Bryan snorted, and sat down across from her. "Ardal was not hurt at all. He believed he had won simply because he knew I would never run any horse along a rocky riverbank. And now Anfa must suffer for it."

"Is he known for such behavior? Why does no one try to stop him?"

"Anfa is not the first horse he has lamed and, sadly, I doubt he will be the last. The other men follow him because he is King Nessan's sister's son, and because he is tall and proud and well-spoken—and confident to the point of arrogance. He wants nothing more than to be the tanist of Cahir Cullen, and he seems to have the following to do just that."

"Ah, I see. He wants to be the one to succeed your king. Does no one else want to do so? A kingdom must have a tanist named long before the king's life ends, in order to allow enough time for any objections to be settled. Does no one else want to be chosen tanist, when next King Nessan and his druids and the free men of Cahir Cullen meet together to choose their prince?"

Bryan raised his chin. "I, too, want to be the tanist. I am a cousin of Ardal and a member of the king's own family. Cahir Cullen has always been my home and I would not see it taken over by one like Ardal."

She tilted her head and studied him. "Are you the only one who does not trust him? Do the other men of Cahir Cullen not see him for what he is?"

Bryan smiled a little, and then shrugged. "He is a man of great accomplishment. It isn't all just bragging. He knows exactly what to say to any man, or to any woman, to instantly win their confidence. And yet . . ."

"Yet?"

"Yet I do not trust him because of the way he treats his horses." He looked away again, waiting for her to mock him for this, as everyone else always did whenever he had dared to share this opinion. *Oh, accidents can happen,* they would say. *A man who would be king must not be afraid to use all of his resources to the utmost—including his horses.*

"A man who would be king must show mercy and care to all who serve him—even his animals," said Niamh. "I would not trust him, either." She smiled at Bryan, and he forgot completely about what anyone else had ever said about anything.

"You would make a queen for any king," he said softly. "You are both beautiful and wise. Perhaps if I do become first tanist and then king, and therefore require a queen, I will come back and ask for you."

He had thought she would be flattered. He waited for her to blush and giggle and protest. But Niamh only stared at him, her expression suddenly very still, and she raised her chin so that her long hair pooled in the grass behind her.

"You well know that your people expect a high-born woman to be their queen. They would never accept a low-born herdsman's daughter who must get her hands dirty each day."

He looked away. "I am sorry, Niamh. I did not mean to insult you. You would make a wonderful queen for my people or anyone else's, no matter what station you were born into."

But she seemed not to have heard him. "And besides— being a queen is the last of all positions that I would wish to hold. As I told you, I have lived all my life among the wild deer and wheat fields. To be shut away from all that, closed in by stone walls and held fast by ritual and duty, would be no life at all for me. You will have to look for your queen elsewhere, Bryan of Cahir Cullen. Perhaps you will find her at the Fair."

He shrugged. "When five kingdoms come together for fourteen nights, it's not surprising that there are more matches made than horses traded or footraces won. But the Fair has not yet started, and on this night I would be happy to sit in the forest with the kind and beautiful lady called Niamh."

She turned and smiled at him again, but this time her lips were tight. "My family would be pleased to have you stay as our guest for the rest of the night—but perhaps we are being selfish. Should you not take Luath and return to the Fianna's camp, to let them know what has happened? They will be wondering where you are, I should think, and I am not sure they will be pleased to have to search you out in the dark of night."

Bryan started to answer, but then paused. He realized that he had gone too far with this woman by boldly announcing that he might someday come back and ask her to be his queen. He had only just met her, for one thing, and for another she was not one of the noblemen's daughters at the *dun* who were used to such harmless flattery.

He sighed, ready to kick himself for such a blunder, and felt only disappointment at the thought of leaving this dark and quiet field by the river where Niamh and her family were camped. "I suppose you are right," he said at last. "Might Leary and Anfa stay with your family until morning?"

"Of course," Niamh said, rising to her feet. "We will tell Leary that we asked for a man of the Fianna to protect us, and that we would like to let Anfa walk slowly behind the ox-cart for the rest of his trip to the Fair. I'm sure he will agree."

"I'm sure he will," Bryan echoed, also standing up. "I thank you for your kindness, my lady. I wish I did not have to leave you now. Perhaps . . . perhaps I will see you at the Fair."

"There are many people at the Fair."

He reached out and gently caught her hand. "I will look for *you*," he said, and began to draw her closer.

She quickly squeezed his hand, and then released it. "You might," she said, and then she caught up her skirts and turned to run lightly over the grass to the bright campfire where her family was gathered.

Chapter Four

Niamh found it difficult to sleep that night. Close beside Aine and the fire, she made a comfortable pallet of two thick woolen cloaks spread out on the grass with another one to cover her, and was quite warm against the cool damp summer night—but her thoughts and dreams were filled with wild and frightening horses that spoke to her of revenge, and of handsome men with shining brown eyes and soft brown hair who galloped in with drawn swords to protect her and her family from the beast.

When the soft light of the cloud-covered morning finally awakened her, she raised her head to see that all was still quiet within their little encampment. Aine still slept nearby on her own pallet. Her parents rested together in their own blankets not far away. The two oxen remained tethered with their ropes thrown high over the sturdy branches of the oak trees, as did the pair of young red-and-white heifer calves, and all grazed on whatever grass they could strain to reach.

Leary, Niamh saw, was still snoring in his place beside the wagons where Dowan and Conn had taken their rest.

Already the two working men were collecting dead wood to build up the fire for the morning meal.

Quickly she sat up and looked toward the river, and then breathed a sigh of relief. Anfa, the lame horse that had come to them last night, stood calmly near the water and watched all that happened in the camp.

There was no sign of any wild and angry *puca*, nor of any handsome warriors on beautiful dark-gold horses. She knew she ought to be glad that, except for one drunken young man and his very lame horse, all was as it had been the day before, but as she set about awakening everyone else in the camp so they could continue their journey, Niamh realized that she had never before been in such a great hurry to reach the grounds of the Lughnasa Fair.

She knew she should not feel this way—she knew that, ultimately, Bryan would prove to be just another arrogant young warrior deigning to flirt with a simple farm girl. But even so, she quickly threw off the covers and got to her feet, rousing everyone else and getting the flour and water to make flatbread for their breakfast.

Thanks to her efforts, it was not long before they were all on their way. Niamh and Aine sat on the rear edge of the second of the heavily loaded grain wagons—the first had the two protesting heifer calves securely tied to the back of it—with their booted feet dangling just above the dirt road and the skirts of their good linen gowns carefully gathered up against the dust.

Just behind them, keeping up with the slow plodding of the oxen without too much difficulty, Anfa walked with uneven steps. Leary walked with him, leading him by the bridle and letting him stop to rest by the side of the road whenever he seemed to need it—or whenever Leary needed it, for he was constantly rubbing what seemed to be an aching head.

Aine looked up at Leary and nodded toward the horse. "He seems to be walking a bit better this morning," she said with a pretty smile.

Leary grinned back at her, apparently forgetting for the moment his throbbing head and empty stomach—he had not touched a bite of the good hot buttered flatbread Niamh had offered him on awakening. "He is indeed a little better. I am just glad to see him walking at all, though I think he would walk all the way across Eire if it meant he could be this close to you."

Aine blushed and looked down at the road that passed beneath them, but Niamh saw her shining eyes and restrained smile. "Ah, be careful now, Aine," she said to her sister. "He is a young man of the Fianna. You know about them, don't you? They are great warriors who spend the days from Beltaine to Samhain riding from border to border throughout their kingdom, hunting and fishing and taking their sport wherever they find it. They are charged with protecting the kingdom from any who might try to invade it, though who protects the young women of the countryside from them I cannot say."

"Why, no one need protect the women from the Fianna! It is our duty to protect them! Never would we so much as touch any who are not willing."

Niamh continued, "And then, when Samhain arrives and the cold and damp of winter set in, they return to their great ringed fortresses and generally make nuisances of themselves with their drinking and endless fighting with each other, until Beltaine finally comes round in the spring. Then they can all be pushed out to roam the countryside again, much to the relief of the fine nobles and druids and warriors trying to live peacefully within those high thick walls."

"But, Lady Niamh, the Fianna must ride and train and

hunt so that they might be the best and strongest of any warriors anywhere! We are the king's own men and will defend him with all the skill we have—"

"So you will, much to the despair of the country folk who must put up with your constant tearing across their fields and flocks. Oh, and then there is the Fair. Aine, you've not been to the Lughnasa Fair before, so I must warn you: On both of the years when I was there, never did I see any men so doggedly pursue the young women as those of the Fianna."

"Oh, but surely you do not believe—"

"Have you ever been to the Lughnasa Fair before, Leary?"

"I have not, but—"

Niamh nudged her sister. "There, you see? This young man of the Fianna has not even been to the Fair yet, and already he walks not five paces from your own wagon and cannot keep his eyes from you!"

"But Niamh—Aine—I am only trying to—Anfa must—"

And with that, both Niamh and Aine looked at each other and burst out laughing, leaving Leary to blush and look away and suddenly pay very close attention to Anfa's limping steps.

Then a new sound caught their attention. From somewhere behind the wagons came the thunder of many galloping hooves, pounding down the road and coming straight toward them.

Niamh caught hold of the high wooden side of the wagon and pulled herself up to see what was coming. She saw a few more ox-carts and pack ponies and people on the road far behind them, more farm folk like themselves drawing closer to the Fair. But all of them were quickly pushing and crowding their slow-moving animals off the road and into the grass to get out of the way of a thundering herd of at least thirty riders who tore down the road at full gallop, kicking up a great cloud of dust that hung in the air behind them.

Niamh's own wagon lurched as the oxen dragged it off to one side of the road—and not a moment too soon. The herd, men of King Nessan's Fianna, stampeded past in a roar of pounding hooves, all shouting to their horses and each other. And at the very front of the pack, outpacing them all, was a handsome man with soft brown hair who rode a beautiful dark-gold stallion. He tore past the wagons without even noticing Niamh.

"Look!" Leary called. "He's winning! No horse can beat Luath! He'll win every race at the Fair, too!"

Niamh could only cough and try to wipe the dirt and dust from her eyes. "I wish I could see them, Leary, but they've kicked up so much dust I can hardly see anything."

Beside her, her sister Aine sneezed. "Will they race like this at the Fair? How will anyone see who wins?"

"Oh, the race won't be held on a dirt road," Leary said. "At least, not all of it. It will be across a wide swath of the country over the grass. Bryan has told me about it many times. You'll be able to see most of the race quite well!" Then Leary's face fell as he placed his hand on Anfa's shoulder. "This horse should be there with them. He was the only one who had a real chance against Luath."

Just then there was the sound of a horse galloping down the road, as though one man of the Fianna was returning the way he had come. And almost before Niamh could turn around, Bryan was dashing past them again and sending up another cloud of dust.

As Niamh tried to shield her eyes from it, she caught a

glimpse of Bryan circling his stallion around and then jogging back toward their wagon.

She drew a deep breath, trying to wave away the dust, and then straightened her very long hair behind her. In a moment Bryan was alongside the wagon and looking down at his brother.

"Leary! I thought I saw you and Anfa as we rode past. How is he today?" But before Leary could answer, Bryan frowned and shook his head. "Not much better, I can see that. Still so lame he can barely keep up with the oxen." He looked up ahead of them, as though looking down the road at someone or something, and his brown eyes hardened. "Someday they will see that man for what he really is."

Then he suddenly looked down at the wagon, and his handsome face relaxed once again. "Niamh," he said, his brown eyes shining. "I hoped I would see you again this day."

"There are many wagons on this road, and many young women. I could have been in any one of these carts or in none of them at all."

"So you could—but I knew that Leary and Anfa would do nothing but stay with the family that had been so kind to them both last night. And I also knew that wherever I found Leary, I would find you, too."

"Well, you are nothing if not clever, Bryan of the Fianna," she said, and at seeing the look on his face had to bite her lip to keep from laughing. It was a look that said he was not sure if he had been complimented or insulted.

He patted the stallion's neck. "Did you see the way Luath pulled away from the pack? Nothing will stop him at the Fair, either. And he is just as good at swimming as he is at galloping. He'll win both races, you wait and see!"

"I believe I did see him, just now," Niamh said, with a little cough.

"And was he not magnificent? Surely you have never seen the like!"

"I have not—but I, and my sister, and everyone else on this road are now covered with the dust kicked up by those fine racing horses of the Fianna, since their riders forced them to gallop along right beside us instead of on the grass."

Bryan's face grew serious. "Oh. I am sorry, my lady. We only hoped to show all the folk of the five kingdoms how strong and fast we really are, and impress them with our—"

"With the amount of dirt you can kick up onto our newly cut grain?" She shook her head. "I am sorry, but we are not impressed. We are merely dusty."

Aine, too, gave a small cough and brushed off her long linen skirts with both hands. Leary's face grew serious and his eyes widened. He quickly glanced up at Bryan, but would find no help there, for Bryan, too, looked completely at a loss as to what he should do or say now.

Also, he was having difficulty keeping the long-striding Luath behind the slowly creeping ox-cart. Abruptly he swung down and took the horse by the bridle. "Would you walk with me in the cool grass, Niamh? Perhaps we could talk, and allow Luath to walk at a more comfortable pace."

He reached out one hand to her, and she took it and hopped down from the end of the wagon to walk beside Bryan and his dark-gold stallion. "I won't go far," she promised Aine, who grinned down at her, and then she and Bryan and the horse walked out along the grass, soon leaving the ox-drawn wagon behind them.

"I am sorry to know that Luath's victory did not impress you," Bryan said. "And I do apologize for the dust."

"The dust is not so bad. And I was indeed impressed with Luath's accomplishment, for he does not run just to impress the onlookers. He runs for the joy of it, and because you ask it of him."

"Do you not think I race for the joy of it?"

"Oh, I'm sure you do, but I think all young men race and compete and do battle for just one reason: to impress young women."

A slight frown crossed Bryan's handsome face. "But do not all of the people of Cahir Cullen ask it of me? Do they not insist that any man who wants to be chosen as tanist show them what he is made of, by racing and hunting and leading the cattle raids? How else could it be done?"

"I do understand that a man who would be a king must prove his worth in every way he can. Doing it just to catch the eye of a foolish young woman would be rather shallow, would it not?"

"Shallow?" He laughed. "It is just the way of young men, to do such things."

"Surely you do not believe that bragging and boasting are what women really want?"

She had thought he would come back with another defense of his position, but instead he only threw back his head and laughed again. "My lady—what man ever knows what women really want?"

Niamh looked up at him. "Is it really so difficult a thing? Too difficult for even a king to know?"

He blushed a little and looked away, carefully straightening Luath's bridle. "I have never known any man, old or young, king or rock-man, who ever claimed to know what women want."

"Well, then. I shall tell you, Bryan, and you will be the first."

He glanced at her, eyes shining. "I would be very grateful if you would do so. I have not known you long, but already I can see that you are a plainspoken lady if ever there was one. Please—tell me what it is that women want."

But Niamh did not respond. Instead, they walked in silence for a time as she gazed around her at the soft cloudy sky and at the tall oak trees lining the road, and listened to the call of the skylarks. She made no move to answer him. After a time, Bryan cleared his throat. "My lady—will you not answer me?"

She sighed. "I have decided not to tell you."

"You have decided not to tell me? I must say, I am quite disappointed. Is that because I was right after all, and no one knows what women really want—not even women themselves?"

"Not at all. It's just that . . . I believe it would be better to let you learn this on your own."   .

He laughed again. "Learn it on my own? I am twenty-five years of age. If such a thing were possible, do you not think I would have learned it for myself by now?"

"Here is what I will do," she continued, as though he had not spoken at all. "I will tell you that there are three things that every woman wants from the man in her life. Perhaps you could take it as yet another contest—another challenge—to see if, by the end of the fourteen nights of the Fair, you can learn what those three things are."

"I do accept your offer. I never turn down a challenge!" Then he paused, looking closely at her with a bright gleam in his eye. "Yet what is a contest without a prize? What have I earned, if I succeed at this challenge of yours?"

"Oh, it is quite simple. You will have shown me that you truly do have an interest in me, beyond the casual glance, by going to a bit of trouble to give me my three answers."

"And that is all? I will have *proved a genuine interest in you?*"

She lifted the end of her long leather belt and looked at it carefully as they walked, brushing away the dust of the road from its tip. "Are you saying that is not good enough? That you have no interest in me, then? Very well. I will go back and ride with Aine, and trouble you no further. Good day to you, Bryan." She turned to walk back to the wagon.

He caught her with a gentle hand on her arm. "Please, Lady Niamh. Stay and walk with me for a time. I will accept your challenge. As I said, I never turn one down. And I never fail."

She smiled, and then went on walking beside him. "We shall see," she said. "I'm sure you will be quite busy at the Fair, what with all of the races and hurley games and javelin throws you will no doubt be competing in."

"Well, that is not quite true. I do not compete in the team contests like the hurley games.

Niamh considered, and then nodded. "I can understand why a man who wants to be chosen as tanist, and then king, would not want to play hurley. Running up and down a field of men, all with wildly swinging sticks, chasing after a little bronze disk and trying to knock it into a hole in the ground? Only a man whose body is whole can ever serve as king, and there is no better way for a man to be crippled, maimed or blinded than for him to play hurley."

Bryan laughed. "That is true. But it is also true that I was the best of the hurley players when I was a boy. It's just that now, I would rather test my strength and skill alone, without the help of teammates."

"So that you might keep the glory of winning all to yourself?"

"So that I can better test myself, of course. Entering only the individual contests is a sign of my humility."

42

"Ah, humility. I am glad to hear that you have it, for humility is a fine thing in a man. So many men cannot stop boasting of how humble they are, and so to meet a man with genuine humility is a rare thing."

"So it is." He reached out and ran his fingers down Luath's mane. "Tell me, then. What is it that *you* plan to do at the Fair? I have told you that I will be racing Luath and competing in the contests, and that I hope to prove once and for all that I am the one who should be chosen tanist. But what do you hope to do while you are there?"

She laughed. "Nothing so ambitious, I am afraid. I go with my family to celebrate the grain harvest, and to watch the races and the contests, and to meet the other young people who have come to gather at the Fair."

"Oh, I understand. You are looking for a husband!"

Niamh hardly spared him a glance. "I am twenty-two years old. That is past the age when most girls are married. Is it so unusual that I may be thinking of a family of my own?"

He shrugged. "I am sure it is not. But . . ."

"But what?"

He looked away. "I must tell you, I have not ever been drawn to the idea of making a marriage."

"You are not drawn to the idea of making a marriage? Why, just last evening you said you would consider coming back and making me your queen should you become Cahir Cullen's next king. I am sorry—I must have mistaken."

He smiled a little. "You were not mistaken when I said you would make a fine queen. But I must tell you, I have seen few couples—maybe none—who seem to be happy together for even a few years, much less for all of their lives."

Niamh nodded, her face serious. "You are right, sadly

43

enough. Yet I will tell you this: If you learn the answer to my challenge, and learn the three things that women want from men, you will know the way to keep a marriage happy for a lifetime."

Bryan looked up at her and grinned. "Will I, now? That would be a reward indeed."

He halted Luath, looking up ahead of him, and then turned to Niamh. "I must return to the Fianna. They're gathering in the road up ahead, for we are nearly at the Fair. I thank you for walking with me this day, Lady Niamh. I promise, I will search for you once we make our encampment, and see you at twilight."

She threw back her head and began to laugh. "I thank you as well for a pleasant walk, but I do not expect—"

Her words stopped as he gave her the gentlest of kisses.

For a moment, everything around her seemed to stop. She was conscious only of a pleasant warmth flooding through her, as though she stood in the warmest summer sunlight. Bryan's lips were softer than she ever would have expected.

She could only stand and watch as he swung up on his horse and grinned down at her. "Until twilight, Lady Niamh," he said, and then he galloped off down the road to rejoin the men of the Fianna.

Chapter Five

At last, as the sun reached its zenith behind the thin clouds of a soft grey sky, the main road curved sharply and became a narrow forest path through tall stands of grey-barked rowan trees. After a brief time in their cool shadows, and with the rushing sounds of the curving river just on the other side, the ox-wagons and their passengers broke through into daylight once more—this time into a wide and seemingly endless tree-studded field. The field stood at the foot of a long, wide mountain that had two widely separated peaks, one long and flat and the other high and conical.

Niamh hopped down from the wagon. "Come on, come on! It's Gathering Day! There's so much to see!" She caught Aine's hand, and her sister too slid down to walk alongside the wagons. Niamh watched the girl's eyes widen at the sights that greeted her, and she laughed. "You've seen nothing yet. They're still setting up and many are only just arriving, just like we are!"

As the wagons swung around again, following the road as it curved up toward the mountain, Niamh's heart leaped at the sight of the huge stone-and-gorse pens on either side of the road—one for the sheep, one for the cattle and one for the horses that would be put up for trade during the Fair.

But most exciting of all were the many tents and shelters going up all over the field, on both sides of the road and under the few scattered trees. As the ox-carts continued to rumble toward their destination, the sound of wooden mallets hammering stakes and poles into the earth filled the air, along with the laughter and calls of the people who waved and shouted out to the new arrivals. All across the field, men and women draped cowhides and sheepskins across the newly raised poles and tied them down to create temporary homes for the Fair.

Some of these shelters were rough and small and serviceable, and would be the houses of farming and herding families like Niamh's; but others were quite large and made of heavy oak timbers hung with slick new cowhides. These were decorated with brightly woven banners and hangings and had well-dressed warrior men outside to guard them. These fine shelters would serve as the homes of the kings, queens, warriors, druids, and other high-born who had come to the Lughnasa Fair from their stone-walled circular fortresses.

The road curved again to pass along the base of the mountain. "Look, Aine!" Niamh said, pointing to a large and isolated campsite ringed by a low stone wall. In the center were three very spacious tents made of solid black cowhide, with fine woolen rugs and new sheepskins covering the grass in front of them.

"There is the encampment of King Conaire and Queen Treise. They have the largest and best camp because this is their kingdom—the kingdom of Dun Solas, which is our kingdom, too! The other four kings will have their own camps scattered throughout the field with their own people around them."

"So if you can learn where King Nessan's encampment is, perhaps you can find Bryan again," suggested Aine.

Niamh raised her chin. "Bryan? He is a man of the Fianna—one who was trying to save his brother from a very strange beast last night, and who happened to come across our camp. Save for a night or two, such men have no interest in we girls who live on the land. They much prefer the brightly clothed women who live in the great fortresses and paint their eyebrows and lips and cheeks. Why would I go and search for him?"

Aine giggled. "Because he is handsome and strong? Because he clearly has an interest in you? Because you have come here to find a husband?"

"That is not the only reason I am here," Niamh argued. "And I have been to the Fair twice before and did not come back with a husband either time, did I?"

"You did not meet a handsome young man of King Nessan's Fianna, either, so far as I know."

"Well . . . I met a few young men, all nice enough and handsome enough, and had a most wonderful time. There is no gathering like the Lughnasa Fair! I enjoyed the games and the contests and the horse trading and the cattle trading and the sheep trading and the bonfire and the storytelling and the music and the dancing and the feasts—"

"And the berry-picking?"

Niamh stopped and turned to her sister. "And what do you know of the berry-picking?"

"Why, I know that it happens on the first night of the

Fair, and that all of the young unmarried men and women take baskets and walk out together just before dusk to climb this mountain." She looked up at it again, gazing from left to right as if hardly able to take in its great size. "And they gather as many bilberries as they can, even if it takes them until dawn!"

The wagons rumbled on past. Niamh took Aine by the arm and they continued walking down the road, with the king's encampment and the mountain on one side of them and the great field on the other.

"Aine, I'm sure you will want to go and gather bilberries, but you and I will go together. You must not be persuaded to become some man's 'Lughnasa Sister' just because he is charming and handsome and tells you how very lovely you are underneath the stars on the mountaintop."

"A . . . sister? What do you mean?"

Niamh shook her head. "A Lughnasa Sister, or Lughnasa Brother, is a partner in love—but only for the fourteen nights of the Fair. If you see a girl on the mountaintop tonight with a circlet of leaves and flowers in her hair, that means she has become someone's Lughnasa Sister."

She sighed. "I know you want to walk out with the others tonight, and so do I, but remember this: I have gone to the berry-picking twice before, and enjoyed a beautiful evening and a bit of flattery from attractive young men. Most of the other young women came back with their skirts askew, their hair full of brambles and their baskets all but empty, but I never came back with anything but a basket full of bilberries."

"But Niamh—did you not *want* to be someone's Lughnasa Sister?"

She smiled as she walked along. "Of course I did," she

answered. "Who would not be tempted, when the man is attractive and the night is magical and so many around you are doing the same? But you must not be in too great a hurry to give yourself to a man, Aine. The women of our family have always known this. That is why I have this beautiful piece of gold to wear in my hair, and that is why someday you will wear it too—if you still want it by the end of this Fair."

Aine smiled back at her. "I will still want it."

"Good. I am glad to know this. Come on, then, we have a lot of work to do before nightfall!"

They followed the road past King Conaire's encampment and nearly to the far end of the mountain, until they reached a row of graceful rowan trees, which separated the camping field from the vast, grassy open spaces that served as the gaming fields and racecourses. The two sisters quickly found their family at a spot at the very edge of the camping field, just beneath one of the fine rowan trees, hammering the poles that would serve as the framework for their shelter.

As she went to drag one of the tightly bound bundles of newly cut straw from the wagon, Niamh looked around and realized that there was no sign of Leary or Anfa. "Where has Leary gone?" she called to her mother.

"Oh, they went straight to the Fianna's camp, over near the horse pens," her mother said, beginning to unroll the heavy red-and-white cowhides that would form the tops and sides of their shelter. "He was quite polite, but he had to rejoin the Fianna and get Anfa to the pens, for he is to be traded at the Horse Fair tomorrow morning."

"Traded at the Fair . . . injured as he is?" Niamh shook her head. "Not even given time to rest and heal." She stole a glance across the great field, but it was filling up so rapidly with the pole-and-hide shelters of some two thousand people that she could not even see the horse-trading pen down by the river.

"Come now, Niamh," Aine said, as she walked past with a stack of good woolen cloaks in her arms and a mischievous gleam in her eye. "Bryan said he'd be back at dusk, didn't he?"

Niamh could only give her a small frown and go on unloading the wagon, determined not to think about who might or might not come to call on her that evening.

The work went on throughout the afternoon, and by the time the shadows began to lengthen, the little camp was entirely set up and ready to provide a comfortable home for the next fourteen nights. A sturdy framework of heavy oak poles supported a draped-and-tied assembly of well-worn red-and-white cowhides, with heavy brown sheepskins thrown over the very top to keep out the worst of the rains that were sure to come.

The grassy earth floor was thickly bedded with newly cut straw fresh from the harvest and would provide a clean dry bed where they could sleep wrapped in woolen cloaks, and where they could sit in comfort to enjoy their meals and conversation if it was too wet to sit outside. A small firepit was dug just outside the tent, shielded by the two big wooden wagons drawn up end-to-end in front of it.

Conn and Dowan would make their beds inside or beneath the wagons, and the oxen would be turned out to graze with the other beasts on the far side of the mountain and collected again when the Fair was over. The two young red-and-white heifer calves had already been led to the enormous cattle pen near the entrance, where all of the cows and calves and oxen available for trade were kept so that everyone might see them and make their choices in time for the Cattle Fair.

From within their tent, Niamh threw back the cowhide hangings covering the open side of it and she and Aine stepped outside into the early evening. The sun had just slipped down behind the mountain and the encampment lay in its cool shadow. Already lighted torches set high on poles driven into the earth began to appear.

"It's never dark here, is it?" asked Aine, standing up on tiptoe to see over the surrounding tents.

"Never at the Fair," Niamh answered, handing her one of the pair of linen-lined, woven wicker baskets she held. "Never dark, and you almost never get any sleep, either!"

"Ah, but my daughters will have sleep, safe in their own fine tent." Their mother Morna walked up to them and inspected them both. One after the other, she took their hands and held them out, smiling in approval as she looked at their fine clean gowns of natural linen and their good leather belts tied off in rings of bronze. She touched their long, long hair—Niamh's dark gold and Aine's soft brown—smoothly brushed back from their faces and held with a single comb. Aine's comb was of polished wood, unlike Niamh's of shining gold worked into the likeness of a sheaf of wheat.

"My girls are as beautiful as any fine lady in her flashing gold and brightly dyed wool, and far more honorable than many of those! Aine, you listen to your sister and do as she does. You will have an enjoyable time, but still think well of yourself come sunrise!"

"I will do as she says, Mother, I promise." Aine laughed. "Are you ready to go, Niamh?"

"I . . . I am," Niamh answered, after a quick glance over her shoulder. For a moment the colorful world of the

Fair seemed to stand still. *He is not here . . . He said he would come, but he is not here. . . .* Then she straightened and looked at Aine. "I am ready. Thank you, Mother. We will be back well before sunrise." The two girls embraced their parents and then set off for the mountain—but stopped as soon as they walked around the wagons and set foot on the already well-worn path.

Bryan and Leary stood before them on the path. "Good evening to you, Niamh," Bryan said. "And good evening to you, Aine. Will you walk out with us to the mountain this night?"

The noise and color of the Fair faded away, and for Niamh the only thing that existed was the sight of Bryan waiting for her and extending his hand. "Leary has not been to the Fair before, either," he said. "We hoped that perhaps you and I could show him and Aine what it's like—and keep an eye on them in the process." He smiled at her, his eyes gleaming, even as Leary caught Aine's eye and grinned.

Niamh caught her breath. She had told herself not to expect that he would come, and now that he was here she was almost at a loss for what to do.

Then she looked at the eager faces of Leary and Aine, and at Bryan's handsome profile as he glanced at the mountain with the glowing evening sky behind it. "We were going anyway," Niamh said. "I'm sure it would be a fine thing if you both walked with us." Bryan nodded to her, his eyes alight, and together the four of them set off through the Fair toward the mountain.

Most of the tents and shelters were now in place and their inhabitants were settling in for the fortnight of the Fair. It seemed that practically everyone had brought something to trade. Families heaped clean straw outside their tents, lit torches and candles against the darkness, and laid out whatever they had to offer. The air was filled with the never-ending sounds of bargaining for the goods so temptingly displayed.

There were spools of brightly dyed thread on wooden rods and stacks of newly woven linen and woolen fabric, some in natural dark brown wool or soft tan linen but others dyed in bright reds or greens or yellows or purples. Some had been woven in stripes or plaids of many colors, fit for any nobleman or even a king or queen. A few clever traders hung the finished pieces of brightly colored cloth from the wooden poles of their tents where they could wave in the wind and catch the eyes of passersby.

Pieces of good finished leather and tanned sheepskins with the dark shaggy wool still in place were offered, along with coils of flax rope and carved wooden yokes for oxen. Those skilled at working in metal set out iron knives with bone handles next to sturdy bronze cauldrons and plates and cups.

In front of many tents were little pens of woven wicker, thickly bedded with straw, where mother dogs nursed their litters of puppies. Some would grow to be enormous fierce hounds brave enough to bring down wolves, and others would be small gentle dogs much loved by highborn ladies as pets. Children were set to guard the puppies and keep them from wriggling out of their enclosures before they could be traded.

And everywhere were displays of that commodity for which there was ever a demand: food. Always there was the good smell of fresh hot bread and roasting meat, ready to be bartered a few slices at a time, along with baskets of hard white cheese and wooden bowls filled with dark gold butter and sweet honey and newly ground flour and fresh-picked clover and watercress.

And after tonight, there would be tiny sweet red woodland strawberries, a few early-ripening blackberries, and—most of all—heaps and heaps of tiny, sour, blue-black bilberries, ready for mashing with a little fresh cream and honey for a sweet summer delicacy.

"I don't think I will ever be content to live out in the *rath* again," Aine said, hardly able to take it all in. "So many people! So much noise, so much excitement!"

"It is true, it can be hard to imagine going back to such a quiet life after being at the Fair," Niamh agreed with a laugh. "But after a fortnight of this, the forest can be quite a peaceful place to return to."

"So it can," Bryan said, walking beside her. "But the Fair is something you never forget, and you will find yourself drawn back to it year after year—just as *they* are."

Near the foot of the great mountain, gathering in little groups and then beginning their trek up the forested mountain, were seemingly all of the young unattached men and women at the Fair. No matter their stations in life, all were dressed in simple linen clothes, with only plain copper brooches to fasten their light woolen cloaks.

"Come with me, my lady, and we'll find all the bilberries you could ever desire," said Bryan. Taking Niamh's hand, he walked with her to the well-worn path that led up the side of the mountain.

Chapter Six

The wide grassy floor of the field rose up to meet the foot of the mountain, and there it gave way to a heavy cover of tall thick grass, thorny dark green gorse, shrub-sized rowan trees and the occasional gnarled oak. Growing wherever they could see the sun were thickets of bilberry and blackberry bushes. And under all of this cover, finding shelter along the ground, were tiny, sweet red woodland strawberries.

The high clouds thinned and parted as the four made their way up the many winding paths, which branched and divided among the grasses and beneath the low trees until they covered the whole of the mountain like a spider's web. In the deepening dusk, they could catch occasional glimpses of other young couples and hear their footsteps and laughter and whispered conversations.

"Oh, look! This way!" cried Aine, and caught hold of Leary's hand as she hurried over to a large stand of bilberries just around a bend in the overgrown path. In a moment both of them were out of sight.

Niamh started to walk after them, but Bryan stopped

her with a touch on her arm. "She will be quite all right on her own," he said. "Aine is a wise girl like her sister, is she not?"

"Wise enough, I suppose," Niamh answered with a wry smile, and shifted her empty basket on her arm.

"Then let her go and enjoy a little time alone with Leary." He nodded toward another branch of the path, and glanced upward. "This one leads to the very top of the mountain. The encampment is quite a sight from there. Would you walk up with me?"

"I will," she answered, and turned to follow him through the brush, mindful of the heavy gorse with its big sharp thorns, and reaching up to brush the delicate low-hanging leaves of the rowan trees off of her hair.

The path wended its way back and forth up the side of the mountain, and everywhere, it seemed to Niamh, young women were beginning to pair off with young men. Here and there she saw a girl who already wore a circlet in her hair made from the woven stems and leaves of bilberry bushes and rowan trees, a sign that she was now someone's Lughnasa Sister.

They reached the top of the peak just in time to look down on the grassy valley on the far side, where the oxen and riding horses grazed and rested until the Fair was over, and to see the sun slip below the horizon. For once, the sky above Eire was open and clear, and it darkened to its deepest blue even as Niamh and Bryan stood atop the mountain and watched the first stars begin to appear overhead and surround the low crescent moon.

"A pretty sight—but look here," Bryan said and placed his hands on her shoulders to turn her around.

"Oh, so it *is* a pretty sight . . . and never the same from year to year."

Niamh looked down on the vast encampment far below, which now lay in the deep night shadow of the mountain with the stars quickly appearing above it. The masses of tents and shelters and wagons were dotted with bright flickering torches from one end of the field to the other, and nearest the mountain was a large bright rectangle marked out in torches—King Conaire's camp. His was the largest and most prestigious, and had the choicest location, for the Fair was being held within his kingdom of Dun Solas.

Far on the other side, just as the world slipped all the way into night, Niamh could see the silhouettes of the horses and cattle and sheep in their three huge separate stone pens, each awaiting its own part of the Fair where it would be put up for trade. And just on the other side of the stone pens, almost hidden beneath the rowan trees, was the faint dark gleam of the river in the starlight.

Bryan came to stand close beside her, so close that his breath touched her ear. "It's almost like coming home, isn't it?"

Her lips parted and she felt unable to move, as though she were held fast between the beautiful sight at her feet and the warm and powerful presence of the man so close beside her. "Home," she whispered. "Home is where the people you love reside."

"And the people who love you in return," he whispered softly, so softly that he barely spoke, but then his lips brushed the bare skin of her neck. She jumped as if pricked with a needle and quickly moved a few steps away.

"I think I will look for some berries," she said, willing her swiftly beating heart to slow down, and deliberately taking long, slow, deep, regular breaths. "I promised Mother I would bring her a basketful, and I told Aine that no self-respecting girl would come down from the

57

mountain on this night without her basket being filled to the brim!"

Niamh crouched down and felt carefully through the bushes, holding her basket out beside them with one hand while combing through the leaves and stems with the other. She became aware that Bryan was searching through the bushes too, a little behind her, and smiled to herself. It was kind of him to help her.

"So, are you finding very many?" Bryan asked, after they had worked together for a time. "There are still a fair number of berries left over here. I suppose it's early, yet. It looks as though not many of the others have come up this high to take them."

She glanced back at him in the darkness and laughed. "You know as well as I that few folk really come up here for the berries. They come up here for . . . for . . ."

"For what, Lady Niamh?" He walked back over to her and dropped a handful of bilberries into her basket, then gently took the basket and set it down. He caught her hand and held it in both of his own. "I am sure you know that as well as I."

"Of course I do." She withdrew her hand. "They are here to pair off with each other, to find their Lughnasa Brothers and Sisters—their lovers for the duration of the Fair."

"So they are." He stepped forward and lightly ran his fingers down her hair. "Niamh . . . I find you to be the most beautiful of all the young women here, both in body and in spirit. And I believe you have enjoyed my company too, ever since our very strange meeting. It seems to me that we would be a perfect match to be each other's Lughnasa Brother and Sister. Will you accept me?"

Niamh took a step away from him, and then crouched

down to resume collecting berries. "I am sorry, Bryan. I hope I did not mislead you by walking up here with you, but you must understand this: I have never wanted to be a Lughnasa Sister."

He sat down on the ground beside her and handed her the basket. "Perhaps you have never had a man like me ask you before—a man of the Fianna, a man who might one day be a king."

Her hands stopped. She turned to look at him. "I have never wished to be *any* man's Lughnasa Sister, whether he is farmer or king." She turned away and went back to gathering berries.

"But . . . why not? Why not accept a man who is greatly attracted to you—when this night is so beautiful, when your skin is as soft and warm as the breeze and when your scent is sweeter than the tiny golden flowers of the gorse . . . Niamh, look at me, please."

Slowly she turned to face him, knowing she should not, and again he was there, right there in front of her, and his lips were again on hers even softer and warmer than before.

Niamh closed her eyes. It would have been so easy to melt into the warmth of his arms, to yield to the heat and life that flowed through her at Bryan's touch—but she made herself stand up. Quickly. Her basket fell over and half the berries rolled out onto the ground. She caught it up and walked several steps away, looking down on the hundreds of flickering torches below.

"I told you that I might be open to finding a man to be my husband—but not for only fourteen nights. Sleeping with him for only that time, only to see him ride away and forget me as soon as the Fair is over, holds no interest for me. I hope to find something far better."

"And I have no doubt you will," Bryan said, rising to his feet. "Though I do not want to think of another man possessing you! Surely, Niamh, for now—for the delightful time that is the Lughnasa Fair—we could make each other so happy, we could have—"

"There are many other young women on this mountain who would be more than happy to take you as a Lughnasa Brother. You should go now, and seek them out, while the night is still new."

"There is time," Bryan said. "I am in no hurry."

She shook her head, still gazing down at the encampment. "You will not talk me into it," she warned. "You should go now and find another, before they are all paired off—so that you do not end up with one of those women who takes more than one Lughnasa Brother and simply does not tell. Or would you not mind such an arrangement?"

Again he took the basket from her hands, but this time he reached down and began gathering up the spilled berries. "I think I would like to help you find more berries, and walk with you and enjoy your company and conversation on this beautiful night, if you will agree."

She turned to look at him. He stood tall and proud beneath the starry night sky, his shoulders so broad that it seemed he would have the strength of two men instead of just one. Any woman would have been drawn to him, to his power and his courtesy and his smooth skin and soft hair and warm, gentle lips . . . and yet he was content to stand waiting for her, holding her little wicker basket and offering to gather berries with her simply because she wished it.

Niamh smiled. "I will agree," she said, and together they set off on the long path that ran across the top of the mountain.

Rising up from the hillsides in the soft starry night

came the giggling and whispering of couples already beginning to pair off with one another, as well as the breaking and rustling of the brush as laughing girls ran through it and young men pursued them. But not everyone had found a partner yet, for just as Niamh and Bryan walked across the centermost part of the mountain they were met by three laughing, giggling, racing young women, each with a few berries in her basket but no circlets yet on their heads.

"Oh!" The first of them nearly collided with Bryan as she dashed up the side of the hill. The other two had to stop short, laughing all the while. "I'm sorry, I didn't see you! But now that I have—" She looked him up and down in the moonlight, hardly sparing a glance for Niamh. "I must say, I'm glad I nearly ran you down. Do I know your name?"

"My name is Bryan, of King Nessan's Fianna," he answered, with all courtesy. "And your name, my lady?"

"A man of the Fianna," she repeated, looking up into his eyes. "And a very handsome one at that. My name is . . . 'Bryan's Lughnasa Sister.'" All three girls burst out laughing. "Does that suit you?"

He shook his head. "I'm afraid it does not. I have my heart set on another." He spoke with great solemnity, but Niamh could hear the mischief in his voice. "Though, of course, your offer is politely appreciated."

"Oh. Well, my name is Urla. I am sorry you don't want to be my Lughnasa Brother. You are by far the best-looking man I've seen here tonight!" Flicking her eyes at Niamh, Urla stretched out her arms to the skies so that her linen sleeves fell back from her wrists and revealed smooth white hands with neatly colored fingernails. Clearly, Urla was not a woman required to work in the fields or in the houses. She was demonstrating to all that she was not low-born like Niamh.

Janeen O'Kerry

The girl sighed. "In that case—I don't suppose you would rather just pick a few berries with me? I see that you already have a basket." And with that, she turned around and quite deliberately bent over to examine a blackberry bush so that her shapely backside was right in front of Bryan.

Niamh felt her face redden as something like anger rose up in her—but then told herself that this was no doubt for the best. Perhaps now she would learn what sort of man Bryan truly was. But he only turned back to Niamh, took her by the hand and led her down the narrow path in the starlight, leaving the three other girls alone by the bushes as if he had not noticed them.

After a moment, he stopped and took her hands. "I am sorry we ran into them. Some women seem to know no other way to attract a man. I hope you were not . . ."

"Were not what, Bryan?"

"Were not thinking that I would turn away from you for a woman like that."

She smiled. "I am glad it happened," she said coolly. "If you are the sort whose head can be turned by a common bush-strumpet who intentionally and publicly presents her arse to a man just to get his attention, I would much rather learn about it now instead of later."

"Then I hope you have learned something about me, and that you will go on walking with me tonight."

"I have. And I will."

As they continued their walk, Niamh took a deep breath of the cool night air as a kind of sweet happiness enveloped her. She had made it plain to Bryan that she would not take him as a Lughnasa Brother, yet he had still turned down the most blatant invitation from a very willing partner. Never had she hoped to find any man like this!

The hill rose up before them to form the second peak,

cone-shaped and high, and after a steep climb up the encircling path they stood on its wide flat top. The surface was almost completely covered with a thick layer of ash and fire-blackened rocks, for this was the place where the Lughnasa bonfire would be lit seven nights from now.

"The folk of five kingdoms will be able to see this blaze," Niamh said. "On the years when work demanded that I could not go to the Fair, always I could see the bonfire far in the distance and know for certain what night it was—the night of Lugh's harvest, the night to honor his foster mother Tailte. The night of Lughnasa."

"I, too, have seen it from a distance," Bryan said. "But I much prefer to be up close." He brushed his cloak aside and took something from his belt—a circlet of bilberry stems and leaves, Niamh saw, neatly woven together. There were even a few tiny pale flowers from the wild strawberries fastened among the stems.

He took her hand and drew her against him once more. "I hope you will not be offended if I ask you again to be my Lughnasa Sister. I have used all of my skills as an artisan—and they are not many, I will admit—to make you this circlet of leaves and flowers. Will you not take it from me, Niamh?"

The words caught in her throat for an instant, but she made herself speak. "I am sorry, Bryan. I cannot . . . though I will thank you for a lovely evening and understand if you decide to go on alone to find the Lughnasa Sister you wish for, and give your pretty circlet to her."

But he only smiled and walked out onto the great ashen surface until he stood right at the center. He placed the circlet at his feet and then walked back to her. "If you do not want my circlet, I do not want anyone to have it at all. Come with me, now, and I'll help you fill that basket."

"You are certain?"

"I am certain. Come, now."

They started down the path that would lead them back across the wide face of the mountain, but just as Niamh left the ashen circle and set foot on the overgrown path, she came to a startled stop as a tall blond man stepped right in front of her. He was blue-eyed and smooth-skinned and quite handsome, though Niamh could feel his arrogance even as she looked up at him. He was in the company of a couple of laughing young women, one on each arm, and he seemed very familiar. She was quite certain she'd seen him before, though she could not immediately remember where.

"Ardal!" Bryan stopped close beside her, frowning up at the man. Niamh quickly remembered where she had seen him.

"You rode the race with Bryan, earlier today, out on the road," she said. "And you are the man who galloped your horse over the rocks and lamed him."

She thought he would be polite and apologetic, but instead he only laughed. "It is of no consequence, my lady. I will get another at the Horse Fair tomorrow. And then you will see me ride another race, one in which I defeat Bryan and his Luath yet again!"

"We shall see about that," Bryan murmured, his voice surprisingly low and ominous.

Ardal ignored him. "But the Horse Fair is not until tomorrow, and there is still plenty of time left for the pleasures of this night." He looked her up and down, his eyes flicking over her body. "Have you a Lughnasa Brother yet, beautiful lady? It would be a great pity if you did not." He spoke as if Bryan were not there.

But he *was* there, close beside her, and Niamh could feel him tense. "I have no Lughnasa Brother, for I do not wish to have one," she said coolly.

"No Lughnasa Brother? Ah, well, perhaps you will change your mind if I offer you this." And even as the girls on his arms frowned and scowled, Ardal held out a circlet to Niamh.

Most of the women would be offered simple circlets made from the wiry stems and soft green leaves of the bilberry bush, just as Bryan had made for her, but the circlet Ardal held also had slender ribbons of fine linen dyed in bright colors of red and gold woven all through it and hanging down the back in long streamers. Fastened between the stems of the wreath and carefully sewn to the streamers were handfuls of the bright white ox-eye daisies that grew everywhere in the green fields at this time of the year.

"Very pretty," she said, and could not resist reaching up to touch one of the long gold streamers with its delicate white flowers.

Bryan went rigid beside her. She cold feel him glaring at Ardal. Niamh drew her hand back, and glanced up at Bryan before smiling politely at Ardal. "I thank you . . . but you should save your lovely circlet for someone who wants to take a Lughnasa Brother. Enjoy your evening, Ardal, with your two ladies. I will enjoy mine with Bryan. Good night to you, now."

For a long moment, Ardal simply stood and studied her, with a kind of cold smile on his handsome face. Then, finally, he stepped aside and let her pass by, moving the two women with him and all but pushing them into the bushes to get them out of the way. "Good night to *you*, my lady. Though it is a pity you will go back with nothing in your basket save a few berries."

Bryan started to turn around, fists clenched, but Niamh caught his rock-hard arm and—to her relief—he stopped. They could hear the laughter of Ardal and his two female companions as they wandered off along the top of the mountain.

Slowly Bryan began to relax. "I am so sorry. It is always the way with him—always the arrogance and crude expressions, all of it masked with a pretty veneer of condescending courtesy." Then he glanced at Niamh and his face grew serious. "But perhaps I should have left you to your own opinion. You did seem to like the very fancy circlet he made."

Niamh laughed. "I doubt he made it himself. It was a pretty thing, to be sure, but something pretty means little if there is nothing of worth beneath it. Did you really think I would go and be some man's Lughnasa Sister just because he offered me a pretty present?"

Bryan looked away. "He is handsome and strong. He thinks he should be our next king. All the women like him."

Niamh continued walking down the path. "Oh, so you consider me no different from 'all the women'?" She stopped, and turned to face him. "I told you that I wanted to be no man's Lughnasa Sister—and if I can resist being yours, I can certainly resist a trinket from a man like Ardal."

She watched his face, and in a moment a slow smile began to appear. "I am glad to know this, my lady Niamh," he said, and took her hand to walk with her down the path once more.

Chapter Seven

Slowly the stars wheeled overhead, only occasionally hidden by a few stray clouds, and slowly the crescent moon set beneath the western horizon. Niamh and Bryan spent their time together wandering back and forth on the maze of paths across the long front of the mountain. Every so often they would encounter other couples, either walking along the path or already enjoying each other's company in the shelter of the bushes.

Occasionally they came across little groups of women who were still unattached and who smiled up at Bryan with invitation in their eyes—but he behaved as if they were not there, and wandered the starlit paths with Niamh until her basket was overflowing with the berries. She covered the top with a handful of tiny white blossoms from the strawberry plants, and smiled up at Bryan. "I think I've got all the berries I can carry."

"If you want any more, I'll carry them for you," he said, and together they set off down the path again.

They had descended perhaps halfway down the mountain when they passed three girls sitting and giggling in a close circle beside a cover of thorny gorse, and Niamh realized that one of them was wearing the very fancy circlet Ardal had offered her earlier. The girl turned at hearing the footsteps on the path, and the man who had been stretched out on the ground in front of her quickly sat up. It was Ardal.

"Urla, come back here!" he said, and pulled the girl down beside him again. The other two girls laughed and reached out to straighten Urla's beribboned circlet. "Do you plan to turn and watch everyone who walks down the hillside?"

Niamh hurried on, covering her mouth to keep from giggling out loud. "What is it?" Bryan asked, rushing to catch up to her.

"Well," she said, a little breathless, "I guess we know now what sort of man is attracted to a girl who bends over in front of him while everyone watches!"

Bryan grinned. "Oh, 'Urla' was that girl? Well, I cannot think of a more deserving man for her than Ardal."

They continued on their way, still laughing, and then Niamh looked up to see Aine waving to her with Leary close by her side. Aine's basket was overflowing with berries and there was not a single leaf or bramble caught in her long dark hair—nor a circlet. "I see you've had a fine evening," Niamh said to her sister, holding out her own well-filled basket. "As have I."

Aine glanced up at Leary, and smiled shyly. "A beautiful evening," she answered. "And a full basket of berries, as you can see."

"I'm glad to see it. And our mother will be glad to have those berries. Please tell her that I will be along soon."

"I will tell her." Aine took Leary's hand, and the two of them started down the mountainside toward the great torchlit encampment.

Just then came the sound of laughter and giggling from

the path behind Bryan and Niamh. A whole group of young men and women walked by, some leaning on one another, some arm-in-arm, all of them with their long hair tangled with bits of grass and brambles.

"It seems *they*'ve had a fine evening, too," Bryan remarked.

Niamh glanced at him. "So they have. But will those young men even remember their young women's names a fortnight from now?"

Bryan turned to her. "I cannot say, but I do know that the Horse Fair begins after sunrise tomorrow. Leary and I will both be there. He is in need of a new mount, since Ardal seems to have borrowed his indefinitely, and I mean to help him choose. Will you walk there with me in the morning?"

After considering for a moment, Niamh nodded. "I meant to go anyway, for I enjoy seeing the horses. I will meet you there as soon as my tasks are done in the camp."

"Then perhaps I can walk with you back to your camp, after the Horse Fair is over."

"Perhaps."

His eyes gleamed. "Best be careful, Lady Niamh. If we spend such time together, all at the Fair will suspect that we are Lughnasa Brother and Sister after all."

She raised her chin. "How could that be? I wear no circlet in my hair, and no sticks and brambles either—and even more important, you have not yet answered my question."

"Your question?" He frowned, and then his eyes widened. "Ah, I remember. You set me the task of learning the three things that a woman wants from the man in her life."

"And have you any answers yet?"

He sighed. "I have none. If I had not already agreed to

accept your challenge, I would tell you it was impossible. But as I said, I never turn down a challenge. I promise you I will do the best I can."

"That is all I can ask of you, Bryan. Let's go now."

They continued on their way, following the downward paths across the wide face of the mountain until they were again below the high peak where the bonfire would burn. Soon they reached the grassy field at the mountain's foot. "This way," Niamh said, following the curve of the mountain away from the encampment. "There is something very special here."

"So there is," Bryan agreed, and walked with her into the quiet darkness.

Away from the noise and glare of the camp, in the deep western shadow of the mountain, a little spring-fed waterfall tumbled down the mountainside into a rock-lined pool. Here the people came to fetch their fresh water, leaving the river to the horses and cattle and sheep and dogs. There was a well-worn path leading from the camp to the spring, but right now all was quiet here save for the gentle splashing of the clear water falling into the pool.

"This is Lugh's Well," Niamh said, and Bryan nodded. She walked toward the spring with Bryan close beside her, and as her eyes adjusted to the darkness she could see that other visitors had already been here. Their offerings of fruit and flowers and grain covered the boulders surrounding both the high spring and the pool below.

Niamh gathered up the fresh white flowers from her basket and spread them out over the rocks, and then took up a handful of berries and placed them with the flowers. "This is a small gift to honor Lugh, the Sun King, the winner of every contest, the victor in every battle, the king of every skill. It is also meant to honor his foster mother, Tailte, who laid down her life to clear the forests of Eire so that we might plant our grain."

From his belt, Bryan took a little bunch of white daisies and placed them atop the berries and flowers Niamh had left. "For Lugh, the winner of every contest, and for his beloved foster mother, Tailte."

The darkness and quiet were a welcome respite from the noise and glare of the encampment. Bryan turned to Niamh, and she thought he meant to kiss her once again, but then he tensed, and looked over his shoulder, and turned around so that she was shielded behind him.

"What is it?" she asked, trying to peer around his broad shoulders.

"Shh! Listen. Do you hear it?"

She stayed close to Bryan and closed her eyes, allowing the sounds of the night to settle over her. She heard distant footsteps and happy shouting and even the faint snapping of torches from the camp, and the slight breeze in the rowan trees and oaks up above them on the mountain—and then, from the deep shadows of the trees and bushes in the darkness at the foot of the mountain, the sound of footsteps.

Not footsteps. Hoofbeats, coming steadily toward them through the trees behind the Well. And then a low snorting laugh, neither human nor animal but something in between.

"It's come back," whispered Niamh.

Bryan pushed her back against the rocks and pulled his iron dagger from the sheath at his belt. "Wait here. If it's that—that *puca* creature again, I cannot allow it near the camp."

"Wait," Niamh said. "If you mean to attack, it will only be provoked. Wait—please!"

71

But Bryan only went striding off toward the shadows, knife in hand, and just as he reached the trees, there was a great crashing and breaking of brush and then pounding hoofbeats as some great beast galloped away.

Silence descended over them once more. "Did I frighten it away?"

"It's playing with you. It will be back."

And even as they stood together in the darkness, the faint sound of deep, rasping laughter drifted toward them on the wind.

"Trot her out for me, will you?"

Bryan stood in the midst of the enormous stone-and-gorse walls of the horse pen, surrounded by geldings and mares and foals. Those available for trade wore rope halters and had their owners standing at their heads, with the many prospective buyers looking them over and making lively bargains. He'd found a small, kind mare of a dark golden-brown color, with a golden mane and tail and just a few white hairs on her forehead, and he watched her now as her owner led her at a trot across the crowded, muddy surface of the pen and then brought her back again.

Bryan glanced up, looking along the walls of the pen for Leary—and for Niamh—but saw neither one. He nodded at the mare's owner. "Thank you. I'll consider her," he said, and turned to walk back to the sliding wooden bars at the opening of the pen.

"Did you not like the mare?"

Bryan looked up quickly as he stepped through the bars, nearly hitting his head on the top one. Niamh stood waiting beside the wall, her long gold hair dark as honey and moving gently on the breeze. "I did like her," he said, rubbing the back of his head. "I just did not want her owner to know. That's no way to get a good trade!"

"She is a pretty little thing," Niamh said. "She might make a fine match for your stallion, come the spring."

"I thought the same. I may look at her later, if she is still up for trade. But right now I'm looking for Leary. Have you seen him, by chance?"

"Right there, she answered, nodding toward the far end of the paddock. "With Ardal."

"Ardal?" Frowning, Bryan started to go around the stone walls, but then quickly stopped. "Will you walk with me, Niamh? I would enjoy your company."

She gazed at him for a time, her hazel eyes bright, and for a moment he thought she would just laugh at him. But instead she picked up the hems of her tan linen skirts and walked with him toward the path that led between the horse pens and the river. "Where is Aine this morning?" Bryan asked.

Niamh smiled. "At home, with our mother. She will be with us this afternoon, at the First Harvest."

"I am glad you could be here this morning. I remember you saying that you always enjoyed the Horse Fair. Do you have horses at your home? I know that not all farm families do."

"You're right. They do not. I have always liked horses very much, though we have never had more than an aged pony or two around our farm. Our time must go to the crops and the cattle; there is little wealth left over to trade for fine horses."

They walked alongside the river, just behind the horse pen, beneath the cool shade of the oaks that grew beside it. "A queen might have as many fine horses as she wishes," Bryan ventured. "A queen might have the very finest of all things."

Niamh laughed, a sound as pretty as any music he had ever heard. "But I do have the finest of all the things that

73

I need, for I have always had a warm bed and well-made clothes and good food, as well as a family who loves me and whom I love in return. What things could be finer?" Niamh shook her head, setting her long loose hair to rippling. "I am no queen, and I am quite sure I never will be."

"You would be, if you married a king."

But she only laughed again. "I do not know any kings—certainly none who would look to me, a farm woman instead of a high-born lady, as a bride. Look! There is Leary."

"And Ardal," Bryan said under his breath.

They left the shelter of the oaks and walked up to the far wall of the horse pen. "Leary," Bryan said, "why did you not wait for me? I told you I would help you find another horse."

"No need, Bryan," Ardal said. "I told him I would show him the right way to choose another animal." He stepped back from the wall. "Ah, good day to you, lovely and golden Niamh. Leary will get a much better horse if I help him, would you not agree?"

Niamh studied the tall warrior a moment, and then she nodded toward a long-legged bay who stood alone in a corner, his rope held by one of the young serving-men of the Fianna. "Perhaps that one?"

Ardal glanced up. "I think not, beautiful lady. That is Anfa, who is now lame and of no further use to me. Come with me, Leary, and I'll show you how to make your choice. We'll find a riding horse for you and a racing horse for me." He climbed up onto the wide stone wall and stepped down on the gorse branches piled atop it, finally leaping down in into the pen below.

Leary glanced quickly at Bryan. "I have to go—he is the senior man of the Fianna. I cannot refuse—"

"Go," Bryan said. "But don't let him do your thinking for you." Quickly Leary climbed up over the wall and the gorse and jumped down into the pen beside Ardal.

Bryan looked back to Anfa, standing with his head down facing the damp bare corner of the paddock, his swollen front leg trembling a bit from time to time. His handler stood leaning back against the cold stone wall and did not seem to care whether anyone showed interest in his charge or not.

"At least he seems to have found a companion," Niamh said. "On the far side, there."

Bryan followed her gaze, and saw Anfa slowly swing his head around to touch noses with a pony who had come up next to the wall to stand alongside him. All he could see of the pony was the lower half of its dark head, and the old flax rope that trailed in the mud from its halter.

"He seems to have gotten away from his owner," Niamh said with a little laugh. "Perhaps he does not want to be sold."

Bryan shrugged. "Someone will come for him sooner or later. It's Leary I'm concerned about. Look at him following Ardal like a baby duck following its mother, searching for yet another racehorse for his master as well as some sort of mount for himself." He snorted. "Ardal ruins a horse at will and thinks no more of replacing it than he would a broken bronze pot."

"Or a pair of worn-out linen breeches."

He shook his head. "I hate to see Leary follow him about and learn his ways, but my brother is newly joined to the Fianna and could not refuse such a demand."

"Perhaps he will learn what not to do."

"So we can hope. Oh, but look—look at who is considering Anfa—" He set his jaw.

Niamh looked at the two men running their hands down Anfa's front legs. The men were rather seedy-looking in their worn clothes and greasy hair, but the young handler spoke to them eagerly and no doubt was extolling Anfa's great speed. "Who are they?"

"I don't know their names, but they—and their type—are to be found at every Horse Fair. They love to trade for fast horses as cheaply as possible and then run them until they drop, making all their profit on wagers. Anfa is exactly the sort of horse they will be looking for."

"But Anfa is lame! He cannot run for them."

Bryan shrugged. "There are ways of killing his pain long enough to let him run."

Niamh shook her head. "Anfa deserves far better."

"He does—but you and I together would not have enough to trade for him, for Ardal would never let me have him." He sighed as he watched one of the two greedy men pick up a handful of cold damp earth and slap it on Anfa's back, indicating that the horse had been traded away. "Perhaps Leary will do better."

But Ardal seemed to have no true care for finding a horse for Leary. He was looking at the best of the racing animals for himself and seemed to be quite taken with a long-legged grey. With Leary at his elbow, he set to bargaining with the owner, and Bryan shook his head. "I can see that this will take some time. I think I will look at the mare again, and if she meets with your approval perhaps I will take her. Would you come and look at her with me?"

"I will. She does appear to be a beautiful little creature."

"Five years old, by her teeth, and broken to ride. And quite pretty, as you say."

Bryan climbed up the wall and stood on top of the gorse, carefully placing his booted feet between the big sharp thorns, and reached down to help Niamh, but she climbed nimbly up the stones, stepped across the gorse, and flew down to the ground before he could straighten up again.

"Are you coming?" she called.

He grinned at her and leapt down to the ground, and together they started across the enormous crowded pen.

Stallions were kept in a stone pen of their own, and so this large pen held the geldings and the mares and the foals. The furry foals were now just old enough to leave their mother's sides, and several already had lengths of rope left tied around their necks and a clod of damp earth rubbed onto their backs to show they had been traded for and were no longer available.

Bryan walked toward the bars that served as a gate, looking for the golden-brown mare, when Niamh touched his arm. "There is Anfa's friend again. Still trailing his rope."

"So it is," Bryan said, just as the black pony's rump disappeared beside another small group of horses being held by rope halters—the same group that held the tall grey Ardal now bargained for. All of the horses nickered softly at the pony's approach and turned around in a effort to touch noses with it before being jerked back again by their handlers.

"I am not surprised to know that Ardal is interested in these horses. No doubt this is where he will find his next racer," Bryan said, nodding toward the group where the black pony stood. "Their horses are young and fast, but they do not last long. They use them until they are nearly worn out and then trade them before they are completely spent. It's exactly what Ardal is looking for—an animal to race and win at the Fair, and to discard as soon as it is over."

"They sound much like Ardal himself, in the way he treats his horses."

"So they are, my lady. So they are." He looked away from them, and then smiled. "Ah, there she is—and she is not yet taken." He walked up to the man who held the golden-brown mare, greeted him, and then looked the mare over once more, walking all the way around her. Then, after a brief discussion, Bryan took a pair of bone-handled iron daggers from his belt, each with fine gold wire wrapped around the base of its hilt. After a bit more discussion, the man accepted the pair of daggers and the trade was done.

The mare's former owner reached down, scooped up a handful of damp earth, and pressed it onto the mare's back. Then he tied a short length of rope around her neck, slipped off her halter and walked away, leaving the mare to stand with Bryan and Niamh.

The horse made no move to leave, turning instead and lipping at Bryan as if looking for a bit of bread or apple. "I'm sorry. I've brought nothing for you," he apologized, gently stroking her face and smiling as the mare closed her eyes in contentment.

"Beautiful mare," Niamh said, running her fingers through the fine gold mane. "What will you call her?"

"I'm not sure. She needs a special name, a mare as pretty as this. What would you suggest?"

Niamh stroked the smooth slick coat. "Perhaps . . . *criostal*, a beautiful shining thing of the earth."

"As all horse are. Criostal it is, then."

Even as the mare wandered away to rejoin her herd-mates, Bryan saw Ardal standing beside the long-legged grey and watching the owner rub a bit of earth onto the horse's back. "Now, Leary, this is a beast meant for racing at the Fair," Ardal said. "He'll serve to win the races, and then he can be traded as an ordinary mount once we've gotten our wins out of him. Do you see?"

"I see," Leary said, glancing over his shoulder as Bryan

and Niamh approached. "I thank you for showing me how to make a trade, Ardal. What mount would you suggest I trade for?"

"Oh, let's see—you don't need much, just something sturdy to carry you along the roads so you can serve the Fianna. Here, now, how about this one? This old fellow's been wandering loose all day, halter and all."

Ardal reached out and grabbed the black pony's trailing rope, pulling its head around to face them. "Come here, you. I think you're just what Leary—"

The pony braced its four legs and leaned back on the rope so hard that Ardal was nearly jerked off his feet. Then it threw up its head, arched its thick neck, and glared at him with red-yellow eyes that burned as fiercely as any fire.

"I will have my revenge," it whispered in its deep raspy voice. Then it spun around, pulled the rope from Ardal's hands and rejoined the herd of racing horses, who quickly surrounded it and nickered their anxious greetings.

Leary turned white as milk. His eyes bulged and his mouth moved, but he could make no sound come out. Even Ardal stood rooted to the spot, blinking his eyes and clearly unable to believe what he had just seen and heard.

Niamh and Bryan took hold of Leary's arms and led him across the pen to the barred gate in the stone wall, helping him as he staggered on badly shaking legs. "It's come back! It's come back for me! Did you see it? Didn't everyone see it? It's right here! I've got to get away!"

"Quiet, quiet!" said Bryan. "No one else saw it. It all happened too quickly. Calm down, now!"

"You are safe here, Leary," Niamh said gently. "And safe from that creature as long as you stay away from it."

"But *it* will not stay away from *me!* It found me last night, and it has found me again today!"

79

Bryan shook his head. "It found Ardal today."

But Leary forced himself to turn his head and look back toward the herd of racing horses. "Where is it now? Is it still with those horses? Where did it go?"

Bryan stepped away from him and began searching the pen, looking among the many groups of geldings and mares and foals both loose and held by halters, but there was no heavy-headed black pony with a trailing rope wandering among them, and certainly no fierce and fire-eyed *puca* to be seen anywhere.

It was gone.

Chapter Eight

Later that day, Niamh stood in the afternoon sun and threw her long dark-gold hair over her shoulder, letting the wind blow it back from her face. Holding her small bronze sickle in her right hand, she grasped a few stalks of wheat with the other and cut them neatly and cleanly near the ground.

Beside her, Aine did the same, and so did the eleven other young women in bare feet, plain linen gowns and unbound hair. All were from herding and farming families, as Niamh and Aine were. They worked within a large circle made of a solid stone wall, built so that this grain might grow undisturbed by the animals and be ready for the ritual harvest at the Lughnasa Fair.

Within the stone wall stood King Conaire and his dark-haired Queen Treise, along with his retinue of druids and warriors. The king and queen watched in silence as the young women worked. When all thirteen of them—one for every full moon of the year—stood with long stalks of grain cradled in their arms, King Conaire stepped forward and spoke to them.

"You have done your work well, you who are daughters of gold—the other gold of the earth, this grain that has nurtured you all of your lives. Now it is for you to prepare and share with your people. Go, and take it to them."

The young women bowed to the king and queen and walked in single file out through the narrow opening in the circular stone wall. The open field outside, on the other side of the mountain from the camp, was the place where the oxen and work ponies usually grazed while their owners enjoyed the Fair—but today the animals stayed well away on the far side of the pasture, for crowds of people waited outside the stone walls. They watched quietly as the women lined up behind a row of wide, flat boulders set into the earth.

The thirteen women spread the bundles of newly cut wheat on the surface of the stones and picked up the willow-wood flails from the grass. As one, they each raised a flail—two thick lengths of wood hinged together with a leather thong—high overhead, and listened to Niamh's words.

"Earth and stone, help us to free this harvest!" And together they brought down the flails on the heads of the wheat, again and again, until the tough husks finally shattered and surrendered their grains. Niamh made a neat bundle of a few bits of the straw and tucked it into her belt.

Thirteen men stepped forward and handed each woman a wooden rake, and Niamh spoke again. "Winds, take the chaff for yourselves, and leave the gold for us!" With that they took up the rakes and used them to pitch the straw up into the air, so that the wind would carry away the light straw and chaff and let the rich heavy grain fall back to the stones.

At this the people surged forward, laughing and laughing, raising their arms and jumping up to catch the straw and rubbing the chaff out of their eyes as it blew over them. When all the straw was gone, the men handed smooth wooden shovels to the women and watched as they were used to toss the heaps of grain into the air, giving the last bits of chaff to the wind. Finally, lengths of coarsely woven linen were brought out, and the wheat grains were sifted to remove any pebbles that might remain.

On the other side of the boulders was a wide shallow firepit, scraped out of the grassy, muddy earth and lined with stones. Coming forward now was another group of thirteen young men, each with an armload of split wood—the smooth and beautiful wood of the rowan tree with its reddish heart clearly showing. Among the men was Bryan, who managed to catch Niamh's eye, and Ardal, who walked at the head of the procession.

Ardal placed his firewood into the stone-lined pit. The other men stacked theirs close by and then surrounded it in a circle. Ardal accepted handfuls of newly cut straw from one of the women, and after sprinkling the dry straw over the wood he turned and took the foremost place at the head of the circle—but it was Bryan who spoke the words to the thirteen women.

"We have brought you wood for your fire, wood from the rowan trees," Bryan said. "These are the trees upon which Lugh's beloved foster mother, Tailte, used the last of her strength in trying to clear them from this very plain. She did this so that we might plant our grain and survive, and in so doing she laid down her life for her people. Even now, the heartwood of the rowan still holds the heart's blood of Tailte."

Ardal took flints and struck sparks onto the wood and straw, and all fell silent while patiently waiting for the first flame to take hold.

In the silence another group of thirteen women came forward, all of them mothers and grandmothers. They faced Niamh and the other maidens across the row of flat boulders and handed a saddle-quern to each—a rectangle of granite hollowed out so that it curved upward at each end, with a thick stone cylinder resting inside. The maidens accepted them, set them down on the stones, and began placing handfuls of the newly harvested and winnowed grain on the querns. Then they set to the task of scraping the stone cylinders across, slowly crushing and grinding the wheat into flour.

As the young women worked, the flames in the pit began to snap and climb, and the crowd became noisy and merry once more. Someone began beating a drum and another played a wooden flute in time to the scraping and grinding, and soon the folk were clapping their hands along with the ancient rhythm of the grain.

The older women brought large wooden trays to the maidens, and soon the trays were heaped high with newly ground flour. Last of all, the mothers and grandmothers handed new waterskins to the maidens.

Niamh accepted the first of the waterskins and then stood straight and faced the crowd once more. The music stopped and the clapping ceased as the people waited politely for her words.

"Water from Lugh's Well, quench the thirst of this grain that we have ground, and allow us to knead it into dough." Each of the young women poured a little water onto her heap of flour and began to work it into a soft and pliable mass. The older women brought around a stone dish of salt and a wooden bowl of butter, throwing a little of each onto each mass of dough as they walked behind the maidens.

When there were thirteen satisfactory mounds of dough on the wooden trays, the women formed them into smooth flat circles and then carried them in a single line to the firepit. By this time, the first pieces of wood had burned down to hot glowing coals and large rounded stones had been placed among them. The women took their places in a circle around the firepit.

"Fire, give our grain the final element it needs to become our bread," Niamh said, and each of them reached forward to place the flattened dough on one of the rocks to bake.

Niamh took up some of the straw she had saved and began to twist and fold it into the rough shape of a person, fashioning body and legs and arms and head. She set it aside on the earth and continued working with the rest of the straw until she had three shapes. From a little leather bag at her belt she took small rags of linen, and began arranging them on the straw figures so that they seemed to be dressed in gowns. When she was done, Niamh stood with her hands together and held out the figures she had made.

"These are the wheat spirits, made from the straw that supported and nurtured our grain right up through this day. We give these to the ones closest to us, for whom we wish long life and everlasting abundance."

She walked to King Conaire and Queen Treise and gave them the first of the wheat spirits, bowing as she did so. "Plant this in the spring with the new crop of grain."

She gave the second to her parents, who stood near the front of the crowd, and said, "Continue the circle of life and renewal."

And for the third one, she approached the young men

who had brought the firewood. Ardal stood taller and took a step forward at her approach, but she moved past him as though he were not there and walked straight to Bryan.

"Take this, and protect it all winter long," she said to him. Bryan's eyes shone as he took the wheat-spirit from her, and covered her hands with his own. But as Niamh returned to the circle with the other young women, she caught a glimpse of Ardal and the cold, angry look he gave to his cousin.

At last the bread was ready, and the young women quickly took it off the hot rocks and dropped it onto the wooden trays. They carried these to the king and stood behind him in a half-circle, and everyone was silent as he spoke.

"For another year, the harvest is complete. The bread is ready to share." King Conaire turned to Niamh, took the fresh hot bread from her tray, pulled it apart and held the pieces high overhead.

"Here you see the living essence of the gods themselves, their gift to us from the oldest of times when they taught us to prepare proper food as all people should do. No longer would men and women eat raw food from the forest like animals! From that time forward, we would combine earth and wind and water and fire to make good bread to enjoy together in our homes.

"The life of this grain has been sacrificed to sustain us, but it will live again next year after sleeping within the earth. Now is the time for all of us to share in this, a sacrificed life, a sacrificed god, and both to respect the knowledge that made it possible and to accept it as the gift it truly is. Share it among you!"

The king tossed the two halves of bread into the crowd, and the people quickly tore off small bits and passed what was left to others with everyone taking a tiny piece. Niamh, Aine and the other maidens each took a small bite of the remaining loaves and helped to pass them out to the crowd, where they quickly disappeared.

When everyone had had a taste of the newly harvested and ritually prepared grain, the king spoke one last time. "You have done well to remember the things the gods have taught you, and to accept and respect this sacrifice of the grain. Go, now, and enjoy yourselves among your families and friends, and take with you the measures of grain that are yours according to the law." He turned to his men, who stood near the base of the mountain where it curved around to the camp. "Bring it out! Bring it out now!"

From around the end of the mountain came the slow and rattling ox-drawn wooden wagons, each one heaped high with one sort of grain—wheat to make bread, barley to make beer, and oats to feed to the horses. The people crowded around them and held out their big leather bags and heavy woolen sacks, while the druids, well-schooled in the law and aware of exactly how much grain each man, woman and child was to be allotted under the law, supervised the distribution with eyes that missed nothing.

As the people jammed together at the wagons, the king and queen stepped back to accept refreshment from their servants, and the women of the ritual set down their tools and walked away to rejoin their families. Bryan took the opportunity to go to Niamh—but found Ardal blocking his way.

"Magnificent, isn't she?" he said, following Niamh with his eyes as she and Aine walked past the stones toward their parents. Her long hair streamed like gold in the sun.

Bryan turned a dark glare on Ardal. "You care nothing

for her. You already have a Lughnasa Sister. You say this only to antagonize me."

"Antagonize you?" Ardal laughed. "Not at all. I would take that one in an instant. Low-born as she is, she's still the most beautiful woman here. What man would not want her?"

A cold anger began flooding through Bryan. "She is not for any man save the one she chooses."

Again the laughter. "Oh, I think she will choose me. I have much to offer, do I not? No woman yet has turned me down! You watch—she will be sitting beside me at the feast tonight. Perhaps her little sister will settle for you instead of your brother."

Bryan clenched his fists. "With the kind of women you choose, I'm not surprised that none have turned you down. They're the sort who will take any man if he but gives them a pretty present."

Bryan thought Ardal would grow angry at those words, but instead his cousin only smiled, a cold look in his eyes. "I hear Niamh is no one's Lughnasa Sister, not even yours. She's already turned *you* down. Why should you care if she chooses me?"

"A woman like her would never choose a man like you."

"Oh, but she very well might. Think about it, Bryan. She has chosen no other, and as I said, I have much to offer her. A girl from the *raths* and fields would certainly find a much more comfortable life with me than she would toiling away year after year to herd the sheep and bring in the grain."

"Haven't you noticed that she does not like you at all? That she will barely speak to you?"

"But that's all part of the game, Bryan. Don't you know that? No wonder you have no Lughnasa Sister. You simply do not know how to handle women. But I do. In fact," he said, looking after Niamh again, "I may well offer her a handfasting. The ritual is only seven nights away. I think I will go and speak to her about it now."

He turned to walk away, but Bryan grabbed his arm. "You will do no such thing."

Ardal bared his teeth in a grin, and threw off Bryan's hand. "Oh, but I think I will."

"Even if she were foolish enough to accept you—and she is not—do you think I would stand back and watch you plan to use and abuse her as though she were one of your horses? It is bad enough that you would even *think* to annoy her with your advances. I will not allow it!"

"Oh, but you *will* allow it. You would need far more than just your single sword to keep me away from her."

Bryan grabbed his cousin's arm again. "That will never happen so long as I stand upon the earth."

Ardal clenched his fists. "Then I will see that you do not stand upon it."

Bryan drew back his arm, thinking to strike Ardal and seeing nothing but his cousin's cold, mocking eyes, but someone behind him caught hold of his arm.

"What are you doing? What are you thinking?" Leary gasped, wrestling his furious brother away from his opponent. Bryan began to notice that many of the people in the crowd had gathered around, most with looks of horror and disbelief on their faces.

"This is the Lughnasa Fair, Bryan, not the Fianna camp with no one else in sight!" Leary forced his brother to turn and look at him. "You will be thrown out of the Fair for fighting, exiled from the kingdom if you draw blood. And if you should kill him—Bryan, has your reason left you completely?"

Slowly Bryan straightened and pushed himself away from his brother. "Not completely," he said, managing a smile as he straightened his tunic. "But you're right. Thank you for stepping in. You're braver than I thought, to interfere with the two best fighters in five kingdoms."

"It's true that Bryan and Ardal are the best fighters in at least five kingdoms—but if Leary had not stopped them, they might well have no kingdom at all by now."

Bryan and Leary looked up to see King Conaire glaring down at them "Have Ardal brought here, too," the king said to one of his men, and stared hard at Bryan while they waited.

In a moment, a much more somber Ardal came striding forward between two warriors to stand in front of his king.

"I want both of you here before me. Stand shoulder-to-shoulder, and not a word from either of you." The king looked around at the murmuring crowd. When total silence fell, he spoke once more. "The two of you are rivals to be the next tanist of Cahir Cullen, are you not?"

Bryan and Ardal glanced at each other. "We are," Bryan said, standing taller and raising his chin.

"You seem to forget that you are standing in my kingdom now, for this Fair is held within the boundaries of Dun Solas," King Conaire said. He glanced over at King Nessan, who stood a short distance away, but the ruler of Cahir Cullen only nodded at Conaire and kept silent.

Conaire turned back to Bryan and Ardal. "Perhaps you will tell me how you propose to be tanist of a kingdom when you are exiled from it, for breaking the King's Peace at his Lughnasa Fair? Or when you are dead, having been executed for killing another man during this gathering?"

The two cousins kept silent and looked down at the ground.

"This rivalry between you must end now," the king

said, "or it will go on and on until one of you is tanist or one of you is dead."

Sadly, he shook his head. "I will order that all the free men of your kingdom be present at my camp tonight, at the Feast of the First Harvest. They will make their choice then and there and not wait for the Equinox. Before the sun rises tomorrow, Cahir Cullen will have its tanist."

Chapter Nine

In the flickering light of torches set high on poles, the noble men and women of both Dun Solas and Cahir Cullen gathered at King Conaire's encampment at the foot of the mountain for the Feast of the First Harvest. The guests sat on cushions and sheepskins along rows of large wooden squares, which rested directly on the grass. These squares had been beautifully set with plates and goblets of either gold, bronze, or copper, depending on how close each guest sat to the place of the king, and were further decorated with little wreaths and circlets of bilberry stems and bright white daisies. And filling the air was the sweet music of bronze-stringed harps and cowhide drums.

The night was beautiful and clear, as clear as the day had been sunny, but for once Niamh had no thought for the beauty of the world around her. She could only sit quietly beside Aine at her own place on the outskirts of the feast and try not to stare at Bryan across the many rows of brightly dressed men and women.

He and Ardal sat on one side of King Conaire and

Queen Treise, while King Nessan and Queen Ernet sat on the other. The two kings and queens conversed pleasantly enough as the feast was served, but neither Bryan nor Ardal appeared to be saying a word to anyone. They looked only at their golden plates, and nowhere else.

Since Niamh and Aine had taken part in the ritual of the First Harvest, they, and the eleven other young women who had been there, were permitted to attend the feast. Because all of these women were from farming and cattle-herding families and were not of the nobility, they were given the farthest places from the king. But King Conaire and Queen Treise were well-known for their generosity, and so Niamh and Aine and the others were served the same newly baked bread with butter and honey and the same roasted mutton with boiled roots of clover and dandelion on their copper plates as the kings and nobles received on their dishes of gold. But Niamh would have traded all of her fine food for a wooden cup of water and a scrap of bread if it had meant she could sit beside the tense and apprehensive Bryan on this night.

At last the feast was over. Everyone sat back with cups of mead and blackberry wine. King Conaire got to his feet and looked left and right, and as he did the conversations quieted and the harps and drumming stopped.

He looked at Bryan and Ardal. "Come here and stand beside me," he commanded, and as they did he placed his hands on their shoulders and turned them to face the people.

"Free men of Cahir Cullen, you know why you are here. Your kingdom is in need of a tanist, a prince to be your next king when the time comes for him, and it is for you to decide who this man will be.

"Both choices are admirable ones. Both men are members of the Fianna. Both men carry the blood of King

Nessan's family. Both men are as skilled and as strong as any king could hope to be—but both are also so fiercely determined to be chosen that I fear they will bring about their own disaster if the choice must wait until the Equinox of Autumn, as was planned.

"They nearly came to blows this day—here at the Lughnasa gathering, here in my own kingdom. That is why I, in agreement with your king and his advisors, have decided that you will choose your next tanist here and now.

"So—free men of Cahir Cullen! Rise to your feet, and come and stand now with the man you would wish to serve as your next king."

Slowly, a few at a time, the men of Cahir Cullen got up from their places and walked toward Ardal and Bryan. Some moved to stand beside Ardal, and some with Bryan; the crowd beside each man grew larger and larger until at last, when the last man had gone to stand beside his choice, both groups appeared to be of equal size.

King Conaire nodded to three of his druids. Quickly they moved to count each group, and then huddled together to discuss the results.

Niamh sat straighter. She tried and failed to keep from biting her lip. But instead of informing King Conaire of their findings, all three druids went back to count once more.

Again they gathered to compare their findings. And again they returned to count the gathered men. Finally the three druids went to stand before King Conaire.

"I am sorry, my king," the first of them said, "but an equal number of men stands with each of these men. We counted three times. No choice can be made."

"So, the rivalry to be tanist ends in a tie," King Conaire said.

"Indeed it does," said the second druid.

"It is for the king to break the tie," added the third.

Conaire glanced up at them. "I am not their king. I have ordered this choosing only because these men brought their feud to my gathering in my kingdom. If anyone is to choose Ardal or Bryan and break the tie, it should be their own king. King Nessan, which man will you stand with?"

But Nessan only shook his head. "I do not want to make that decision. It is for the free men of Cahir Cullen to decide, not their king."

"But they have not been able to choose," said Conaire. He turned back to his druids. "And neither has King Nessan, and neither have I."

"Then who will break the tie?" the first druid called. "Cahir Cullen must have a tanist! They have waited too long already."

Conaire studied the two men who stood anxiously waiting for his words, and then looked up at the mountain rising up behind them—up at the point where the bonfire would burn—and then turned to gaze out over the vast, torchlit encampment stretching all the way to the river.

"We are gathered here for a festival to honor Lugh, who was the master of every skill and the victor of every contest. Perhaps we should let Lugh decide this question for us."

"Let Lugh decide?" the first druid asked, taking a step toward the king. "How do you mean to do that?"

Niamh did not think that Bryan and Ardal could look any more tense, but as they strained to listen for the monarch's next words their faces grew a little whiter and their fists clenched a little more tightly. Finally, after pacing a few slow steps across the grass while gazing down at his boots, Conaire stopped and looked at the two young men who stood surrounded by the druids and warriors and craftsmen of their kingdom.

"We are here, in part, to watch the games and contests that are held in Lugh's honor. These two men are here to win whatever of those contests they can. I propose that we name three of the most difficult of the individual contests—the javelin throw, the horse-swimming race, and the cross-country horse race—and see which of these men is the first to be victorious over the other in any two of them. That man, I believe, is the one favored by Lugh to be a king."

Conaire looked at King Nessan. "Is this agreeable to you?"

"It is, King Conaire."

He stared hard at Bryan and Ardal, and at the men surrounding them. "And to you?"

All of them nodded and murmured their agreement, though Niamh did not fail to catch the cold hard glare that Bryan and Ardal exchanged between them. Never had two men been more competitive or more determined—and never would anyone see a Lughnasa contest like this one.

The men of Cahir Cullen returned to their places at the wooden squares on the ground, but still the tension hung close and ominous over the gathering. Quickly King Conaire waved a couple of servants over to him, whispered something in their ears, and sent them off again. Then he went to take his own place beside Queen Treise, but before he could even settle himself, a couple of ox-drawn wagons came rattling up to the tables.

Instantly the mood of the entire gathering changed. A

great cheer went up, and all the men and not a few of the women grabbed their gold and bronze and copper cups and dashed over to the wagons.

"It's the beer! At last, the beer is brought out! Come on! It's the beer!"

"King Conaire is indeed a wise king, I should say. He knows how to make a decision, and then he knows how to put everyone back in a good mood so they'll forget what's ahead of them."

Niamh looked up to see Bryan standing over her. She took one last bite of buttered bread and quickly stood up, walking a short distance away from the gathering so that she stood in the shadows at the edge of the light cast by the torches.

Bryan followed her. "What is it?"

"Bryan," she said, turning to him, "so much has changed now! The games are no longer just games. I wonder if this is what the Lughnasa Fair was meant to be about."

"But it makes no difference, do you not see that?" There was amusement in his voice, and even in the shadows she could see the gleam in his eye. "I would have won all of my contests anyway. The king's decision makes no difference to me at all!"

"I'm sure Ardal would say the same," Niamh said, glancing over her shoulder.

"It matters not at all to me how he feels. I am going to win, and that is all there is to say about it. I'm glad that King Conaire has decided that the choice will be made through the games. Besides," he said, stepping toward her, "I thought you had no interest in who the next tanist of Cahir Cullen is. I thought you had no interest in the idea of ever being a queen."

"You are right," she said calmly. "My concern is for the tone of the games. They should be joyous and fun, with their purpose to bring the folk of five kingdoms together. Winning should be important only to those who will celebrate and brag about their victories over their beer that night. And for only that night. With so much at stake, how can the games ever be the same?"

He stroked her hair, then leaned down to kiss her on the forehead. "They will be no different, beautiful Niamh, for I will win them all whether the prize is a kingship or a good cup of beer."

His lips still moved over her forehead, as sweet and soft as the sun-warmed petals of a wildflower. Niamh closed her eyes and brought up her hands to rest on the hard muscles of his arms, arms so large and strong that her fingers would hardly fit halfway around them, and allowed herself to rest her head on his shoulder.

For a long moment, all was warm and quiet and perfect . . . and then Niamh's eyes flew open as she thought she heard heavy, pounding hoofbeats trotting through the brush on the mountain up above them.

Bryan braced against her and caught hold of both her arms. Their eyes met, and she knew they both instantly had the same thought:

Has it come back?

But the sound was gone almost as quickly as it had come.

"Perhaps it was just a work pony who found his way out of the field," Niamh said.

"Or just Ardal chasing after his Lughnasa Sister," Bryan said, and both of them laughed.

"Bryan—would that creature come so close to so large a gathering at night?"

"I don't know. It was very bold today, walking among the horses at the Fair and having no fear at all about showing itself when Ardal touched its rope."

"I only wish I could understand what it wants," Niamh

said. "It is very angry about something, and I keep hearing the single word it spoke: *revenge*. I do not believe it will stop troubling us until it gets what it wants."

"Well, so far it has not done any real harm—it just frightened Leary out of his wits, which may not have been such a bad thing." Bryan smiled down at her. "I'll bet he will never again get on a horse that does not belong to him—especially when he's been trying to drink with someone like Ardal."

"Perhaps not." Niamh returned his smile. "This creature may be one of those mysteries of nature that we will never fully understand, but I think I will watch for it nevertheless. I will always be curious about it."

"If anyone could understand such an animal, it would be you. But please—do not think of it now. It will come when it will. Come and sit down with me now, and enjoy the rest of the evening with me. We'll try the beer and sample the fresh bilberries with honey, and listen to old Seamus tell his stories of the past heroic winners of the Lughnasa games."

"And hope that perhaps you might one day be among them?"

He drew back in mock indignation. "'One day'? What do you mean, 'one day'? I won plenty of contests last year, and the year before that, and I—"

He stopped as a tremendous shouting rose up from within the main encampment. It seemed to come from the direction of the river, and rolled in a wave toward the mountain and King Conaire's feast.

"Stop that beast! Stop it!"

"Someone drive it off!"

"It's trying to get into the horse pens!"

For an instant Bryan and Niamh stared at each other,

and then together they turned and raced through the camp, dodging cowhide tents and agitated people and frightened children and excited dogs in a mad dash to the horse pens.

"Niamh, go back! I will see to this! Go back where it is safe!"

"I will not go back. If the *puca* has returned, I may be able to help. I am the only one here who does not fear it and who is not trying to kill it. I am the only one who is not a threat to it! I must try to speak to it again!"

In moments they had made their way to the thick stone walls of the pen with the stacks of heavy, thorny gorse piled on top. The only way for a horse to get out was if someone slid back the three heavy oak logs which barred the narrow opening in the wall—but as Niamh and Bryan skidded to a halt just outside the pen, they saw the *puca*, black as the night sky with eyes glowing a fierce yellow, pick up its left front foot and step down on the bottom bar. The heavy oak log snapped like a twig.

As the people watched in horrified silence, the creature put its right front foot on the second bar and snapped that one, too. And finally it threw its great heavy head up high, reared on its hind legs, and with stiffened forelegs smashed right through the top bar.

The crowd gasped. Everyone fell back a few steps. But as the *puca* lowered its head and charged into the horse pen, the men all surged forward again, shouting and cursing and brandishing their iron swords and javelins and wooden pitchforks and shovels.

Niamh started to go toward the pen, but found herself suddenly shoved back the way she had come. The angry crowd had been forced to turn back as all of the horses in the pen stampeded out through the narrow gate and swung hard toward the river.

The first horses out were the strongest and fastest, and they sped by in a heartbeat. Niamh caught a glimpse of Bryan's small dark-gold mare as she raced with the others, now wide-eyed and sweating as she galloped with the herd.

The horses disappeared into the night. Niamh could hear them splashing through the ford in the river as they made their escape. And then, once they were gone, there appeared at the gate all the horses that could not keep up with the others—those that were old and those that were lame. Some seven weary animals limped and staggered through the gap in the stone wall in a heartbreaking effort to keep up with the rest of the herd.

Among them was Anfa—and right behind Anfa was the snorting, glaring *puca*.

A few bold men rushed forward and tried to get hold of the stragglers, but they were driven off by the angry *puca* as it flattened its ears and bared its teeth and snapped at them, swinging its heavy head and roaring at the men in its rage.

The path around it cleared. The *puca* slowed to keep pace with Anfa, who struggled along at the rear of the little herd. All of the people kept well back, but as the limping horses disappeared into the darkness beneath the oak trees and the first ones took their tentative splashing steps into the ford, Niamh turned and hurried after them before Bryan could catch her, running to catch up to the horses in the shadows beside the river.

"*Puca!*" she whispered.

The creature swung its head around and turned its baleful yellow gaze on her.

102

"Speak to me," Niamh said, taking a step toward it even in the face of its malevolent glare. "Tell me why you are here. Tell me what you want. I promise you, I will try my best to help you."

The *puca* looked back toward Anfa, now splashing into the ford, and then toward Niamh again. "*The cave in the rowan grove. Across the river,*" it said in its harsh rasping voice—and then it raised its head as if to look behind Niamh.

She turned to see Bryan hurrying toward her, with the agitated crowd of people beginning to surge after him, but when she turned to the *puca* again, it was gone. The only sounds were those of Anfa's painful climb up the far side of the riverbank. Then the night was quiet once again—until the crowd at the encampment recommenced their shouting.

"Men of King Conaire!" one man cried. "And all others who wish to help us! We are going to get the horses. Meet us out on the road!"

To Niamh's relief, the people turned away from the river. Instead of trying to follow the *puca* and the runaway horses, they all scattered to see to their friends and families, or started toward the road to join the king's warriors in the search. Bryan came to stand before Niamh and placed his hands on her shoulders. "I will go with them. We must get the horses before they are lost within the deep forest."

But Niamh shook her head, and reached up to grip one of his hands. "The others will find them. I need your help. Please, Bryan—will you come with me?"

He glanced quickly at the stream of men beginning to leave the camp and head out toward the darkness of the road, but then he looked back to Niamh and smiled.

"They seem to have plenty of help. Since you ask, I will go with you."

She held tight to his hand. "First come back with me to my family's camp. There are a few things I need." Together they hurried back through the encampment, dodging angry, frightened people at nearly every step.

Chapter Ten

"It said, 'The cave in the rowan grove. Across the river.'" Niamh walked carefully through the heavy darkness of the forest, trying to follow the faint path by the intermittent light of the waxing half-moon while steadying the large, sloshing wooden bowl she carried. "Do you know of any cave in this part of the woods?"

"I do not. I have never been here, across the river. There was never any reason to go."

"I have never been here, either. But wait! Listen . . ."

They stood together, barely breathing as they strained to take in the sounds of the deep forest at night—and coming to them on the nearly imperceptible breeze were the faint sounds of horses moving about and occasionally giving a low nicker to one another.

"This way—but slowly," Bryan whispered. "We cannot know if this is the main herd or just the few cripples that went with the *puca*."

Niamh nodded and followed him closely through the darkness.

After a time they came to a clearing in the trees, an

open space where a little of the moonlight could shine down whenever the clouds allowed it. "These are rowan trees," Bryan said.

"And there . . ." Niamh nodded toward what looked like a great looming shadow at one side of the grove. "A mound. Is there a cave in it? It almost seems to have a faint light within, as though the full yellow moon were shining straight down upon it—but that is not possible tonight."

"I don't know about a cave, but there are horses here. They are standing still and silent, watching us approach. I can feel them. I can smell them. They are here."

"And so is the *puca*."

The clouds parted over them, and the faint yellow gleam Niamh thought she had seen became the glare of the *puca*'s eyes. It seemed to climb up out of the ground, out of a hole in the mound, and Niamh saw that the "cave" was really a large depression carved out of both the side of the mound and the earth below it—an excellent place for any creature to hide.

The *puca* halted just outside the cave and stood watching them. The seven lame horses that had escaped with it continued to watch from near the mound and under the rowan trees. Anfa took a few halting steps toward Bryan, who reached out and gently scratched the beast's neck. But Niamh continued to approach the *puca* and held out her wooden bowl.

"We have brought you a small gift," she said. "We have come here because we want to understand you. We have no wish to harm you."

It took a step toward her.

"Here. We have brought you this. We hope you will accept it."

106

The creature lowered its head, and the yellow light in its eyes began to dim somewhat. For a moment it looked almost like a normal horse. Niamh set the bowl down on the ground and waited quietly. After a moment, the *puca* walked forward the last few steps and put down its head to eat from the bowl.

Though her heart beat very fast, Niamh slowly reached out with one hand and touched the creature's neck. The rough black hair felt cool and damp, and she gently stroked the thick neck and coarse, heavy mane.

Slowly the *puca* raised its head, its muzzle dripping with thick milk and honey, and swung around to look at her.

Niamh took her hand away from its neck. "Please," she said to the beast. "You can see that we have come as friends. Tell us what it is you want. Tell us why you are angry. We will do all we can to help you."

She hoped it would speak to her again, and she waited for the chilling sound of its deep rasping voice—but instead it reached out with its nose and gently lipped her hand, leaving her fingers damp with milk.

Niamh could not help but smile. "You do understand," she whispered, as relief flooded over her. If the creature was growing to trust her, and would accept her friendship, she could find out what it wanted and put a stop to its destructive rampaging.

The *puca* lowered its head again. Niamh turned and peered into the darkness beneath the rowan trees, searching for Bryan. "Did you see? Did you see?" she said softly to his shadowed form. "Surely this is all it wanted. A bit of kindness works wonders with any animal." She reached out to touch it again. "Surely this will—"

The *puca* was gone, leaving only the empty wooden bowl at Niamh's feet. And as Bryan came to stand beside her, they both heard all around them the sound of a great powerful beast tearing through the forest, snorting wildly and voicing a terrible rasping cry that sounded all too much like laughter.

It was very late that night before she and Bryan finally returned to the camp. Their journey was a long one, with seven lame and aged horses to bring in; and when they arrived home they found that all of the other horses had already returned, trotting quickly for home as if something were herding them.

No one asked any questions as to what might have driven them back.

Once the animals were safely in their large pen, with newly cut logs placed across the space in the stone wall and several guards standing watch, Niamh walked with Bryan to her family's tent and went straight to her bed of clean thick sheepskins on a pile of new wheat straw.

After what seemed like the longest night Niamh could remember, dawn finally lightened the skies to the east and the camp began to come alive once more. Everyone got through their morning routines of dressing and eating and washing up as quickly as possible and then began moving to the far side of the playing field downstream of the river. They gathered as near to the banks as they could and laid claim to their favorite spots, for this morning would see the first of the three contests that would determine the next prince of Cahir Cullen: the horse-swimming race.

From the moment she arrived at the river, the tension began to build for Niamh. As she had said to Bryan, the Lughnasa games would no longer be the same.

Now she stood at the edge of the crowd on the highest

side of the field, as near to the river as she could get. The crowd had separated itself into two parts, leaving a wide strip of the grassy field open straight down to the widest part of the river. And on the far side of the water was another open space with a single large rowan tree at the center.

Niamh took a deep breath and pulled her dark woolen cloak close around her. Always before she had enjoyed the competitions, but so much had changed now! Not only was there the matter of Bryan and Ardal having these contests to decide which of them would be the next tanist of Cahir Cullen—but now she began to remember the breakneck pace of the horse-swimming race, the terrible chances the riders took, the aggressive tactics which always came into play.

Before this, it had all been rowdy good fun. But as the sun began to burn the mist away, the crowd caught sight of a red stallion appearing at the far end of the field and sent up a great roar, and a chill came over Niamh even in the soft summer morning.

King Conaire entered the open pathway on his small but powerful red stallion, flanked by two of his men. And following in single file were ten bare-chested, barefooted men riding their fastest, strongest horses bareback with only flax-rope halters on the animal's heads and nothing but knee-length woolen trews on their own bodies.

The crowd shouted at the riders and jostled each other to get a good look at each of them, for the wagers were flying fast and everyone wanted to be sure that their horse and rider looked like the best choice on this particular morning.

Niamh stepped up on a rock and stretched as far as she could to see over the heads of the surging, shouting crowd. From her precarious perch she could see eight jogging, snorting horses shaking their heads and lunging against the scant control of the rope halters, and being pulled back into line by their very forceful and determined riders. The ninth rider was Ardal, sitting tall and smug on his new long-legged grey while the animal nervously threw its head, and there, finally, the very last in line, was Bryan on the dark-gold Luath.

Niamh's heart, already pounding, beat a little faster at the sight of him. Bryan sat relaxed and ready on Luath's bare back, gazing out over the crowd as calmly as though he were just riding down to the river to let his mount drink.

As King Conaire and the first of the riders reached the river, they turned around and continued their slow parade before the crowd, going back the way they had come. As Luath arched his neck and slowly jogged along, Bryan looked from side to side and his eyes flicked over the crowd—and when at last he passed Niamh standing perched upon her rock, he smiled and then nodded politely to her. After that, he looked neither right nor left but just continued on behind Ardal as they rode back to the far end of the field.

Finally all of the riders crowded their horses together so they could line up side-by-side across the field, and held their eager mounts as still as they could while King Conaire swung his own horse around to face them.

"Riders!" he cried. "You have gathered this morning for the horse-swimming race. It is not enough for a warrior's mount to be swift over land; Eire is filled with rivers and lakes, and your horse must bear you through water just as easily as he carries you over roads and fields."

He jogged his red stallion to the sidelines and the

crowd fell back to make room for him. The way was now clear in front of the line of horses. The snorting creatures began to dance and half-rear as their riders struggled to hold them.

"You know the course!" King Conaire said. "Across the river, once around the single rowan tree, and back across to the line where you now stand! So, now, if you are ready—"

The crowd held itself to a tense murmur. The horses snorted and tried their best to leap forward. Niamh held her breath.

"Go!"

Like a roll of thunder, ten horses charged down the field between the shouting, screaming crowd, tearing up bits of grass and earth as they went. There was barely enough room for ten horses abreast, and Niamh could see the animals slamming against one another as they galloped down the narrow course, with some of them inevitably forced to the rear of the pack.

Luath ran near the front. Niamh caught a glimpse of Bryan pulling one leg up to keep it from being crushed between his own mount and the horse beside him. How he stayed on, Niamh did not know, but stay on he did, and then the first of the riders sent their horses leaping down the banks and into the river with a tremendous splash. The wild clatter of horse hooves on rocks echoed beneath the trees overhanging the water.

The riders all shouted to their mounts and to each other as they leaped in, but soon the splashing eased and the ten men settled in for the deceptively long swim across the cold river.

The horses all but sank down out of sight as they swam. Only their heads were visible, their teeth bared as they curled their upper lips to keep the water out of their nostrils. Their riders clutched tightly to the animals' manes and let the reins hang loose, guiding them only enough to keep them swimming straight toward the bank nearest the lone rowan tree.

Niamh could see that speed over land did not necessarily mean speed through the water. Not all the riders knew the trick of holding on only to their horse's mane and floating above him as he swam; some of the men still clung with legs and arms while their mounts struggled to keep their own heads above water. Some of the first horses in were now slipping toward the rear, their nostrils red and flaring with the effort of trying to obey their shouting, clinging riders' demands for a faster pace.

Luath held his place near the front, with Bryan leaning far down over his mount's ears and holding tight to the golden mane so he would not drift back and be left behind. Ardal and his grey were just behind. Another horse, a black one, held the lead by some half a length as they approached the deep center of the river, his rider maintaining a position just past Luath's head.

But on the other side of the black horse, a man on a blaze-faced bay was determined that the black horse would not overtake him. As the crowd roared, he reached out for the black horse's rope halter even as the other rider tried desperately to punch his arm away. But the bay's rider succeeded in getting hold of the rope reins and all he had to do was throw his weight against them. The black horse was immediately pulled over on his side, his head disappearing beneath the water and his wildly kicking four legs thrashing above the surface.

The riders behind him were forced to go around the capsized black horse, who finally threw his head above the surface and made straight for the bank with a wild look in his eye, snorting frantically to get the water out of his head. His rider made a grab for his passing tail—and missed. The crowd roared with laughter as all the other horses swam right past him and the man had no choice but to swim toward the bank himself, trying to keep his head above the churning, muddy water.

Luath was now neck-and-neck with Ardal, but the blaze-faced bay was still close to his other side. Niamh saw the bay's rider steal a glance at Bryan, but Bryan only glared back at him and took a shorter wrap of his rope reins.

They were nearly to the bank.

In a moment the three riders popped above the surface as their horses' backs rose up beneath them. The animals began to clamber out of the water and onto the rocks and mud of the riverbank.

As soon as Luath was out, Bryan pulled him hard to the side so that his shoulder struck the still-struggling bay. The bay horse staggered, uninjured but knocked off balance, and as his rider clutched hard at the rope reins in an effort to stay on, the confused animal spun completely around. Luath shot past him, as did Ardal and his grey, and together the two sets of horse and rider galloped toward the lone rowan tree.

They were far ahead of the other horses. Luath and the grey seemed relieved to be out of the water that forced them to move so slowly, and tore over the grass as they headed toward the tree. Luath was on the inside as they made the tight turn around it, passing so close to the trunk that Bryan had to pull his leg up once again to keep from getting hit.

Both horses slipped on the tight and muddy turn around the tree. Niamh caught her breath. But the two horses stayed on their feet and raced back down to the river just as the last of the other riders struggled out of the water onto the bank.

Once again, Luath and the long-legged grey splashed into the river and started to swim, driven hard by their riders and encouraged by the idea of heading for home. Luath swam at a strong and steady pace, almost seeming to respond to the roar of the crowd, and his straining head started to pull ahead of Ardal's grey.

Niamh's fists tightened. "He'll win! He'll win!" she cried. Her voice was lost in the shouting of the crowd, but she did not care. "Bryan will win!"

Slowly but surely, Luath drew ahead. He and Ardal's grey were halfway across the river before the rest of the riders began forcing their mounts back into the water. But then Niamh froze as she saw Ardal reach out for Luath's halter rope.

Quickly, but with great caution, Bryan steered his mount away. But the young grey instinctively followed, bringing Ardal ever closer, and the man reached out again for Luath's rope.

Bryan struck hard at his arm. This forced Ardal to pull back, but only for an instant. Again Ardal reached out— he was nearly there—another swimming stride and he would have the rope . . .

Bryan grabbed hold of Ardal's wrist, locked his legs around Luath's body and yanked with all his strength. Niamh knew she would always remember the shocked look on Ardal's face as he fell into the river with a tremendous splash, his feet flying high over his head as he disappeared beneath the muddy brown water.

Bryan nearly lost his own balance. Quickly he dropped his horse's reins and released his legs so he would not pull Luath over. For a moment he floated far to the side of Luath, with only a handful of mane connecting him to the horse, but he swam hard with one arm and both feet and got himself back over Luath just as the stallion's hooves reached the sloping river bank.

Niamh cried out to him, even as everyone else in the crowd shouted to his or her favorite. "Ride, Bryan! Ride! You have the lead! Ride! Ride!"

And ride he did, taking a short wrap of the reins and galloping hard over the grass. Ardal's tall grey stayed right beside him, but it did not matter; his rider still floundered in the water and without him, the horse could not win. Luath's wet coat shone in the morning sun as he flew down the straightaway between the screaming crowds, and he crossed the finish line just ahead of the other beast. The other riders were still struggling to get out of the river.

The crowd broke ranks and swarmed across the field to surround Bryan and Luath. The open straightaway was gone, but no one cared. The race was over; the crowd had its winner and the losers would just go back to their camps to dry off unnoticed. Some of them, like Ardal and the rider of the black horse, would have the further humiliation of having to catch their mounts first.

Niamh struggled to get through the surging, shouting crowd. She could still see Bryan upon Luath, sitting tall and waving to his admirers, the horse remaining calm even with the masses of people pressing in on him. Finally Niamh pushed through to Bryan's side just as King Conaire made his way through the crowd on his red stallion.

"People of the five kingdoms!" he cried. "I give you Bryan of Cahir Cullen, the winner of the horse-swimming race—and the winner of the first of these contests between him and Ardal to become the next tanist of their kingdom!"

At the king's words, Bryan swung Luath around and the crowd quickly fell back, pushing Niamh back with them. As she struggled to keep him in sight, he reached down and accepted the shining gold goblet that was the winner's prize and held it up high overhead. He waved to the crowd as Luath snorted and danced, but kept scanning the faces as though looking for someone.

"Bryan!"

He saw her then, hearing her voice even over the noise of the crowd, and halted Luath so that she could hurry over to him.

How handsome he looked, sitting tall and wet and bare-chested on his beautiful young stallion in the morning light, surrounded by cheering throngs who would follow him anywhere and who were just as thrilled with his victory as he himself was.

He looked like a man who would someday be a king.

Chapter Eleven

That evening, as a swollen half-moon hid behind soft thick clouds, Bryan sat at the center of King Nessan's torchlit feast and took in all the praise and adulation that his own king and his own people could heap upon him— not to mention enjoying the choicest of the loin cuts of beef, the most perfect of the broadbeans boiled in salt and drippings, and the very best of the sweet honey wine.

He also looked to be enjoying the fact that Ardal was nowhere to be found. As one of the losers of the race—a loser who had also been publicly humiliated by the winner—Ardal would not be seen until it was time for the next contest. This night belonged solely to Bryan.

Niamh sat beside him on a fine leather cushion. This time she, too, sat at the king's row of boards instead of on the outskirts as before. Yet she was acutely aware of how her placement was not the only thing different at King Nessan's feast as compared to King Conaire's.

That one had been held at the base of the mountain on the edge of the encampment, so that one could still see the trees and sky, but here, they were right in the center of the vast main camp. The walls of the tents and shelters rose up all around them and shut out the sight of the trees, and any stars that might have been visible behind the drifting clouds were drowned out in the glare of hundreds of torches.

She knew that it would be no different within the high walls and torchlit grounds of any king's earth-and-stone fortress. Yet at this moment Niamh could almost wish for stone walls to hide her from the curious stares of King Nessan's warrior men and from the noble-born, well-dressed ladies who sat beside them. Each time she stole a glance at any of these people she found them staring at her in cool fascination or whispering to one another as they watched her, and she would quickly look away.

Pretending to gaze down at her cup of sweet honey wine, she could hear their soft comments—all politely kept low enough so that the king and queen would not hear, of course.

"Who is that woman sitting with Bryan? No one here knows her."

"She's not from Cahir Cullen, nor from Dun Solas."

"One of the other kingdoms, perhaps?"

"Of course not! Look at the way she is dressed. This is a low-born woman of the fields. She must be his Lughnasa Sister. No doubt Bryan will see the last of her as soon as this Fair is over!"

Niamh glanced up at Bryan, but he was looking away from her down the boards at some other man and woman who were regaling him yet again about his great victory. "And then after I pulled him off, his new horse ran away from him!" laughed Bryan, and all the others along the boards joined in the merriment.

Niamh smiled too, but touched his arm to get his at-

118

tention. "Will you walk with me?" she asked, and to her relief he nodded to the other guests and got to his feet.

As they left, she looked again at the other women who sat in the king's row. All she saw were bright colors and heavy gold. These women wore soft linen gowns and beautiful cloaks of wool made light as a cloud, some in glowing solid colors like purple and blue and some in bright intricate plaids of red and yellow and green and white. Their rectangular cloaks were held with shining brooches of gold, some with inlays of amber or jet or quartz, and all of the women wore more beautiful gold on their fingers and wrists and even hung delicate designs from their ears.

Niamh glanced down again at her own clothes. She had made every piece herself, from spinning the flax into yarn and weaving it into lengths of linen fabric, to cutting out her long bleached-white undergown and shorter cream-colored overgown, to stitching the pieces together. The wool of her dark brown cloak was made from sheep she had helped to raise and whose fleece she had clipped from their backs. She and Aine had spun the clean brown wool into good sturdy thread, woven it into cloth and cut and stitched the cloaks.

But as all women did who were born in and lived among the forests and farms and fields, she left the fabrics in their natural tones of tan and cream and dark brown and occasional bleached white, and wore only the simplest of jewelry—a copper brooch or armband, perhaps, and sometimes only a heavy wooden thorn to fasten a cloak at her shoulder.

"What is it?" Bryan asked, as they walked between the tents and out onto one of the main paths.

"I am not sure I should have been sitting at the king's

row at this feast," she said, stepping onto the grass beneath the row of trees that grew along the path.

"What are you saying?" he asked with a laugh. "There is no one I would rather have shared my victory feast with."

She stopped, and placed one hand on the rough grey-black bark of a rowan tree. "It's just that . . . I am not like the other women who were sitting there. I am not one of them; I do not look like them; I do not dress like them. I am sure I must be only an object of curiosity among them."

He stared at her with puzzlement and concern in his eyes. "You are no object of curiosity—unless it is the curiosity of shining ravens for the simple skylark who sings far more beautifully than they. And if you would like to wear a bright and beautiful cloak when next there is a feast or a gathering where you are my guest, Niamh, I would be most pleased to—"

She pushed away from the tree and took a few steps on the grass. "Bright colors are only for the high-born. Everyone knows that. Even the laws agree, for no one who is not of the noble class should pretend to be what they are not. I have never disagreed with this."

"Neither have I. But Niamh, no one is concerned with what you wear at such things."

She laughed a little, but her face was serious. "I have never had any interest in being anything but what I am and what I have always been proud to be—a woman who lives near the earth. I understand the earth, and how to coax life from it, in ways that the pampered women living closed away behind high stone walls will never know.

"I am very different from the women you have always known—and I would not change any of what I am. How

120

could I ever have faced the *puca* and understood what it was, if I had not trusted the knowledge gained from a lifetime spent side by side with the spirits of the earth and of the forest? No high-born warrior could have done so, any more than I could have killed such a beast with a sword." She shook her head. "Never would I want to give that up. Never would I want to be anything else."

"And I would never want you to be anything else. You are the most beautiful of women. You need no bright clothes or heavy ornaments, for they could never match your beauty anyway."

"It is true that I, Niamh, do not need them. But a queen would need them. And I know that it is impossibly bold of me to think of such things now, when we have done no more than share pleasant conversation and sit beside each other at a feast—but I do have reason to think of them."

"Pleasant conversation, indeed, and oh, I seem to recall that we also faced a monstrous supernatural beast together on more than one occasion," said Bryan with a casual wave of his hand, and both of them laughed. But Niamh soon turned away from him again.

"It is not where we are that worries me," she said. "It is where we are going. Or rather, where I am going."

"I do not understand."

She threw back her long hair and looked him straight in the eye. She could feel the blood pounding in her ears, but he waited quietly. "I cannot say how you will feel about me when this Lughnasa Fair is over. But I know that for myself, if we continue with our pleasant conversations and our sitting at boards together—and, even so, our facing of strange and frightening magical beasts together—for myself, I will find that I have grown to love you . . . and if someday you should ask me to be your wife, I may not be able to refuse without a great deal of suffering."

"There is no reason why you should suffer at all." Bryan placed his hands on her arms, even as she continued to stare up into his gentle brown eyes. "Why should we not continue to enjoy each other's company for as long as we can? I will do all I can to please you, and you have certainly made this Fair the best I can remember. Why worry about what might happen some distant time from now, when we can enjoy ourselves now for as long as the Fair goes on?"

"Bryan . . . do you want to leave the Fair knowing there is a woman who loves you, and whom you might love in return, who would find it very difficult to live the life of a warrior's wife and who could never be a queen?"

He cocked his head and tried to smile. "Are you so certain, Niamh? There are many fine things about being a queen. Even if you do not care for rich clothes or heavy gold or fancy furnishings, would you not like the chance to serve and care for the people of your kingdom the way you now care for your own animals and your own land?"

She laughed, but there was no happiness in it. "A queen is a woman who serves a king. I am under no illusions about that."

"Niamh . . . I have no doubt that should you become a queen, you will serve where you choose and help those who need it most. That is what you do now."

He tried to take her hand, but she only stepped away from him. "If I continue to see you, Bryan, I will come to love you, and I do not want to love a man with whom I could never have a future."

"Could you not learn to be the wife of a warrior? You

could still spend much of your time outside the walls of the fortress, and you could keep your love of the flocks and fields."

"And especially for those who live among them."

"Does not a queen serve all those who live in her kingdom?"

Niamh smiled. "Some are more worthy of a queen's time than others. Everyone knows this. And as I said, first and foremost a queen serves her king." She laughed a little. "You may as well take a sheep from the field, dress it in plaid linen and gold earrings, and proclaim it a noble lady. It would be easier to do that than make a queen out of a wild and ungroomed spirit like me."

"Were I only a warrior, we could find a way to live between the worlds."

"But you will be far more than only a warrior, Bryan."

"Are you so sure I will be king? Are you one of those fey women who knows the future, Niamh, as well as being strong and brave?"

She looked up at him, and shook her head. "If ever there was a man determined to be king—a *good* king—it is you. You are fearless. You are honest. You are a natural leader. You even have a care for the horse that carries you. These are all fine things in any man, and they are vital in a king. Truly, I hope you do become tanist, Bryan, for your kingdom will be the better for it."

"Do you not think I might have the wisdom to look for what is best in a queen?"

"You are not there yet. You may well change your mind when you see the looks on your people's faces at hearing that you want to take a woman of the fields and make her their queen."

He paused. She could almost see the thoughts turning

over in his mind. "The choice would be mine and mine alone. I do not know what the future holds, Niamh, but I can say that any man would be proud to have you as his wife—and that any king would be honored to have you as his queen."

She drew a deep breath, and then turned away and smiled. "I do not know why I have concerned myself with such thoughts," she said, shaking her head. "Have you yet brought me the answers to the question I posed to you?"

Bryan frowned. "Question? You did not—oh . . . so you did. You asked me what it is that a woman wants most from a man." He tried to laugh. "I would hope that what a woman wants is a bold man who can take victory for himself even under the most difficult of tests—and still do it with honor. I did drag Ardal from his horse, it is true, but only because he was doing his best to grab Luath and pull him under the water. The race was a fair one."

She nodded quickly. "It was. But I see that my question remains unanswered. Until you can . . ." She turned and started to walk away.

"Niamh." He caught her arm. "Is it that you truly want an answer, or do you merely use this as an excuse to walk away from me?"

"I . . . I don't . . ." She paused. "I cannot allow this to go further. I cannot wake up and find myself in love with a man with whom I could never share a life. That would not be fair to either one of us."

"Niamh—"

"The Lughnasa Fair is still young. There is still time for you to find a companion to enjoy for the rest of it. You are a good man, Bryan. I do not regret the time we spent together. I hope you do not regret it, either. But you do not, and I cannot . . ."

She turned and hurried away from the glare and noise

of the encampment, searching for peace and solace in the quiet of the forest.

She slept little in her family's tent that night, for even in her dreams she thought she heard Bryan's voice calling her name. She kept seeing him galloping out of the river on Luath with the water streaming off of both them in the sunlight. She would awaken suddenly, but then find herself in the darkness and quiet of the cowhide tent. She could only lie down again on the sheepskin-covered mound of straw and hope that sleep might come.

All the next day she stayed close to her family, grinding grain and baking bread and keeping the campsite clean. Twice she picked up the family's waterskins and took them to the well at the far end of the mountain, but saw no sign of Bryan even though she told herself she was not looking for him.

That night was much like the previous one, and the long day that stretched before her held little attraction. Aine and their parents left to go and watch the hurley games out on the field where the horses had raced, but Niamh felt no interest in joining the raucous, shouting crowds. She braided her long hair into a single plait that hung down her back, and then did her best to line up tasks to keep herself busy: spinning the basket of dark brown wool she had brought with her, shaking out the fleeces and hides that covered the floor of the tent, endlessly grinding grain.

The grinding was hot work in the still, heavy air of the late afternoon. Niamh wiped her brow with the back of her sleeve and tried to throw the loose strands of her braided hair back from her face. At last she sat back and caught up a scrap of linen to dry her hands, thinking that perhaps she should take the grinding stones outside and work where there might be a breeze. She stepped outside to try to catch a breath—and then she heard it.

It began as a hissing and a rustling high upon the mountain in the distant oaks, rowans and grasses. A strong wind had begun to move through them. Niamh could see the trees bowing low and folding their branches almost to the ground, then springing up as the wind drew in its breath, and then being forced down again. And all the while the hissing grew closer and louder, and the movement of the trees rippled down the mountainside like a wave moving through the water.

And rising up behind the mountain was a boiling, ominous cloud, bright white where it billowed at its height but a deep blue-grey underneath. Even as she watched, a streak of lightning flashed from the dark cloud and the deep rumble of thunder spread instantly through the camp.

Other people stopped and looked toward the mountain. And just as they did, the hissing in the trees on the hill raced toward them and grew to a roar just as the wind struck the encampment.

The wind was cool and fresh and carried the clean metallic smell of rain, but it was so strong that small things began blowing throughout the whole campground. A bouncing stampede of wooden buckets, small brass cauldrons, sheepskins, pieces of cloth and tunics left out to air went flying past the tent, surrounded by whirling torrents of loose straw, dry leaves, and stinging dirt lifted from the well-worn paths.

Niamh moved to grab hold of the sheepskins thrown down on the straw in front of her family's tent, then tried to gather as much of the rapidly disappearing straw as she could. Stuffing it all into the tent, she stood inside and took a moment to think.

Storms were commonplace during this time of year.

She'd ridden out more than a few in this safe shelter. This tent had always remained standing and was so thick and heavy that it hardly leaked at all; the shallow trenches dug around the edges and the thick bed of straw inside served to keep the flooding rainwater out and the floor mostly dry.

Her parents and Aine were all out in the fields watching yet another hurley match. Conn and Dowan were probably there too, as were at least half of the people at the Fair. No doubt they would return, but it would take some time for them to work their way through the crowds and get back to the encampment from the distant meadow. It would be up to Niamh to keep their little campsite safe.

The light faded, as though the sun was setting much too fast. Then a bright flash and a shaking roar of thunder sent Niamh outside again—and one look toward the mountain made her catch her breath.

The storm cloud had risen up from behind the mountain, and Niamh realized that the billowing white she had seen was only its tip. Now a monstrous grey-black cloud stretched from far past one side of the mountain to far past the other, and as it stretched out to cover the huge encampment it rippled with lightning and shook the whole world with its thunder.

This would be no ordinary storm.

Quickly Niamh checked the outside of the tent as raindrops began to fly. The heavy flax ropes attached to the thick cowhides were firmly staked to the ground. The tough ragged sheepskins along the top supports of the tent were firmly lashed down with more ropes. Climbing into first one wagon and then the other, she found that their wheels were properly blocked and everything inside them—all of Conn and Dowan's possessions—were stowed away in heavy wooden boxes.

Niamh smiled, even as the rain began to make a drumming noise on the earth and on the nearby tents. Her father had always insisted on a good secure camp, even where others were more careless.

More brilliant flashes. Thunder shook the earth. And then the wind roared in the trees and lashed the whole encampment with its fury, driving the rain into her face and soaking her gowns and braided hair.

Jumping down out of the wagon, she dodged more flying debris and a large piece of cowhide. Someone's shelter must have come apart already. Well, she would be safe within her father's tent, and she would ride out the storm there and wait for her family to return.

Just as she turned to go, a movement up in the air caught her eye. Something large and waving, like another big piece of hide, flew high in the air and made a black silhouette against the angry deep grey sky. But it could not have been just cowhide—before she could move out of its path, the wind grabbed it and drove it down hard into her forehead, harder than any piece of hide would have felt.

Bryan ran through the camp with one arm over his head, trying to shield himself from the howling wind and driving rain, and from the pieces of blowing wood and hide and straw. He had been standing down near the river at the playing field watching the hurley match, but also doing his best to watch for Niamh from a distance. He had spotted her family not far from the river, but had not seen her.

When the storm broke, the players reluctantly left the field, but only after lightning struck a tree halfway down the mountain and the shock of it knocked three players unconscious. Bryan had started toward the encampment, but he was on the far side of the field and it took some time for him to push his way through the crowds.

Summer storms were as common as breathing in Eire, and just as fleeting, but this was one of the worst Bryan could remember. As he hurried through the camp, all around him the tents and shelters went crashing to the ground. Most fell flat as their wooden structures broke in the driving wind and rain, or turned on their sides in the mud. A few were actually pulled right out of the sodden ground as the wind grabbed the tightly stretched hides and sent them and their wooden frames soaring high in the air, forming dangerous flying missiles.

At last he reached the place where Niamh and her family had their camp. If she had not gone to the hurley match, she would most likely have stayed at the campsite to keep an eye on things. She would certainly have come there when the storm came up.

Yet the whole camp was taking such a beating from the storm that, for a moment, Bryan was not sure he was in the right place. As he continued to run headlong into the wind, he was constantly dodging the people coming at him—mothers with crying children in their arms, families trying to get out of the way of flying debris, and frightened dogs and puppies racing away from the wind and the rain and the wildly blowing hides and sheepskins and household possessions.

Most of the people ran down to the river, where they huddled together to get what shelter they could from the trees and boulders and from each other. But Bryan turned away from the sight of them and pressed on through the cold lashing rain.

Another bright flash. Another explosion of thunder.

He looked around frantically for Niamh, but all he saw were more people running past him for the river while others stood outside their tents and held fast to the ropes in a last-ditch attempt to keep their dwellings from collapsing in the wind.

"Niamh! Niamh!" he cried, but of course she would never hear him in this storm. He looked around frantically for the large red-and-white cowhide tent that was her family's . . . and there, he saw it at last, still far ahead of him just behind the two wagons sitting face to face.

He dashed over the rain-drenched ground toward the tent. Just as he turned past the last of the other still-standing tents, he stumbled and nearly fell over something heavy in the mud.

"Niamh!"

Chapter Twelve

She lay on her side in a puddle of water, with an enormous red dirt-splattered mark on one side of her forehead. Bryan crouched down beside Niamh, scooped his hands beneath her and lifted her up, turning so that his body sheltered her from the worst of the wind and raising her head so that he cradled it against his chest.

Water poured from the hems of her gowns. Her face was cold and pale. Yet he could feel her chest rise and fall against his as he carried her, and saw that her little golden comb still gleamed in her wet braided hair.

He was glad to know she had not lost it.

At last they were inside her family's tent. The wind whipped and tore at the cowhide walls, and a little water dripped here and there, but though it rattled in the wind, the heavy oaken framework looked to be secure. Brian set Niamh down near the center of the tent on one of the sheepskins atop a thick pile of straw. The trench dug around the outside was managing to hold off the worst of the water, and most of the straw was still dry, as were the wooden storage boxes and bags and baskets of food.

Bryan grabbed a heavy wool cloak and threw it over Niamh, tucking it close around her. Wool would always keep a person warm, even when it was wet. "Niamh," he whispered, bending close to her. "Niamh . . . wake up. You're safe now. You're home. Please, open your eyes."

Her head fell back a little, and her lips parted. For a moment Bryan thought his heart would stop, as he feared the worst. But then he could see that her chest still rose and fell, and that a faint beat of life still showed at her throat.

Quickly he searched through the tent and found a folded linen mantle. Holding a corner of it up to the roof of the shelter, he allowed the rainwater to soak through it and then turned back to Niamh, using the wet linen to clean the dirt away from her forehead as gently as he could.

Niamh moaned, and she tried to turn her head away, but he went on working. Beneath the dirt was a large smooth lump that seemed to turn from red to purple even as he looked at it.

"Niamh," he said again. "Open your eyes. Look at me." Her eyelids fluttered. Slowly she turned her head toward his voice, blinked a few times, and then gazed straight at him. "Bryan," she whispered. "What are you doing here?"

She tried to sit up, but only moaned again and brought one hand up to touch her forehead. Bryan eased her back down to the straw. "Lie still," he said as the rain continued drumming on the tent's cowhide walls. He covered her hand with his own. "I found you out in the storm. Something struck you, left you unconscious."

"Oh," she murmured. "The storm. I remember now." Her eyes flew open wide. "Oh—my family! Where is my family?"

"I saw them at the hurley match. They may have taken shelter in the forest, down near the river. Many folk went there."

"Near the river," she echoed, and then she tried to smile, though he could see the little twist of pain that went with it. "I thought you did not care for hurley, Bryan."

"I don't. I was . . . I was looking for you."

"For me?" Her brows drew together in puzzlement and she once more grimaced in pain. "I thought we would not see each other again. I thought we agreed that . . ."

Bryan released her hand and reached for the wet cloth. "I agreed to nothing," he said, smiling down at her. "I know that since last we spoke at King Nessan's feast, you have stayed near your family's camp—though you did go to the well twice yesterday. And I am not sorry I know this, for since you were not at the hurley match with your family I knew you must be here. I am glad I knew where to find you, for you were the first thing I thought of when the storm struck."

The wind seemed to be easing. The trickle of water through the cowhide roof slowed to a drip. Niamh smiled back at him, and reached for his hand again.

"Thank you for helping me," she said, closing her cool fingers over his. "I am not sure what might have happened to me if you had not come."

"But I *had* to come." He took her hand in both of his. "I think I have finally learned the answer to the first of your three questions. Women want to feel safe when they are with the man they love. Is that right?"

She smiled again, and this time a soft glow came into her eyes in spite of her pain. "It is."

"I hope I helped you feel safe today. I hope you know

that you will always be safe in my company, for as long as you are with me."

"I believe I will, Bryan. I can only thank you again." She gazed steadily into his eyes, and a little color started coming back into her cheeks and lips. Gently he brushed a strand of hair away from her face, and then found that he could not resist bending down to kiss her.

Her lips were as sweet and hot as woodland strawberries warmed by the sun. And to his surprise and delight, she returned his kiss with equal gentleness.

"*Niamh!*"

Bryan drew back. The cowhide flap at the entrance flew open, revealing soft grey skies and a steady drizzle of rain—and the faces of Niamh's family.

"Niamh, what happened?" Morna asked. "Are you hurt? Oh, *oh!* Look at your head! Oh, my dear, I'm so sorry—let me help you!"

Niamh sat up a little and reached for her mother's hand. "It's all right, Mother. Bryan was here. I am safe. I will always be safe when I am with him."

Niamh slept deeply all that night, lulled by the soft sounds of her sleeping family and by the soothing patter of rain on the cowhide walls of the tent. When she finally awoke, the sun was fully risen and her family had already gone outside to greet the new day. She sat up, putting her hand to her head. It was still very sore and scraped from the piece of broken wood that had struck her during the storm, but she felt much steadier and much clearer-headed than she had yesterday.

Aine stuck her head inside the tent. "Are you awake yet? Are you well enough to go to the Cattle Fair? It's about to start!"

"Of course I'll be there. Just give me a moment."

"All right. But don't be too long! Rua and Geal are waiting!"

Aine disappeared again. Niamh threw off the cloak that covered her, stood up, took a deep breath, and got herself ready to go out.

The day was cool and fresh and clear, for the tremendous storm had driven away the heat and heavy clouds. As Niamh walked across the campsite, with Aine beside her, she breathed deep of the sweet fresh air and felt her head clear a little more.

"I will be sorry to see them go, won't you?"

Niamh smiled at her sister. "Rua and Geal? I will. They are two of the prettiest calves we have raised. But it is the way of things that they must go to new owners so that we might trade them for something we need more—and so that there will be room for two new calves next spring."

"Oh, I understand. I know it must be done. But I will still miss them."

On this morning, all activity seemed to be centered on the enormous rectangular stone pen that held the cows and calves and oxen brought for trade, with another smaller stone pen nearby for the bulls. A steady stream of men and women and children made their way to the pens, where a large crowd had already gathered.

"Do you suppose Bryan will be here?" Aine ventured.

"I do not know. No doubt he will be practicing for the javelin throw to be held this afternoon. It is one of the tests that will determine the next tanist of his kingdom."

"Well, surely the practice will not take too long. Perhaps he will still be here. There are no other games or contests scheduled for this morning."

"Of course there are not," Niamh said, keeping her voice calm and steady. "The Cattle Fair is where the real profit is made, for both king and herdsman alike. Anyone with any sense would rather have cattle than gold. Will gold give you good milk, or butter, or cheese, or meat? Gold is pretty, but not when you are hungry!"

"You will get no argument from me," Aine agreed with a laugh. "I just wondered whether we might see—"

"Look! There are Geal and Rua, right near the gate." Niamh caught up her skirts and hurried the rest of the way to the enormous cattle pen.

As she had thought, the two small red-and-white faces with huge brown eyes were indeed her family's two young heifers, and both of them bleated at the sight of Niamh and Aine. "There, there," Aine called, catching up with Niamh and trying to soothe the pair of calves. "Oh, it is going to be hard to see you go!"

The two women stepped between the horizontal bars blocking the entrance to the cattle pen, and quickly caught hold of the two long ropes that trailed from Geal and Rua's flax-rope halters. They led the pair out toward a fairly dry spot near the center of the stone-walled pen and waited to see who might want to trade for the pair of fine young heifers.

Niamh and Aine each took out the piece of rough woolen cloth she had brought and began to use it in small circles on each animal, rubbing hard to clean away the dried mud and old hair so that their fine sleek coats, good flesh and fine bone structure could be easily seen by any who might walk past. But as Niamh worked on Geal, she glanced around and took a closer look at the other cows and calves in the pen.

Most were fine animals. Full-grown cows and strong heavy oxen stood placidly at the end of their ropes and eyed the many strangers with some suspicion, and lively young heifers and weanling bull calves leaped and frolicked at the ends of their ropes, surrounded by more people and commotion than they had ever seen in their young lives. But others, whether young or old or in-between, were bony and rough-coated and had burrs deeply matted into the long hair of their fetlocks and tails. A few showed sores and old wounds that had clearly never been tended to.

"Why would anyone bring such poor animals to the Fair?" whispered Aine, following Niamh's gaze. "Not all of them are old, but they look to be on the point of death! What sort of trade can their owners hope to get for them?"

Niamh shook her head. "It is always so. For some it's easier to simply trade away an old or sick or injured animal than try to heal it."

"It's a poor trade they will get."

"It is indeed. But some would rather have a poor trade than have to care for a sick animal."

As they watched, a man near them accepted a dented bronze cauldron from another man and handed him the rope of a lame cow with a running sore on her back. "Off to the knife, then," said the former owner. "Only five years old, but already lame and no calf this year. I suppose she'll taste fine enough when she's been boiled up with a little onion and watercress."

"That she will," said the new owner, and led the cow toward the gate where a few others stood waiting. Niamh knew they would lead the animal into the forest and dispatch her right away.

"That cow was not old," Aine said. "She was only neglected. Surely she could have been made well and had several more fine calves before meeting her death when it came to her in good time."

"I do not doubt it," Niamh said, scratching Geal's neck. "But for some, slaughter is the only healing they know."

137

She looked around the vast pen, hoping to spot someone who would make a fair trade for Rua and Geal—someone who would allow the cows to live out their lives on good pastures and become mothers to many fine new calves. Standing in the pen, she thought she heard heavy hoofbeats from the other side of the stone wall, along with a raspy, snorting laugh.

Niamh froze. Tossing Rua's rope to Aine, she quickly climbed up the side of the stone wall and peered over—but saw only people and horses and cattle coming and going along the wide dirt path. There was no sign of any large black pony, nor of a glaring, angry *puca*.

She stepped back down to earth. Perhaps she had only imagined she'd heard the mysterious creature. But as she looked again at the lame, thin, ill-treated cow being pulled away towards the forest, she knew that none of them at the Fair had seen the last of the beast.

The sun rode high behind broken grey and white clouds as Niamh and Aine joined the people gathered on the gaming field. This time the crowd all stood in a great throng that faced the mountain and curved all the way across the open space, leaving perhaps half of the grassy field wide open. Lined up across the field were seventeen men, each with a rowan-wood javelin in his hand and each vying for the prize that Queen Treise held out before them now—a long slender belt made entirely of heavy gold links. But everyone knew that two of the men lined up across the field were competing for far more than just the pretty gold belt.

"Here is the javelin throw," King Conaire called from beside his queen, "and here also is the second of the three contests that will determine whether Ardal or Bryan shall be the next tanist of Cahir Cullen. Whether they win the contest outright or no, whichever of them outscores the other shall add this test to his wins toward being named tanist. If Bryan outscores Ardal, the test is over, for that would give him two wins—but if Ardal scores the better, the tests will continue with the cross-country horse race.

"Now then!" he continued, as Queen Treise and her ladies started toward the sidelines. "All of you know the rules. Each man will get three attempts to throw his javelin as far as he can. The man with the farthest throw is the winner. Show us your skill!"

The king and his men left the field. Ten of his warriors spaced themselves out in a long line down each side of the open meadow, some ten paces apart. Niamh stood not far from the king and queen, right at the front of the crowd, and waited.

The first man stepped forward. Niamh did not know him. He raised his worn javelin with its dull rusted-iron tip, took three running steps, and hurled it with all his strength in the direction of the mountain.

Niamh had not expected much from such a plain-looking weapon, but the throw was a good one. It went nearly as far as the eighth man out in the line and stuck hard in the grass, the long shaft waving back and forth in the intermittent sun and shadow.

Two more men threw, and though they did well, neither throw went as far as the first man's. Then it was Bryan's turn to step forward.

He glanced toward the king, and as he looked away his eyes met Niamh's for just an instant. Beneath his look of concentration she could see the start of a confident grin. He raised the javelin to his shoulder and pointed it straight at the mountain. Its shaft of polished red wood from the heart of the rowan tree gleamed in a ray of sunlight, as did the long sharp tip of polished flint. Then, after drawing a deep breath, he took three great running strides and sent the javelin flying.

Niamh held her breath and followed the weapon with her eyes. It flew and flew, out beyond the first two javelins until it reached the farthest one—and dove down to rest perhaps one pace in front of the other.

The crowd erupted in cheers. "A magnificent throw! Did you see that? Never have I seen any javelin go so far!" Bryan glanced at Niamh again, and she could not help but smile back at the sight of the gleam in his eye.

Three other men made their throws, and then it was Ardal's turn. He made a nice show of bowing to the king and queen, and then turned and raised his javelin.

It was a beautiful weapon. Its shaft was made of gleaming red rowan heartwood like Bryan's, but this one had a beautiful leaf-shaped tip of shining bronze. Ardal raised it up and let it go—and the shining weapon leaped from his hand, overtook all the others, and dove into the earth some two paces in front of Bryan's.

Again the crowd shouted out, slapping each other on the back. The wagers were flying thick and fast. The rest of the men made their throws, but none was even close to Bryan or Ardal's javelin. Now the second round would begin.

The men ran down the field to retrieve their weapons. Ardal pulled a scrap of red linen from his belt, placed it on the grass where his javelin had struck, and weighted it down with a stone. When the men ran back to the line with their weapons, they turned to see the bit of bright red fabric far down the field, taunting them as it waved in the wind.

In the second round, the first man did not throw nearly so far. Bryan sent his javelin flying nearly as far as the red scrap of linen—and this time, Ardal's throw did not go quite so far as Bryan's.

Niamh let go of her breath and closed her eyes. One more throw—or miscast—of a javelin was all that remained between Bryan and kingship.

She did not know which she should hope for.

The men walked out to get their weapons. This time Bryan marked his winning throw with a scrap of yellow linen.

One more round to go. The first two men made their throws, but fell far short. Then Bryan stepped forward again.

He kept his gaze fixed firmly on the bright yellow linen waving far down the field. Holding his javelin up level to his shoulder, he took his great running steps, one, two, three, and hurled the weapon with such force that it seemed he meant to throw it straight through the mountain.

The javelin fell quivering just past the waving yellow linen. Bryan had outthrown both his own first mark and Ardal's.

Niamh twisted her hands together. One more throw—Ardal's—and it would be over.

But she had forgotten about the other competitors. Three more men had to make their throws before Bryan's cousin, and with each it seemed to Niamh that never had any man taken so long to simply throw a javelin. None was even close.

Finally, Ardal stepped up to the line.

Niamh closed her eyes. If he failed, Bryan would be the next tanist. But if he succeeded, Bryan might eventually go back to his life as one of the king's warriors, free to live either in the great dun or roam the countryside as he

141

chose. As a warrior, Bryan might live with his wife in the forest if he wished, where men were always needed to guard the king's lands—but a king could live nowhere except in his fortress of earth and stone, forever at the call of his druids and advisors whenever he might be needed.

Ardal raised his javelin. No doubt the sight of the yellow linen taunted him, as did the shaft of Bryan's javelin just beyond. He drew back his arm and let the weapon fly, and Niamh caught her breath as the javelin streaked down the field. It struck the waving shaft of Bryan's weapon, tumbled end-over-end, and then came down with its shining bronze tip firmly embedded in the earth—just one pace closer to the mountain than Bryan's.

The crowd erupted in yelling and cheering as they surged forward to surround Ardal, slapping him on the back and, of course, collecting their bets from one another.

A group of the king's warriors pushed their way through the crowd, opening up a walkway for the king and queen to make their way to Ardal. He approached them both, dropped down on one knee, and accepted the beautiful, shining belt of gold links from the queen.

"I thank you, Queen Treise," he said. "But if I may, I would like to offer this prize to the one who inspired me to win this day."

"By all means," said the dark-haired queen with a smile, and she stepped back as Ardal began to search the crowd.

It was not long before he stood in front of Niamh.

"My lady, I would like to give this to you. It was thoughts of your beauty that let my javelin travel on wings today. The prize should be yours."

She could only stare at him in shock, even as everyone in the crowd turned to look at her. "Thank you," she said, "but I do not wish to take your prize. You won the contest, and so it belongs to you."

"So it does. It is mine to do with as I wish. And I wish to give it to you."

A sudden movement in the crowd caught Niamh's eye. Pushing his way through, with a set jaw and a determined, angry look on his face, was Bryan.

She had to do something quickly. All eyes in the crowd were quickly shifting from her to Bryan and Ardal, instantly excited at the possibility of a fistfight at the Fair, and at the certainty that both of the combatants would be exiled, or worse.

Niamh glanced through the crowds. There, not far away, stood Urla, Ardal's Lughnasa Sister, dressed in a long gown of heavy green-and-purple plaid wool with a greenish bronze brooch holding the too-large neckline closed. She watched the action closely and never took her eyes off Ardal—except to turn a spiteful glare on Niamh.

Niamh looked quickly at Bryan and held up her fingers just for an instant, and to her great relief he paused and stood waiting a few steps from his cousin, clenching and unclenching his fists.

"Ardal," Niamh began in her sweetest tone, "I see that Urla, your Lughnasa Sister, is here in the crowd today. I am sure you actually meant to give your lovely prize to her." She looked straight at Urla, folded her hands, gave her a polite smile, and then simply stood waiting— which, of course, caused everyone in the crowd to turn and look at Urla too, and then to stare at Ardal, waiting for his reaction.

Even the king and queen stood gazing at him expectantly.

There was little else he could do. With a tight smile, Ardal faced Urla and forced himself to hold out the gleaming, shining, very valuable belt of gold links. "Will you accept this?" he asked, his knuckles almost white from gripping it so tightly.

"Oh, I will!" Urla answered, managing to pull it out of his hands on only the second try. "I most certainly will." Urla threw a cold glance at Niamh and held the belt against her own brightly colored dress. "Look how nicely it sets off my beautiful gown. It would be lost on a plain shift of undyed linen!" She held it up and examined it closely, seeming to inspect every shining link, and then wrapped it around her waist and fastened it with the hook at one end. "I will see you later, Ardal," she said with a coy smile, and then turned and hurried away with several of the other girls, all of them laughing and giggling and squealing as they caught up the ends of her new belt and hugged her in delight and victory.

Bryan walked past Ardal, whose face was reddening with anger and embarrassment, as though his cousin were not there. He went straight to Niamh and took her by the hand.

"I am sorry I could not win for you today," he said softly, looking down into her eyes. "If anyone deserves such a prize, it is you."

"It means nothing," she answered. "I need no prize." She gazed up into his shining brown eyes, and then he gave her what she truly wished for; he bent down to kiss her again, his mouth warm and soft on her own.

Chapter Thirteen

The deep grey of twilight was just giving way to the blackness of night as Niamh walked through the camp toward the great stone cattle pen. Once there, she climbed a couple of steps up the side of the stone wall and peered over the top, looking down on the scattered cows and calves and oxen in the wavering light of the surrounding torches and into the darkness of the forest beyond the pen.

"And are Geal and Rua happy with their new owners, my lady Niamh?"

Bryan stood on the ground just below, looking up with a sly grin and a gleam in his eye. "How did you know I was here?" Niamh asked, stepping down to the ground.

He took a step toward her. "I walked to your family's camp to see if you might like to walk out with me for a time. Aine told me you had come here to see how the two heifers were faring. You did trade them, then?"

"I did. They went to the herd of King Irial, and we made a fine trade. We got a loom for weaving, and three new large bronze cauldrons, and a set of iron tools for the fire, and two newly made iron-shod wooden wheels for the wagons."

"You will miss your pretty calves, though, I am sure."

She nodded. "I will. But they will be well cared for in King Irial's herd, and we must have a way to trade for things we need and cannot easily make ourselves. All is as it should be."

"I see . . . but if that is so, why are you here? Simply to see them one last time? I know that you do love your animals, Niamh, as you love all creatures."

She smiled. "So I do. But I must confess, I have no worry for the calves. I came here to watch for . . . something else."

"Something else?" Bryan stopped, and his eyes flicked past her shoulder into the dark woods. "Do you think . . . do you think the *puca* might return?"

"I do."

"Why do you believe this? Have you seen it again? Did it speak to you?"

She held up her hand. "I have not seen it. But this morning, while the Cattle Fair went on, I saw several animals who had been poorly treated and were traded only that they might be slaughtered—so that their owners need not go to the bother of giving them decent care."

"I thought the *puca* was only drawn to horses, since it is some sort of unnatural horse itself."

Niamh shook her head. "I cannot say. But I thought— I do not know for certain, I only *thought* that I heard it trot past the cattle pen this morning. It was laughing."

"Laughing?"

She looked up at him. "I do not know whether it will return. It is only a feeling I have. That is why I came out here tonight . . . only a feeling, Bryan, and nothing more."

He smiled and took her hands. "There is no harm in that. I was going to ask you if you would walk with me tonight. Will you still do so? I promise, we will stay near the cattle and keep one eye on watch should any strange creatures approach."

"I will walk with you," she agreed, and together they started down the well-worn path that ran along the outside of the cattle pens.

The three-quarter moon rode high in the sky by the time Niamh and Bryan had made their circuit of the camp, walking all the way around it on the outer paths, and finally she looked up and found herself at the far end of the cattle pen once more.

"There. You see? Another ordinary night in the camp, with folk keeping each other company and enjoying their meat and bread and beer. There is no unnatural *puca* come to trouble us. I am just glad that you and I could have a bit of time together."

"As am I," Niamh said, and turned her face up to his. But just as she closed her eyes, a terrible cracking sound split the night.

Bryan and Niamh instantly turned toward the barred gate of the cattle pen, and saw a monstrous creature standing just in front of the gate. It turned around and kicked out violently with both hind feet—once more, twice more—breaking the heavy wooden bars with every kick and shattering them into little more than kindling. Then it trotted inside the pen, shaking its head and sending waves down the long rope trailing from its halter, and began to drive the bawling cattle out of the pen.

"Niamh, stay here! I've got to stop it!" cried Bryan. As the people nearest the pen saw what had happened and began to shout in warning, he rushed to the gate and stood in the path of the escaping cattle, spreading his arms and cloak wide in an effort to frighten them back inside.

"Back! Back!" he cried, and to Niamh's great relief the beasts hesitated and stood staring at him, tightly bunched in the opening. But then an enormous black shadow came soaring out of the pen, making a leap over the cattle and over Bryan's head, and landing on the torchlit open earth behind him. As the people fell back in shocked silence, the *puca* raised its head and glared at them all, its red-yellow eyes shining fiercer than any torch. Then it turned back toward the pen, half-reared and leaped up into the air again, clearing both Bryan's head and the frightened cattle, and disappeared within the milling herd in the darkness of the pen.

"Get back in there!" Bryan shouted at the cattle, and he was quickly joined by several other men. "Get back! Get back!"

But in the next instant Bryan and the others were leaping out of the way for their lives, for all the cattle came stampeding out through the open gate as though absolutely terrified, bawling and stumbling and jamming their way through the opening in the stone wall until they were pouring out in an earthshaking stream.

Niamh climbed up the side of the stone pen and reached down to grab Bryan's arm, hauling him up beside her. His face was pale and his eyes were wide, but there was determination in them, too.

"You were right," he said as the cattle continued to scrape past the walls just below them. "And this time we've got to find a way to stop it."

Niamh looked down into the dark and shadowed pen. As the last of the cattle ran out, she could see that the pen was empty. "Perhaps it will go back to its lair. I will try to speak to it again—"

"Too late! We tried that. You were right. It is still up to its tricks. Stay here, Niamh, where it is safe. We'll get the cattle in, and then we warrior men will track that creature down and do away with it once and for all."

Shouts and screams filled the camp as a great herd of terrified cows and calves and oxen lumbered through it, knocking down tents and scattering belongings and careening past frightened, angry people. But without their mischievous tormentor goading them on, the cattle soon slowed and stopped and allowed themselves to be herded back to the great stone pen.

But the damage was done. Though no one had been injured, the camp was once more in a shambles. And just as soon as the animals were safely penned up again, with several men set to guard them, word spread throughout the camp that all of the warrior men were to get their horses and meet with King Conaire at the foot of the mountain.

As Bryan sat astride Luath, riding him toward the meeting with the king, Niamh walked alongside with long strides and placed her hand on Bryan's knee.

"Please," she began, as they made their way down the crowded, torchlit path and carefully avoided the still-anxious people trying to gather their belongings and put their trampled camps back together. "Please do not harm this creature."

"How do we even know it *can* be harmed?" he asked, reining Luath in as he started a nervous jog. "It is in no way a real or normal beast, not in the way I understand such things. It comes when it pleases. No one ever sees it leave. There may well be nothing that any man can do against this monster, no matter how fine a warrior he might be."

"Listen to me," Niamh said, hurrying to keep up with Luath's nervous strides. "It has the look and substance—and the sympathies—of a horse. A real horse. Your brother touched it. He rode it. The other horses treat it exactly as one of their own. It does have some very strange and supernatural qualities, to be sure, but that does not mean it cannot be injured or killed."

"All the better, then! Look at what it has done to our camp and to our people, twice now, even after you tried to befriend it! Why should we not kill it if we can?"

"Because it does not deserve killing. It does not deserve harm."

"After all it has done to our people?"

"Think, Bryan! It has harmed no one. It terrified your brother and managed to frighten Ardal—but it did not attack them. It has tried only to protect the horses and the cattle. I think it is angry only because of the mistreatment of some of these animals."

Bryan set his jaw. "It is an unnatural animal. It *speaks*. And when it does, it says only one word: *revenge!*"

They were nearly at the mountain. More and more men rode past into the brightly lit circle of King Conaire's camp. Niamh reached up for Bryan's hand, and reluctantly he halted Luath and swung his mount around.

"Please. Do not kill it. Do not harm it. Let me have a chance to reason with it once more."

Bryan shook his head, and he glanced over his shoulder at the gathering riders. "I cannot promise you that I will not kill it should I get the chance. I will not wait until some innocent is run down and killed, either by this beast or by one that it has loosed."

He looked down at her and tried to smile. "I will come

NAME: _____

ADDRESS: _____

_____

_____

TELEPHONE: _____

E-MAIL: _____

____ I want to pay by credit card.

__ Visa   __ MasterCard   __ Discover

Account Number: _____

Expiration date: _____

SIGNATURE: _____

Send this form, along with $2.00 shipping and handling for your FREE books, to:

Love Spell Romance Book Club
20 Academy Street
Norwalk, CT 06850-4032

Or fax (must include credit card information!) to: 610.995.9274.
You can also sign up on the Web at www.dorchesterpub.com.

Offer open to residents of the U.S. and Canada only. Canadian residents, please call 1.800.481.9191 for pricing information.

If under 18, a parent or guardian must sign. Terms, prices and conditions subject to change. Subscription subject to acceptance. Dorchester Publishing reserves the right to reject any order or cancel any subscription.

back as soon as I can." She pressed his hand and then released it, stepping back as he rode into the circle of the king's encampment.

The campfire burned brightly at King Conaire's camp. He stood just before the flames on an open swath of grass, and lined up facing him were some one hundred men on horses. They had swords in their hands and grim determination in their eyes.

"You have all seen the strange creature that troubles our camp," the king said. "And even if you did not catch a glimpse of it, you have surely seen the damage and destruction it has wrought. Twice, now, this unnatural beast has loosed our animals, terrified our women and children, and all but destroyed the whole encampment! It must be stopped, and stopped now, and so it is that I charge all of you!

"Divide yourselves into groups, one for each direction of the winds, and destroy this ravaging beast before it can return again! Your people are waiting for you to defend them from this monster that destroys the peace of the Lughnasa Fair. Go, now! All of you! Go!"

And with that, the warriors all turned their horses and found their four groups—one for each of the four kingdoms, with Conaire's men remaining to patrol the encampment—and each of the groups rode off in a different direction.

One group circled around to the far side of the mountain, one went straight out across the playing fields, the third headed across the road and into the forest, and the fourth, with Bryan at its head, rode across the ford of the river and into the woods.

Though the king had been right to send men out to every corner of the land surrounding them, Bryan felt certain that his group would find the *puca* near the cave where he and Niamh had encountered it on the night of the Horse Fair. He led his twenty men across the river and into the dark tangled forest, and though they were forced to slow their pace, it was not long before they reached the rowan grove with the mound and the deep cave within.

Bryan halted, as did the others. "Here. Here is where we will find it." But as the drifting clouds parted overhead, the waxing white three-quarter moon showed them that the clearing was empty. There was only silence and stillness to be found in this place.

"Well, Bryan," said Ardal, riding up alongside him. "You seem to have led us nowhere. Do you not recall King Conaire mentioning that it was important for us to find and destroy this creature?"

"It is here," Bryan said through clenched teeth. "It's playing with us. This is its lair."

"How can you be so certain?"

"I saw it here once before. When it took the horses."

"You tracked that monster here that night? And yet you told no one that you knew of its hiding place?"

"There was no need! It attacked no one. The horses were all recovered. How was I to know it wanted the cattle, too?"

Ardal shook his head. "As I said, Bryan, you are as weak as any twelve-year-old girl. A fine king you would make. But at least we know that will never come to pass—not after the horse race. Not after—"

"This way!" Bryan cried, cutting off the stream of his cousin's words, and spurred Luath into the forest once more.

He pressed on through the dark and tangled woods,

every sense strained to the limit for any trace of the beast. He did feel like the fool now, for not going to King Conaire once he knew where the *puca* kept its hideaway. Perhaps Ardal was right. But Niamh had been so sure she had won the creature's trust, that she had persuaded it not to trouble the Fair again, that he had gone along with her wishes. Surely if anyone could charm a monster into leaving her alone, it was Niamh.

But the beast had come back, and now the clever *puca* was nowhere near its lair . . . nowhere to be found.

Near the back of the twenty-man line, now forced to ride single-file through the dark forest paths, Bryan heard the soft nicker of a horse along with a few curses from his men. Instantly he halted. "What is it? What's going on back there?"

"It's nothing, Bryan," one of the men called. "A couple of the horses tried to turn around and go back the other way. Their riders set them straight quick enough."

Ardal laughed. "Well, do try to keep your mounts headed one way or the other, won't you? What with Bryan leading us and your horses turning tail, we'll be lucky if we can find our own backsides by the time this night is over."

Bryan gripped his reins tightly and glared at Ardal in the darkness, but instead of answering sent Luath on down the path again and went back to searching for any sign of the *puca*.

They did not get far before there was again the sound of whinnying horses and of more curses and slaps from the men. "What is wrong back there?" demanded Bryan.

But there was only silence. It seemed that no one even breathed—none of the men, that is. But then all of the horses, even Luath, set to whinnying as though welcoming a long-lost herdmate. They all began trying to turn around and go back down the path the way they had come until their riders angrily jerked them back in the right direction.

Suddenly Bryan allowed Luath to turn all the way around, and he kicked the steed's sides to send him crowding past all the others. "It's behind us! It's followed us! This way! Follow me!"

And just as all of the men allowed their horses to turn and start trotting down the dark and narrow path, a deep, rasping, terrifying laugh echoed through the forest. It was enough to make the bravest man's blood run cold.

Then they saw the pair of huge, glowing red-yellow eyes shining out at them from the darkness.

Bryan braced himself, steadied his breathing, and pulled his sword from its wooden scabbard. "This way!" he shouted again, and pushed past the last of the men so that now he was at their head once again. Luath was already quite eager to gallop after the pair of evil, smoldering eyes, as were all the horses, and so all their riders had to do was let them go.

In a moment they were at the clearing in front of the mound. Once again it seemed to be empty, with no red yellow eyes, though the horses continued to nicker and call. Bryan slid down to the ground, gave Luath's reins to Leary, who rode behind him, and walked straight to the cave—but it was empty, too.

Then a laughing snort made them all look up.

The *puca* looked down on them from atop the mound. The creature was a deep black shadow with malevolent fiery eyes. It reared on its hind legs, throwing its heavy head up high, and laughed its terrible, deep rasping laugh once again.

"There it is!" shouted Ardal. "Up on the mound! We've got it surrounded! Come with me. We'll ride up there and kill it!"

All of the riders swarmed around the mound and up the sides. Bryan swung up on Luath as he trotted past and grabbed the reins from Leary, his heart pounding as they galloped up the side of the hill. Would they have no choice but to kill it? Could they not frighten it away, drive it deeper into the forest and banish it from the sight of men?

Bryan had been as determined as all the others to destroy the *puca* once and for all . . . but the rest of them did not have Niamh asking them to spare the monster's life.

The men had it surrounded, high atop the mound. The creature stood directly over the cave down below. For a few heartbeats twenty men faced down the beast—and then it laughed at them again.

"*Leave here*," it said, in its terrible voice.

"*You* leave, monster!" shouted one of the men. From out of the darkness came the whistling sound of leather cutting the air, and then the *puca* threw its head to one side as a sling-stone struck it hard in the neck.

"Ha! I hit it!" cried Ardal. "It *can* be hit! Let loose on it, now!" And a hail of stones came whipping out of the darkness and slammed into the creature's head and neck.

It staggered to its knees. "Look! The blood drips from its wounds! It can be hurt! And now I'll finish it!" Ardal leaped from his horse and drew his sword. He raised the weapon over the *puca*'s neck with both hands and prepared to swing straight down, a blow that would sever any horse's neck and prevent it from ever rising again. It would be a death blow if ever there was one.

Janeen O'Kerry

In an instant, Bryan was on the ground and running to Ardal—and as the sword came down, it struck Bryan's weapon instead of the *puca*'s thick black neck.

Ardal turned and looked at Bryan in shock. "What have you done?" he cried. But his surprise quickly turned to rage. "Get back! Get away from here! If you're too much of a coward to kill it, then leave it to me!"

But as Ardal raised his sword again, the *puca* threw its heavy head up, regained its balance and lumbered to its feet. Bryan flinched as drops of its blood flew onto him. In a single terrifying move, it struck out with one forefoot and sent Ardal's sword flying end over end.

In the moment of tense silence that followed, the *puca* regarded them all with its malevolent red-yellow stare. Blood ran in streams down its face and neck. "*War*," it said to them—and then it turned around and leaped out into the darkness, straight out over the cave and down to the clearing far below.

Some of the other men quickly turned their horses and raced down the side of the mound after it; but Bryan stepped to the edge and looked down into the clearing. He saw only shadows and moonlight, and heard only silence.

The men would find nothing.

Chapter Fourteen

The next morning, King Conaire cancelled the hurley games and sent every available man and horse out on patrol to continue the search for the *puca*. Those without horses were set to keep watch from the mountaintop and around the outskirts of the camp. The people stayed close to their own camps and left only to fetch water from the well or to take care of other such necessities.

The air was tense, though Niamh could not decide whether it was more from the threat of a supernatural beast or from the hurley games being put off. Bryan was gone again, off with the patrols. She had seen only a glimpse of him this morning as he rode away at dawn, and had been horrified to see the spots of dark blood on his cloak and tunic, but there had been no time for him to explain to her how it had happened.

The king had ordered them to go out and find the *puca* if they could, but Niamh knew they would not find it. A creature like the *puca* would be seen only when it wanted to be seen. When it had a reason to be seen. If the men had managed to wound it, as she feared, no doubt it would hide itself until it could heal. Then it would truly take its revenge, just as it had said it would on that very first night when it had captured Leary.

As the day wore on, and there was no sign of the patrols—or of the *puca*—the conversation turned to the ritual of the bonfire. It should be held that evening, for this was the first night of the full moon, the high point of Lughnasa.

"Do you think they will call off the bonfire?" asked Aine. She and Niamh sat on sheepskins in front of their tent, working at spinning and sewing. Aine looked anxiously at the high peak of the mountain. "I have never seen the Lughnasa bonfire! Surely they would not call it off!"

"I cannot imagine such a thing," Niamh said to her sister as she worked at spinning more of her family's good brown wool into thread. "An entire herd of *puca* would have to stampede through the camp, and even then . . ." She smiled at her younger sibling. "Do not worry. The men will return and the celebration will go on as it always has, and you will have a wonderful time."

"If that creature does not return," Aine said, with a brief glance over her shoulder.

"I do not think it will—and even if it does, Aine, surely you understand, as I do, that it is still a creature of the earth, even if there is some strange magic involved. It does what it does for a reason, as all creatures do, and we have only to find out what that reason is."

"If anyone could find out, it's you," Aine proclaimed, and leaned over to hug her. Then she drew back. "Oh, look! They've returned! The men are coming home!"

Just as the sun began to set behind the mountain, the patrols poured into the camp from each of the four directions. Niamh hurried to the path and searched the faces of the riders, and it was not long before she saw Bryan riding toward her with Leary right behind him.

"Niamh," Bryan said, jumping to the ground. "I am so glad to see you. It has been a long day."

"So it has," she agreed, slipping her hand into his. "Did you find anything?"

"Nothing but oak trees and grass and falling leaves," he answered. "I take it the creature did not show itself here?"

"Not a trace."

Just then, a couple of King Conaire's serving men came walking through the campsite. Looking left and right at the people, they cried out, "The bonfire will be held at moonrise! All must attend the bonfire at moonrise!"

"Moonrise," Bryan said, looking down at Niamh. "I will be back for you before the daylight fades."

"I will be waiting," she answered, and after a gentle kiss she stepped back to watch him go.

The clouds cleared just as twilight fell, so that the folk of the Lughnasa Fair could see the first stars appearing against the deep blue-black sky. A steady stream of people left their campsites and climbed up the sides of the mountain, or else found a place to gather at its base. Last of all came a line of nine druids bearing torches, and then a line of warrior men, and then King Conaire and Queen Treise.

At the highest point of the long, wide mountain—at the conical tip sitting high on one end—Niamh and Bryan stood together with a great crowd of people, looking up at the enormous stack of wood piled up in front of them and watching as the king and his queen came to stand before it, with their warrior men behind them and the nine druids in a row in front of them.

As the last light faded from the sky, the chief druid

stepped forward and raised his torch high. He spoke ritual words. "We have gathered here on this mountaintop, we, the people of five kingdoms, to celebrate Lughnasa. This is Lugh's own Summer Fair, held in honor of his foster mother, Tailte.

"In those ancient days, she was one who used her powers to clear this plain of heavy forest so that her people might grow their grain and tend their animals and build their protected houses. So great was her care for her people, as it was for her foster son, that she never ceased from her labor until at last it tore her heart and ended her life.

"And so Lugh, who loved his foster mother, started the tradition of this gathering at this time to celebrate the land that Tailte laid down her life to clear for them.

"That is why we bring our grain to share amongst ourselves.

"That is why we bring our animals to trade.

"That is why some of those among us seek out companions for love and for marriage.

"All of these things were made possible by Tailte's determination to make the land ready for ones such as us to live on. We honor her memory by doing all of those things, for they allow us to live and even prosper."

He turned to face the east, looking out over the great encampment, and everyone else did the same. "And this is how we know it is Lugh's own night. The full moon rises, this, the second full moon after the summer solstice." He raised his torch, as did the eight druids lined up behind him, and a silence fell over the mountain as a great yellow moon showed its glowing edge just above the trees.

The people stood and watched until it rose all the way

up and showed them its full round shape, casting its shining yellow-white light onto the entire campsite. Niamh could not help but think back to the many years that her own ancestors must have stood here and done this very same thing, years and years uncounted, all the way back to the days of Lugh and Tailte.

"Lughnasa," said the chief druid, as the enormous moon continued to glide above the trees. "Lughnasa!"

He turned back to face the waiting stack of wood. "Let everyone in the five kingdoms know what night this is! Let all who see these flames know without doubt that this is the night of Lughnasa!" And he sent his torch flying high in the air so that it landed right in the center of the huge stack.

Eight more torches flew high, and they all came to rest amid the logs of rowan and oak and the scattered dry twigs and leaves. The kindling quickly took hold and spread flames throughout the pile of logs, and in a moment the crowd was forced to step back as the fires swelled and bloomed into an orange-red mountain of heat and light.

"All those who have something unwanted in their lives, give it now to the flames. And when you have done so, go and enjoy this night with those you love," commanded the druid. "This night is for celebration and merrymaking! Go and enjoy it!"

Niamh stood close beside Bryan, holding his hand and leaning against him as they looked up at the billowing flames. "Do you have anything to give to the fire, Bryan? Something that you do not want in your life any longer?"

"Well, let me see . . . do you suppose anyone would mind if I tossed Ardal into the bonfire?"

She laughed, as much from shock as anything. "I did not expect you to say that! Do you have nothing else?"

He shrugged. "Something smaller, perhaps?"

She giggled, and finally had to put her hand over her mouth to make herself stop. "Think, Bryan. Do you not have something that weighs down your life? Something that you wish to be rid of? Look, there, at the things the others are throwing in."

A few at a time, the people walked as close as they dared to the great wall of heat surrounding the bonfire and tossed in the small objects they held. "Look," Niamh said. "This woman has a piece of red linen. Perhaps it belonged to someone she no longer wants in her life—a troublesome woman, a cruel, neglectful man." They watched as the scrap of linen floated high above the bonfire, held on the hot drafts of air amid the flying sparks, until at last the fire pulled it in and consumed it.

A second woman walked up with a handful of strange items—a broken and crumbling piece of board, a length of half-rotted rope, a badly rusted scrap of iron—and threw them one at a time into the flames. "Weakness," Niamh guessed. "Those things are all symbols of weakness. It must be that she wishes for greater strength in her life, and is trying to rid herself of her own personal signs of weakness."

A man stepped forward, tall and proud, and from his belt took a heavy stick of gorse. It had been stripped of its dark green leaves and tiny yellow flowers, leaving only a bare stick covered with long sharp thorns. He threw it up high so that it dropped directly into the center of the great fire.

"And what would that represent to him?" Bryan asked.

Niamh shrugged. "Cruelty, perhaps. Arrogance. Selfishness. Whatever it is about him that drives away those who try to love him, the way the thorns drive away any who would try to touch the branch."

162

"I see." Bryan nodded toward the man. "And it looks as though you were right." As the man stood silhouetted against the brilliance of the bonfire, he was joined by the form of a woman who slid into his embrace, rested her head on his chest, and stood motionless as he pressed his lips to her hair.

Niamh smiled. "Perhaps their lives will start anew this night."

From a small leather bag at her belt she drew out a flat bronze cup, ancient and battered, and held it out before her in both hands. "What is this?" Bryan asked.

"It is an empty cup. A small cup, but empty nonetheless."

She drew a deep breath, and continued gazing down at the little cup. "For the most part, my life is the best that any woman could have. I have loving parents, a dear sister, a warm and simple home among the most beautiful forests and fields to be found anywhere in Eire. And yet . . ."

"And yet?"

"And yet I do know what loneliness is. I have reached the point in my life when I should find a man to love, and yet I am alone. I know what it is to long for something, and yet fear to pursue it too quickly so that I will not end up with something not right for me—with something that might cause me far greater loneliness than any I might know now."

"I do not want you to be lonely, dear Niamh." Very gently, Bryan lifted the cup from her fingers and walked with her to the edge of the fire. "An end to Niamh's ever being lonely," he said to the flames, and sent the cup flying high. It dropped into the fire with a bright flash.

Niamh looked up at him, smiling as she brushed her long, dark hair back from her shoulders. "Thank you.

That was kind of you," she said. "But are you sure that you yourself have nothing to give to the Lughnasa bonfire?"

He thought for a moment and shook his head. "Nothing. Except, perhaps . . ."

He unfastened the heavy gold brooch that held his cloak, handed the brooch to Niamh, and pulled the rectangular green-and-gold cloak of lightweight wool from his shoulders. Holding it up, he examined it closely and then held out one end of it to Niamh.

"Here. And here. Do you see? Those are drops of blood from the *puca*, from last night when the other men tried to stone it."

"Stone it," she repeated in a whisper. "You tried to kill it?"

"Not I," Bryan said quickly. "We had it surrounded atop the mound over its cave. The others were determined to kill it if they could. First they drove it to its knees with sling-stones, and then Ardal meant to strike it down with his sword—but I blocked it with my own."

"Then you saved it," she breathed. "And what did it do then? Did it attack the men?"

Bryan closed his eyes. "It did not. It said only a single word—*war*. The sound of its voice would make your blood run cold. And then it leaped down into the clearing and we did not see it again."

She touched his arm, looking up into his eyes. "I am glad you did not kill it."

He gave her a tight smile, and shook his head again. "I still do not know whether I did the right thing. But either way, I do not want to walk about with the blood of this creature upon me. Ardal might enjoy having it on his own cloak as a mark of honor, but I do not think of it that way."

Bryan rolled up the cloak and turned to face the fire. "Take the blood of this creature—whatever it is—and take it from my life. May it never trouble me again." And with that the cloak went soaring into the fire, which consumed it with a great flaring and snapping and a thick torrent of smoke.

Niamh rested her head against his shoulder as they watched the smoke rise up into the darkness. "Peace to you, Bryan," she said. "You deserve it."

"And good company always to you, Niamh," he answered, "for you deserve it as well."

He looked down at her and smiled. "Walk with me—out on the mountain, where the air is cool and fresh and the sky is filled with stars instead of smoke."

"I will," she answered, and together they left the enormous bonfire and started out across the long stretch of the mountaintop.

The sky stayed clear, with only a few high clouds for the full moon to shine upon—a moon so bright that its white glow masked whatever stars might have been near it. Niamh and Bryan walked away from the great bonfire up on the peak at the far end of the long wide mountain and started across the top toward the darker, quieter end.

Many people stayed gathered around the fire, but others sought out a dark and quiet refuge among the gnarled oaks and rowans and bushes high above. As on the evening of Gathering Day, there were many young couples who sought each other out under the safe cover of the trees and brush, where only the stars and clouds and brilliant full moon could look down upon them. But this time, Niamh could feel that something was different.

Gone were the lusty chases and giggling conversations. On this night, the height of Lughnasa, these couples had no eyes for any but each other, had no desire to be anywhere save close beside their lovers.

Niamh found a spot just off the main path that ran along the spine of the mountain, and sat down on the grass. A tight row of thorny gorse screened them, but it still allowed them to look over at the bonfire or gaze down on the torchlit campsite.

"I would have spread my cloak on the grass for you, but I gave it to the bonfire instead," Bryan apologized, laughing a little as he sat down beside her.

"No matter, Bryan. The night is warm and soft, and the grass is thick. And I am glad you gave a blood-marked cloak to the fire so that you will not carry the pain of it with you."

"And I am glad you gave the last of your loneliness to the flames." He moved to sit close behind her, and with infinite care slid his hands beneath the long loose hair on either side of her neck. "You are right. It is a warm night. Let me lift your hair off of your shoulders for you, so that the breeze might cool you."

His fingers smoothed the damp skin of her neck as gently as the summer sun might caress the rain-damp earth. Niamh closed her eyes as he lifted up the long, heavy length of hair and placed it over her shoulder so that it fell down into her lap. He smoothed away the last loose strands so that her neck was entirely bare, and then she could feel his breath on her skin, light and soft, as he slowly moved his lips from her ear all the way down to her shoulder, leaving the lightest of kisses as he went.

A great warmth flooded through Niamh, as if the heat from the Lughnasa bonfire had entered her veins. It made her feel heavy and soft all over, so heavy that she could not have moved even if she had wished. She leaned back against Bryan, settling her body against the solid strength of his chest and shoulders, and raised her chin so that her head fell back against his shoulder. She could not help but sigh as he kissed her neck all the way down to the curving neckline of her linen gown.

Slowly, gently, she reached up with one hand to touch the skin of his face, to marvel at the surprising softness of his neck and his smooth brown hair. He turned his head to kiss her searching fingertips, and then reached up to take her hand in his own.

"Look about you, Niamh," he whispered, and slowly she opened her heavy eyes. "Listen to the sounds of this night."

At the other end of the mountain, she could hear the faint snapping and popping of the blazing bonfire. And she became aware of the soft sounds of couples all around them, of the faint laughter and quiet rustling and soft moans. . . .

"Listen to them," Bryan whispered, his lips moving light as air against her skin. "They have grown close to each other since Gathering Day. They spend their time with no other. Many began as Lughnasa Brothers and Sisters, and now they have begun to form a bond. Tomorrow those couples will stand before the druids and make the marriage of a year and a day."

"A year and a day," she repeated. Her eyelids grew heavy again as the warmth of his body enveloped her and invited her to move closer, closer, so close that she would become a part of him and never leave him, never be alone again. . . . "A year and a day."

Bryan raised his head, but he continued to hold her close, and rested his cheek against her hair. "Think of it, beautiful Niamh. A year and a day. I am one who you feel safe with—you told me that. And I am also one who you find comfort with. Is this not true?"

She could not help but smile. "Indeed I do find comfort with you, Bryan, whenever I am with you . . . and never more than here, never more than now."

He held her even closer, and rubbed the side of his face against her hair. "Tell me if this is true. I believe I have found the answer to the second part of your riddle. I know that a woman wants to be safe, both in body and in spirit, when she is with the man she loves . . . and I believe she wants to feel comfortable as well."

"So she does, Bryan. So she does."

"Comfortable . . . so much so that she knows she can open herself to him whenever he is there, and that his touch will never be anything but a caress that will make her close her eyes and sigh, and wish that he might never cease to touch her . . ."

"Never cease," she repeated in a whisper. Niamh tightened her grip on his hand, and in a moment his lips were on hers in the warmest and softest of kisses, a kiss that lingered for a very long time.

She lay back, and he eased her down until her head rested on the grass. Then he lay across her body, his lips on hers again, and she welcomed the new and unfamiliar sensation of his warmth and weight holding her snugly against the soft earth.

For a long moment she returned his kiss, and felt as though she were floating away on a great wave of heat and desire, never to return.

Then, quickly, she sat up. Bryan caught his breath and rolled away from her, leaving a distressing wave of cool air where the warmth of his body had rested. Never had she felt so empty or so cold.

"What is it?" he asked. His voice was calm, but his breath came quick and ragged. She could still feel the great tension in him, even though he lay apart from her.

"I am sorry. I should never have done this."

Chapter Fifteen

Bryan sat up and reached for her hand. "Why should you not do this, Niamh? You are a beautiful young woman. Why should you not enjoy this night with a man who cares for you, who wants only to spend his time with you . . . ?"

He leaned forward to kiss her again, but she managed to stop him with a gentle finger against his lips.

"I cannot. Bryan, I cannot. I am sorry. I should never have come here with you."

He tried to smile, still holding on to her hand. "But if you had not, perhaps I would not have learned the second of the three answers you require. I know, now, that women want to feel both safe and comfortable when they are with the man they love. Are you not pleased that I have learned this much?"

"I am," she breathed. "Most men would have laughed and walked away the minute I asked them such a question."

"But I did not." He raised her fingers to his lips and kissed them, his mouth warm and soft.

She closed her eyes . . . and then gently withdrew her

hand. "You did not. But there is still one more answer that I must have before I can—before I can give myself to you completely."

He sighed, but raised her hand and kissed it again. "I understand. You told me as much when we met."

"And I understand, too." Niamh gazed out over the many camps of her people, and made her voice remain steady. "You will be leaving now."

"Niamh—"

"I will understand if you choose to go and find another. I said that I would not be yours without your being able to tell me all three answers . . . and I meant it."

"I know you did."

"Then why would you stay? You have learned only two of the answers. You may never learn the third. You are surrounded by young and beautiful women, any of whom would be happy to be with you on this night or any other . . . why not go to them now?"

He smiled. "Because as I said—for one thing, I considered your riddle to be a challenge, and I never turn down a challenge."

Niamh felt as though the first breeze of winter had somehow stolen through to the first night of autumn and touched her heart with icy fingers. "I am sorry I am no more than just another challenge for you."

"Not at all! Not at all," he said quickly. "I would not have accepted had I not had good reason to want to . . . though I must admit, I do not know that any man can ever know *all* of what a woman truly wants."

"So you have said."

He nodded, and then smiled at her. "Since I do not know the third answer, I will make you another offer."

He moved around to face her, and took both her hands in his own. "Tomorrow, as the sun rises, many of the couples who surround us now will stand before the druids at the base of this mountain and pledge fidelity to each other until next year at Lughnasa."

Niamh's heart beat a little faster. "They will. I have seen the ceremony. When it is done, they will live as husband and wife for one year. At next year's Fair, the day after these marriages are made, they have only to stand back-to-back before the druids and walk thirteen paces away from one another to dissolve the contract."

He nodded. "Some do this. And some stay together for many years. A few stay together forever."

"But most do not. Most go their separate ways the following year, some after taking a new partner the day before. They are not supposed to do it that way, but everyone knows that they do. Such arrangements can hardly be called 'marriage.'"

"But some do stand before the druids on that same day and make a contract of *permanent* marriage." He moved a little closer to her. "Niamh—you did not want to be a Lughnasa Sister, and I respected your decision. Will you, then, consider making a Fair Marriage with me, and be my wife for the following year?"

She turned to look into his soft dark eyes, and though her lips parted she could not find the words.

At her hesitation he said, "It would only be for one year. If it does not suit you, you have only to walk away at the end of a year."

"Only to walk away . . ." Niamh made herself look away from him. "Could you walk away so easily, Bryan? Perhaps you could. Many men find it easy. But I could not do such a thing. My heart is not so cold." She raised her chin. "No, I cannot accept a Fair Marriage. Not with you, not with anyone."

"Oh, Niamh . . . please don't turn me away again. Why

would you reject this offer? It's not that I would find it easy to walk away; it is just that I understand some things must be tried and tested before anyone knows if they are suited. That's what the Fair Marriage is for.

"Look at me, Niamh. We are good together. It could be a very fine year. What would you have to lose by accepting me? Surely a year spent with me would be far less lonely for a beautiful young woman than to spend that same time with only her family and the woodland creatures for company!"

She shook her head firmly. "I cannot do this, Bryan. I *will* not."

"Do you think I do not truly care for you?" He paused, lost in thought. "With all of my men watching, I stopped Ardal from destroying the *puca*. They believed I would only help him kill it and still do not understand my actions . . . yet that is something I did for you, because you asked it of me, and because I believed you when you so firmly said that this creature should not be harmed."

She took hold of his hand once more. "I do believe you care for me, Bryan. I am glad to know that you had such respect for my thoughts that you spared the life of what seems to be a monster.

"Yet you have not spoken of love. You have not spoken of any wish to be married to me beyond the time of next year's Fair. And you will almost certainly be a tanist and then a king. If that should happen, what will you do then after one year?"

He shifted a little on the grass. "Who can say how they will feel about another after such a time? No man knows the answer to that, not even a king. That is the purpose of the Fair Marriage, is it not, to let couples see whether or not they want to make a permanent bond?"

Niamh laughed a little. "I think most couples make the Fair Marriage because they already know they would never want a permanent relationship with each other, but are glad enough to have some easy companionship for a year. Sometimes men do this in order to keep freedom to seek other partners. Sometimes women do this in order to have the child of a strong and handsome man without the trouble of having that same man underfoot once the child is born—a man who may well want to leave her later for yet another partner."

She shrugged and continued, "If you expect little, you will not be disappointed. And so it is with the Fair Marriage. Were I to accept you, I would still be alone with my family and the woodland creatures after one year. Quite possibly I would have a child to raise, and I would know that I am nothing but just another woman to that child's father.

"Why should I wish to do such a thing to myself, when I already know it is not what I want? When I already know that you are not a man who is inclined to make a permanent marriage?"

He looked away. "It is true," he said quietly. "I told you as much. I have seen what happens to so many couples after they have stayed married—or tried to—for more than just a few years."

Niamh turned to him and gave him a slow smile. With some effort, she got up from her comfortable spot in the soft grass and stood looking down at Bryan. "Come with me," she said as he got to his feet. "I will show you how things can be."

They walked together down the shadowed mountainside, past more couples spending the evening together beneath the trees, and into the brightness of the torchlit camp. There were couples here, too, most of them older than the nineteen- and twenty-year-olds on the mountain. These were husbands and wives who had been together for five years, ten years, even twenty years or longer; Niamh knew many of them, and even with those she did not, she found it easy to read their faces.

They passed one large campsite where the men gathered in a group, standing about, drinking and boasting and laughing, and the women in another, sitting on sheepskins on the other side of the camp, while children ran and played near their feet. On the other side of the path from them, Niamh paused in the shadows between the torches and took a careful look at the women.

"Study them, Bryan," she said. "What do you see?"

He was silent for a moment. "Older women," he said at last. "Mothers and grandmothers. Thirty, forty, even fifty years of age. They are like so many of the women I see who have been married for some time. They are smiling and talking now, but underneath they have that bitter, wary look that is so common among them—as though they were worn out by life and dried out by age and children." He shrugged. "It is simply the way of things."

"Is it?" Niamh looked back toward the women again. "Watch, now. The men are coming over to them."

They could not hear what was being said, but as the men approached, the faces of the women changed. Where they had been relaxed and even smiling, they became grim and tense and guarded. Two of them got up and followed their husbands back to their tents; the rest of the women stayed to enjoy each other's company, but did not relax until their men had wandered off in search of more beer.

"It is the way of things," Bryan repeated. "I do not

176

know why it should be so. I only know that when women grow older, when they have been married for a time, they become cold and distant, bitter and harsh. It is true for nearly all the women I have ever encountered. It is the way of things, and so I wanted no part of it. I did not want to marry a young, vital, beautiful woman, only to watch her grow dry and bitter with the years."

"Well, then," Niamh said lightly, "perhaps we could find a very ugly girl to marry you, and then you would not have to worry about such things."

He glanced at her, and then smiled. "I do not think that would solve the problem."

Niamh looked back toward the remaining women. "If you have a garden of herbs, or a field of wheat, what will happen to if you merely plant your seeds and then turn your back on it? Or, perhaps, if you spend your time tending to someone else's field, and leave your own to take care of itself?"

"Well . . . it may grow poorly, or not at all, if it gets no tending."

"You are right. The herbs will be thin and dry and bitter. The grain will be scant and poor."

"Of course. Everyone knows that."

"Of course. But will you then be annoyed at the herbs for being bitter, or angry at the grain because it gives you no nourishment? Will you then turn your back on your own starving field and go in search of another, since you cannot understand why your own grows so poorly? Will you then be just as angry at your new field when it, too, becomes dry and bitter and poor?"

Bryan kept silent, but he looked closely at the women and then back to their men.

"Come with me," Niamh said, and together they continued through the encampment.

They walked down toward the far end of the field, down near the cattle pens, which were well-guarded but otherwise quiet. Niamh watched for couples along the way, and quietly pointed them out to Bryan.

"This man and woman walking toward us—I know them. They live in a *rath* not far from our own." She nodded to them as they passed, and the couple smiled at her in return. "See how they carry that bucket of water together? They are companions. They work as a team in all things. Because of this, she will always be there for him whenever he needs her, just as he will always be there for her. Neither of them ever needs to fear that the other will not be there."

"How long have they been together?"

"Eight years. Her hair shows a little grey, her face a few lines. Her body is no longer slim as it was, after two children. Yet her eyes are as bright and as hopeful and as loving as any eighteen-year-old girl. Did you see it when she passed us?"

"I did," he answered. "But eight years is not so long. The change will still come over her, sooner or later."

"Will it, now?" Niamh smiled a little, and shook her head. "I have one more gathering to show you."

They continued around the camp, and stepped off the main path toward the river. There beneath the oaks on the wide grassy bank, listening to the singing sounds of the water, were many small groups of people and many couples. Niamh walked along the edge of the grass looking carefully at the gatherings.

"Here, Bryan," she said, stopping beside one of the heavy branching oaks. "Look at these people."

Not far from the water's edge was a circle of some five couples, all wearing simple clothes of plain linen and dark wool just as Niamh was, all passing around cups of beer and listening with much laughter and low humor to a story one of them was enthusiastically telling.

"Watch the man and woman sitting nearest the river," Niamh said. "The woman with the long grey braid, and the man with the light brown hair and beard."

Bryan glanced at her, frowning a bit in confusion. "I see them."

"Watch the way she stays always near him, always with her hand on his arm or on his knee. Watch how he always keeps her comfort in mind, sharing his cup with her or placing his cloak around her shoulders against the cool air from the river."

Bryan nodded. "They seem very happy, as do all of the other couples in this circle."

"So they do. Now look at the faces of these women. You may see lines in them, and the wear of years and hard work; you will see grey hair above them and not the blond or red or soft brown of youth. But with these women, you will also see peace and contentment, and even love. Why do you suppose that is?"

"Perhaps ... perhaps they are happy with their husbands."

"Indeed. But what is it that makes them happy? It is not wealth; these men and women are all people of the land, as I am. They have no riches, no luxuries. They have no shining gold brooches. They have no beautiful swords with fine bone hilts. They have naught but a few head of cattle, if any. What do these women have to be happy about?"

He could only shake his head, and Niamh smiled. "These men—these few, simple men—learned long ago that the way to reap a beautiful golden harvest of wheat is to tend the field each day and provide it generously with whatever it might need. They also learned to give the same to their wives, to give them the same care and attention now that they gave them during the first days of their knowing one another. And they reap a harvest here worth more to them than any amount of gold."

"I can see that." He paused, studying the couples again. "If you do not mind telling me—what is the age of that woman you pointed out to me? The one with the long grey braid? If you know her age, of course," he added quickly.

"I do know it. She is fifty-one years of age."

His jaw dropped. "Fifty-one? She cannot be fifty-one. Forty, perhaps, at most. I cannot believe she is fifty-one!"

Niamh laughed. "But I can tell you for certain that she is. She is my mother."

"Well, of course. I knew that the moment you pointed her out to me. So I do suppose you would know her age, but I never would have guessed it."

Niamh reached up and touched him gently on the cheek. "If you want to know what a man is truly like, you have only to look upon the face of his wife."

With that she turned and walked away, back to her encampment alone, her fists clenched with the effort of forcing herself to leave him standing there.

Chapter Sixteen

Just past dawn, with the grass still damp with dew and the air soft beneath cloudy grey skies, a crowd gathered on the open playing field beside the great encampment. Near the center of the field stood the same nine druids who had presided over the ritual of the bonfire the night before. Now they stood in front of a tall stack of small smooth river rocks, at the top of which rested a very unusual stone.

This was a wide, flat stone that must have rested for many, many years beneath the edge of some waterfall, for it had a large hole worn all the way through the center of it—a hole large enough for a man to place his fist through. The stone had been placed on its end on the pile of rocks, and wedged down into it so that it stood up straight.

Niamh stood with Aine at the edge of the crowd. Her eyes flicked over the people, but to her relief she saw no sign of Bryan.

"He's not here," Aine whispered. "I've been looking,

too. But it's mostly women who like to watch the Fair Marriage ceremony."

Niamh tried to smile. "Of course he is not here. I only came because you said you wanted to watch."

"And why do you think I wanted to watch?"

Niamh started to answer, but just then the druid began to speak. "Gather 'round, all of you who wish to make the Fair Marriage," cried the chief druid. "Stand together, side by side, men behind men and women behind women, here at the edge of the Marriage Stone."

The ten couples lined up as instructed, all of the women dressed in new linen gowns, plain like Niamh's, and the men in new dark woolen breeches and plain linen tunics. The women carried sprays of bright white daisies from the fields and long slender twigs from the rowan trees, their green leaves just beginning to turn to red. The colors were bright against the soft cream hue of their gowns.

"You are here because you have chosen to make a temporary marriage. If indeed this is still your wish, then the man and the woman of each couple shall stand on either side of this stone and place their hands through it, clasping each other's wrists. Then they shall repeat the words, 'I pledge to you my fidelity until the time of the next Lughnasa Fair, when we shall either renew this vow to each other or else walk away and end it.'"

The first couple stepped forward and placed their hands through the stone. "*I pledge to you my fidelity . . .*"

Strong but gentle hands took Niamh by the shoulders. "Come with me, please, this way, and speak to me for a moment." Bryan began walking toward the end of the line of couples, all but carrying Niamh before him, and before she could think she found herself walking with him. A quick glance over her shoulder revealed only Aine's delighted smile.

"Bryan, whatever are you doing?" Niamh asked, suddenly breathless. "Why are you here? I came only because Aine wished to see the ritual."

"... *until the time of the next Lughnasa Fair* ..."

He turned her around to face him. "Make the Fair Marriage with me, Niamh. There is still time. We can go and stand with the others right now."

She glanced at the line of couples lined up at the stone. "I cannot," she whispered. "You know that I cannot."

"... *when we shall either renew this vow to each other* ..."

"I have never offered this to any woman before." Bryan took both her hands in his own. "How long will you make me wait?"

"One more answer, Bryan," she whispered. "You must find my last answer and then decide if you still want me."

He pressed her even harder. "Let me be the one to take away your loneliness, as you wished at the bonfire. Let me be the one."

"... *or else walk away and end it.*"

She could only shake her head. "If I marry you this day, I will still be alone at the end of one year. I know it." She looked up into his eyes, eyes that were filled with warmth and desire for her and only for her. It would be so easy to yield and go with him now, so very easy. . . .

She pressed his hands together and then released them. "I thank you for your offer. I do not take it lightly. But I wear this golden comb in my hair for a reason. I must have my last answer."

And Niamh closed her eyes then turned and walked away, all the way back to her family's campsite. She went to the cowhide tent and sat down inside it and closed the front cover, shutting out the sight of the Lughnasa Fair and the handsome young couples who could place their hands through a hole in a stone and pledge their love to each other for just one year.

That afternoon, the air hung close and heavy over the camp. Niamh stepped out of her tent and looked out toward the field where the Fair Marriages had been made that morning.

She saw only a great shouting crowd lining both sides of the field, watching yet another game of hurley. The couples were gone, as were the druids and the magical stone with the hole worn through it.

She blinked as a few drops of cold rain touched her face. She looked up and saw that while the sky overhead held only a few puffy white clouds and the sun shone down on the encampment, a soft grey wall of cloud moved slowly toward them and was already sending its contents down to the Fair. Niamh brushed the loose strands of her hair back from her face and started down the main path of the camp, heading toward the sheep pen.

The third and final great trading session of the Lughnasa gathering was the Sheep Fair. As the grey cloudbank crept overhead, dropping its light misty rain even as the sun continued to shine, Niamh reached the sheep pen and found that the trading had already begun.

Her family had no lambs to trade this year, so ordinarily she would have had little interest in the Sheep Fair. There was always plenty of work to be done at the camp if she was in need of something to pass the time. But on this day she wanted to take a close look at the Sheep Fair for herself, for now she had a much more pressing reason to want to see how it was being conducted.

The vast rectangular stone pen meant for sheep was built like the ones for the cattle and the horses, but had been further divided up inside by the haphazard placement of piles of thorny branches of gorse to keep the animals separated by owner into little flocks. The pens were very busy even as the light rain continued to fall. The shaggy brown animals, some of them with their fleeces at half-growth after having been shorn for their wool that summer, continuously bleated and darted and bunched up together, and tried to avoid the noisy men looking over the sides of the pens while driving bargains for the animals.

Niamh watched it all very closely from her place at the wall. As with the cattle and the horses, most of the sheep and lambs seemed to have been cared for well enough. These were fat and lively, even beneath their thick matted coats of brown wool. But others huddled close and still and hung their heads near the center of their pens, suffering the aftereffects of brutal and careless shearing. They carried long half-healed knife cuts that had never been tended, and wide scrapes so deep that the wool would no longer grow there. As with the cattle, these thin and suffering animals were traded for a few poor items and taken away for immediate slaughter.

Niamh's fingers tightened on the wall. While she heard no sound, no rasping laugh or guttered neigh, she knew where she would be this night.

In the darkness before moonrise, Niamh crept through the shadows along the deserted riverbank, watching the long stone and gorse walls of the sheep pens. They were blazing with light from what seemed like the hundreds of torches surrounding them, and every few steps stood an armed man looking out into the night.

It seemed she was not the only one who expected the *puca* to return.

She started to step out from behind the trees, but then caught her breath. Walking along the path by the sheep pen, with Leary beside him, talking to the men who stood guard, was Bryan.

Niamh melted back into the welcome darkness. She had not wanted to see him again this day, not after turning down his twice-made offer of a temporary marriage. Tomorrow, perhaps, but not tonight. Tonight she had other things to think of, and for that she was almost grateful.

Suddenly Bryan stopped and looked directly toward the river. Leary almost bumped into him. Niamh's heart leaped into her throat. He had seen her! She thought she had been so careful. Now she would have to speak to him; now they would have to engage in the strained and uncomfortable conversation that was bound to follow such a day. . . .

But then she realized that Bryan and Leary were not looking at her at all. They were peering into the deep darkness on the other side of the river, and quickly Bryan sent Leary dashing off toward the other men.

Finally Niamh turned to look behind her, and there, in the deep forest on the other side of the river, were two small, glowing red-yellow spheres of light.

It is here. It is here!

Niamh turned back to look at Bryan, caught up her skirts and began to run to him. But he had already raced toward the gate at the far end of the enclosure, barred with logs like the cattle and horse pens, and just as Niamh reached the path, she saw a great black shadow gallop out of the night and head directly toward the gate.

"Get back! Go from here!" Bryan yelled. He grabbed a torch and whipped it back and forth in front of the *puca*. "Do not make them destroy you!"

The beast reared up high in front of Bryan, its enormous hooves waving over his head. Then, still standing tall, it launched itself through the air toward the gate. The gate was blocked with a line of torches directly in front, and so the *puca* landed before the gate—but was immediately met with a hail of sling-stones aimed straight at its head.

With a screeching roar of rage, the *puca* turned and leaped back onto the path, flinging its head and sending drops of blood flying over its tormentors. With a chill of fear, Niamh watched the great black beast gallop away, straight down the main path of the camp.

She ran after it, hoping against hope that somehow she could get it to listen to her, that somehow she could persuade it to leave them all alone—but she found herself caught up in the crush of angry, shouting men who were just as determined to find and destroy the *puca*. She was jostled and bumped by their elbows and shoulders, and left gasping for breath as the heat and smoke from their torches rolled over her.

Niamh halted and let them push past her. Finally alone on the path, she breathed deeply of the cool night air, caught up her skirts and hurried around to one of the outer paths leading into the camp. She could tell where the creature was by the huge glow of torches that followed it—but just as Niamh rounded a corner, the beast came straight toward her and forced her to step aside as it galloped past.

Sheer pandemonium broke out in the camp. Women screamed and caught up their children, men shouted out and threw torches and stones—but none of it deterred the *puca*. Unable to get inside the heavily guarded sheepfold, the creature tore through the main camp and set its furious red-yellow sight on anything made of wool.

It leaped over tents and kicked them down if they had sheepskin covers on the top. Any woman who abandoned her weaving or her spinning of wool would find the loom smashed and the wooden spools of thread crushed into the ground. And most terrifying of all, it would race up behind anyone wearing a woolen cloak, grab the cloak in its teeth and race off, dragging the victim down the path until either the fabric tore or the cloak's brooch pulled free.

Niamh touched a hand to her own soft cloak of dark brown wool and dashed out onto the path as the creature raced past. "Stop!" she pleaded. "Stop and speak to me! Let me help you!"

But after a quick glance from its burning eyes, the *puca* ignored her and went after yet another wool-wearing victim. And then Niamh's attention was caught by a team of six men running up to it with javelins raised—and one of them was Ardal.

"Do not! *Do not!*" Niamh cried, running to get in front of the men. She knew they would not throw if she was there—but in an instant something struck her hard on the shoulder and sent her spinning and falling onto the dirt path. Raising herself up and brushing the dirt from her stinging hands, Niamh heard a terrified scream—and looked up just in time to see the *puca* lower its heavy head, charge up behind one of the javelin-wielding men and throw him up on its back. Then it whipped around on its hind legs and tore off through the camp in the direction of the river, leaving behind only the screams of the man on its back as he was taken away into the night.

Like everyone else, Niamh raced through the camp after the *puca*, but by the time she reached the sheep pen, the creature was gone. All that was left was its frightened, sobbing rider, a strong man who had seen many battles and laughed at any other danger—but who now lay begging for help in the thorny gorse walls of the sheep pen, right where the *puca* had thrown him before it disappeared.

"Go after it!" King Conaire shouted to his men, his face red with anger and frustration. "All of the warriors save one small troop to guard the camp will go after it now! You know its blood can be shed. You know where it makes its lair. I want it destroyed this night! Do not come back without it!"

Chapter Seventeen

A few moments later, Niamh stood with her back pressed against a rowan tree, waiting while a great mob of horses and riders galloped past on either side of her and splashed across the shallow ford of the river. They charged headlong into the forest in the direction of the *puca*'s cave and she caught a glimpse of Bryan as he galloped past her on Luath. Their eyes met for an instant, but then he was gone.

She knew he had no choice but to ride with the king's men, but she also knew that those men had no chance of finding the *puca* again this night, not at its lair or anyplace else. If anyone was going to meet with the *puca* tonight, it would have to be her.

Niamh picked up the wooden bowl and the small leather bag at her feet, and turned back toward the camp. She needed just one more thing.

It was never easy walking through a deep and unfamiliar forest, especially when the clouds hid the rising moon, but it was even more difficult, Niamh learned, when she had a heavy leather bag dangling from her belt, a large wooden bowl in one hand, and the halter rope of a young and skittish mare in the other.

Criostal followed her willingly enough, but was understandably nervous and excited about being out alone at night in the forest. She tried to crowd close to Niamh for security, the way she would bunch up close with her own herd if they had been near, but this only caused Niamh to hastily get her own feet out of the way so she would not be stepped on, and to constantly steer the mare's head away from her again and again.

Her arm was growing tired.

On and on they went. Niamh alternately looked down at the faint path and gazed up at the veiled rising moon whenever its faint glow could be seen behind the clouds and through the tops of the trees. And then, at last, the forest thinned and there was grass under her feet instead of damp earth, and she and the mare were out in the clearing that held the grassy mound and the *puca*'s cave.

As she had expected, all was silent here, though she could see that the grass was much damaged and the earth newly cut up by horse's hooves. The king's patrols had come here first, but of course had found nothing, and were now tearing on through the forest in an effort to hunt the supernatural creature as though it were a hare or a deer.

Near the center of the clearing, in the soft light of the cloud-veiled moon, Niamh set down the wooden bowl and dropped the leather bag from her belt. Criostal snorted and paced in a circle around her, the horse throwing her head high as she tried to determine where she was and why she was there—and most of all, what might be looking back at her from the blackness of the forest.

Niamh got the mare stopped and then ran her fingers through its golden-blond mane. Criostal touched her nose to Niamh's shoulder as if to reassure herself that she was not alone, then sighed deeply and lowered her head a bit as Niamh continued to comb through her mane in a soothing manner.

Finally the mare reached down and began to graze, and Niamh set the lead rope down in the grass. "Wait for me. You will be safe here. I won't leave you." She stepped back calmly, and when the mare continued to eagerly crop the green grass, Niamh picked up her wooden bowl and leather bag and walked to the enormous, grass-covered mound.

It was cold near the mound, as though a chill breath billowed from within the dark and featureless cave. Niamh placed the wooden bowl directly before the opening. From her leather bag she took out a second smaller bag, set it aside, and emptied the oats in the large leather bag into the wooden bowl. The smaller bag contained honey, which she poured over the oats and stirred with the first finger of her right hand.

In her left hand she still held the long blond strands she had combed from Criostal's mane. She arranged them in a circle around the wooden bowl, rose to her feet, and stepped back from it.

She glanced over her shoulder to look at Criostal. The mare raised her head to look at Niamh, but then quickly went back to grazing. Niamh turned back to face the cold dark cave and held her hands above the wooden bowl.

"Spirit who lives in the place," she whispered, "show yourself to me now. I have brought you three things that all horses love: I have brought you oats, I have brought you honey, and I have brought you a companion—a sweet-tempered and well-treated companion. Show yourself to me, and let me help you, before the men find and destroy you."

Long moments passed. The only sounds were the mare's tearing and grinding of the grass with her teeth, and the soft breeze blowing high in the trees.

Niamh closed her eyes. If she could not find this creature and find a way to reason with it, it would either continue its attacks or the king's men would kill it—and a feeling of dread came over her at the thought of it being destroyed. She was certain, somehow, that its death would not be the end of it.

She took a deep breath. "Spirit who lives in this place, show yourself to me now. . . ."

There was a soft deep nicker behind her.

Turning, Niamh saw Criostal looking off to the side of the mound, still grinding a mouthful of grass. Niamh walked a few steps to look in the same direction—and froze there.

Glowing yellow eyes gazed back at her from the darkness. Before she could speak, the *puca* ambled past her and went straight to Criostal, who touched noses with it and then went back to her grazing. The *puca* turned and approached the cave, but its only interest seemed to lie in the oats and honey, which it ate greedily. Finally, licking the honey from its lips, it swung its great head around to look at Niamh.

"*Why are you here?*" it asked in its deep sepulchral voice.

Niamh stole a glance at Criostal. The mare swished her tail and went on eating. Niamh drew a calming breath, and turned to face the *puca* once again.

"I am here because there is an entire army of men

searching this countryside for you. They will not rest until they find and destroy you."

The creature tossed its head and made a raspy, throaty sound, and Niamh realized it was laughing. "*They will not find me if I do not wish to be found.*"

Niamh shook her head. "They are waiting for you now at the camp—waiting and watching every moment. If they see you, they will make every effort to destroy you."

The *puca* made no reply. Niamh gathered her courage and took a step toward it, and then another, until she was near enough to touch it.

She ran her fingers along the heavy arching crest of its neck. The creature stood quietly with a lowered head. When she looked at her fingers, she could see the dark traces of blood on them by the soft light of the moon.

"I know you are a spirit," she said quietly. "But it has always been said that some spirits can be injured. Some can be killed. You are one of those. How long can you avoid such a fate, if you keep coming around the world of men?"

It twisted its neck to glare at her, its ears flattening. "*I will never stop coming around the world of men. Not until I have my revenge.*"

Niamh withdrew her hands and folded them together. "You will be destroyed," she said quietly. "I came here to help you. If you will tell me why you want revenge, and why you are so angered, I will try my best to reason with the men . . . but if you refuse to tell me, there will be nothing I can do. They will destroy you, sooner or later."

"*If they do,*" the *puca* said, "*I will be gone for a time, but then I will only come back stronger and more determined than before.*"

She nodded. "I thought as much . . . and you saw that

Bryan spared you, protected you from the other men, because I asked him to do so. Now, then . . . tell me what you want, and both of us will help you if we can. That I promise."

The *puca* began to walk away. "*Follow me*," it said, and then disappeared into its cave.

Slowly, cautiously, Niamh followed the *puca* into the dark and yawning hole in the side of the mound. She could see nothing but blackness, feel nothing but the muddy earth beneath her feet, and hear nothing but the *puca's* clomping hoofbeats as it moved ahead of her into the cave. "This seems like a foul place for a horse," she said, keeping one hand stretched out in front of her to feel for the cave wall. "Dark. Cold. Wet. Lonely."

"*Not so*," said the *puca*, and it sounded to Niamh like it stomped hard on the ground three times with its massive hoof. "*See it with my eyes*," it said. Niamh blinked as a soft glow began to fill the cave, as though the moon were shining right inside it.

She could see now that the cave was as large inside as any fine house. Perhaps twenty people could have easily stood together within. And then she could only catch her breath in astonishment as she watched a rivulet of mud on the floor transform itself into a clear stream, and the wet earth spring up with fresh green grass, and the cold rock walls glow with what seemed to be soft and misty sunlight. Even the air felt warm and comfortable now.

"*A fine place for a horse*." The *puca* stood watching from the very center of the cave, an enormous, black, and very ugly pony with spots of red blood on its heavy neck. But at least its eyes had lost most of their fire and now looked solid black, as black as the cave had looked just a few moments before.

"Please," Niamh said. "Tell me your story."

"*Watch. Learn,*" the *puca* said, and used its powerful left forefoot to strike the ground.

A kind of faint misty fog rose up from the grass and filled the cave. Niamh could still see the black form of the *puca* through the mist, but the stone walls disappeared into the fog. And then Niamh saw the form of another horse, another black pony, which seemed to be walking across the cave—walking just in front of the mist—walking down a quiet road with a rider on its back and a tall forest on either side.

Chapter Eighteen

"*See with my eyes. See with my memory,*" the *puca* said—and Niamh realized that the creature intended to show her what had happened to it, show her why it wanted revenge.

An aging black pony with a rope halter on its head walked down the road in the lengthening shadows, burdened with a large heavy man. Great wrapped bundles of the man's belongings hung down over both of its shoulders and on either side of its rump, bumping and rattling as the pony trudged along. But the creature did not falter or protest; it simply labored on with a lowered head and a patient, uncomplaining look in its old brown eyes.

As Niamh watched, twilight fell over the forest road where the old pony walked. His rider repeatedly raised a large wineskin to his mouth. He teetered and wobbled and nearly fell off, but at every shift of his rider's weight, the pony stepped under him and saved him from sliding off in a heap.

Finally the rider seemed to doze off for a time. The

pony kept to his course, no doubt glad to be heading home. The darkness was falling and there would be wolves about. . . .

Suddenly the rider sat up. "It's dark!" he shouted, dropping the wineskin in the dirt. "I'll be late! The party! The celebration! The wine, the beer! I'll be late! Get me home, you ugly old piece of bone and hide! Get me home now!" And with that he kicked the black pony hard in the sides with both heels, and caught up the trailing halter rope and began lashing him with the end of it. "Get me home!"

The old pony raised his head and with great effort pushed off into a shambling trot. The bags and bundles bounced and flailed and rattled against him as he went, sending up a noise certain to attract the attention of every wolf in the forest.

"Get me home! Get home!" the man shouted, continuing to lash the pony's sides. "Have a gallop, and get me home!"

The twisted flax rope continued to cut his sides, so the pony finally lumbered into a canter. Right away he began huffing and puffing for breath, but his drunken rider forced him on. "Get home! Get home, now!"

Into the darkness the old black pony galloped, his head stretched out low and his nostrils flared red from the terrible effort he was forced to make. Dirty white foam covered his sweating neck and flanks and the air was filled with the sound of his loud rattling breath. Soon his eyes glazed over and his mouth opened with exhaustion and strain. He tried to slow down, but his rider only kicked him on again, and then gave the halter rope a violent jerk and forced the pony off the road and onto a narrow forest path.

"It's faster this way! Come on, you ugly old beast, get me home so I will not be late!"

The pony tried to stop, clearly confused by the sudden change of direction. It did not seem to recognize this path at all and tried to continue down the road. But another mighty yank on the rope and several more cuts on its sides were enough to force it galloping down the strange path through the darkness.

"Home soon! Home soon!" shouted the drunken man, even as the forest thinned and the ground grew more and more rocky.

And then the pony sensed what was coming but could not stop in time, for its legs and muscles trembled with exhaustion and it could not brace itself strongly enough to halt right away. The momentum of its own weight, and the weight of its rider, and the weight of the many packs and bundles it carried, were more than enough to send it stumbling down the precipice and falling over the steep drop and tumbling end over end into the blackness of the valley far, far below.

Its rider's screams echoed off the rocky sides until at last all was silent once again.

Slowly the mist began to clear. Once again the soft glow of moonlight filled the cave. The clear stream ran through the soft thick grass on the floor. Niamh stood quietly as the *puca* lowered its head to drink, though her hands trembled and her heart beat fast. "I am so sorry that this happened to you," she whispered. "It was a terrible thing. No horse should be treated so."

The *puca* raised its head from the stream. Bright drops of water fell from its black muzzle onto the lush grass as it walked to one side of the cave and stood watching Niamh, its eyes beginning to glow with yellow light.

"*I was only an aged horse, long broken through hard years of work, trying my best to please my master. But he was a selfish, drunken lout who had not a care for the tired beast who bore him.*

"There is nothing to be done for me or for him—but now, I will do all I can to see that no other animal suffers at the hands of men. I will not endure having them exist at the mercy of those who own them. I will not let them stay with men who love only shining pieces of metal and care nothing for living creatures.

"I will see that the animals are set free. I will destroy what I must to do so. And any drunken man traveling the roads at night will get a ride on my back he will never forget. Never again will he want to gallop any horse through the darkness and put its life in peril. I will see to that."

"So you have," whispered Niamh. "And I cannot blame you."

The *puca* snorted—a deep and frightening sound that echoed off the cavern walls. "You may not blame me, but the rest of the men care no more for their own beasts than my master cared for me. They will not rest until I am destroyed."

"Do you want all animals set free, then, so that none are ever used by men again?"

"I do not. Men should care for the animals they raise. I never objected to my work, when I lived as a horse. I wanted only fair treatment in life and mercy at the end—and I got neither."

Niamh took a step toward the *puca*. "If I could promise you that no other animals would receive bad treatment— at least, not while they are at the Lughnasa Fair—would you, in turn, promise to leave the Fair in peace?"

Again the raspy, eerie laugh. "I make no promises. I want only to know that no other beast will suffer the wretched life and miserable death that I endured."

She nodded. "I think I know a way. We will show you that at the Lughnasa Fair, all animals are treated as fine as any king, and that all men and women who attend may therefore be left in peace. Watch tomorrow, *puca*, and you will see that my words are true."

The creature snorted again. The soft light in the cave began to fade. The grass disappeared into the rising dark, and once again the floor was only dirt cut through by a rivulet of mud. Quickly Niamh hurried outside, walking out onto the grass of the moonlit clearing just as the cave vanished into darkness behind her.

She walked up to Criostal and caught her trailing rope. Niamh patted the mare's shoulder and then leaned her head against the warm neck. "I understand at last. I know what we can do," she said, and sighed. "All I have to do now is persuade King Conaire."

As first light began to turn the sky from black to grey, Niamh stood waiting beside Lugh's Well at the foot of the mountain. On one side of her was Bryan, and on the other was King Conaire, and standing on the grassy open space between the well and the main campsite was a good-sized crowd of sleepy, yawning people, each one holding a clean wooden bucket.

There had been no games or markets planned for this particular morning, the eleventh morning of the long, arduous and very exciting Lughnasa Fair. The tenth day was always set aside for the most exciting of the hurley games and many folk had stayed up very late to celebrate with beer and meat—at least, all those who were not ordered by the king to either ride out after the *puca* or keep guard at the encampment.

The warriors had returned empty-handed, and the guards had been told to leave their posts. Most had planned to get some extra sleep, but they had been roused before dawn by order of King Conaire. Now everyone stood blinking in the first light of day, fighting either lack of sleep or the effects of a long night's drinking, or both.

Niamh felt lightheaded too, but it was from the rare combination of fatigue and excitement. She fairly trembled as she stood beside the king, listening as he gave his final instructions to the gathering.

"Each of you will take your bucket and fill it from the well—from Lugh's Well, right here." The only response was a puzzled silence from the gathering. The soft splashing and falling of the water could be heard in the stillness, as could the early-morning calling and singing of the birds.

"Go now!" shouted the king. He had had no sleep either, Niamh knew, for he had waited all night for the return of either his warriors or the *puca*. "Go and fill the buckets from the well. Then take them around to every animal in this camp, and let them drink what they will. Take special care to offer this water to any creature that might be injured or weak. Go! Go *now!*"

Slowly the crowd began to shuffle off toward the well, their buckets banging together while their low grumbling filled the air. And Niamh's excitement quickly faded, replaced by a sinking heart as she heard what the people were saying.

"Why are all the animals getting water from Lugh's Well? Has the river run dry?"

"That is supposed to be our well!"

"Why are we all hauling water at dawn, instead of sleeping?"

"That *puca*-monster only does its damage at night. There's no danger from it now."

"Why is the king letting an ignorant farm girl tell him what to do? What does she know about it?"

"I think I'd trade my next nine-days' ration of barley beer for a half-day of sleep!"

But they did gather around the well to fill their buckets, and began carrying the sloshing wooden containers back through the camp.

As they worked, King Conaire glanced over at Niamh. "I am not certain your idea will make any difference," he said. "Neither are the druids. And you can hear how the people are reacting."

"I can," she said, looking down at the worn grass beneath her feet. "They do not believe that someone like me—someone who has never even seen the inside of one of the great *duns* and is no more than a low-born servant—should tell the king how to handle such a threat."

Bryan took a step forward. "If anyone can understand this creature—this *puca*—it is Niamh. All the men of five kingdoms together could not find and destroy it last night. Perhaps we should try another way."

Niamh looked up at Conaire. "I am sorry, my king, to put everyone to such trouble. I know that one such as I has no place offering advice to the king. But I truly believe this will show the *puca* that there is no need for it to protect the animals of the Fair any longer, and then it will leave us in peace."

The king shook his head, but he continued to watch the line of people carrying wooden buckets filled to the brim with the clear sweet water from Lugh's own well. "I hope you are right, Lady Niamh of the Forest. If it continues to invade our camp and run rampage through the people, it is only a matter of time before it badly injures someone—or kills them."

Niamh, too, looked out at the people. "That will not

happen. I am certain of it. I promise you, my king, as I promised the *puca*, I will not let that happen."

By the middle of the morning, all of the horses and cattle and sheep in the pens of the encampment had been offered water from Lugh's Well, and most had accepted it right away. Any that had been suffering from injuries or sickness did seem stronger after a long draught of the water.

Now, with the sun rising ever higher, a very strange procession left the riverbank. It began to make its way through the main road of the camp, heading straight for the mountain.

Leading the way were five musicians—three pipers and two drummers—who looked a bit uncertain, but played merrily nonetheless.

Niamh was next, and beside her walked Anfa, for the king had commanded that she could choose whichever horse she felt was best-suited to this task.

Anfa himself looked very different this day. After drinking the water from Lugh's Well, he did not limp so much. Even the look in his eyes was softer and clearer, as though much of his pain had left him. And hanging from his neck, tied there with a strip of the finest blue linen, was a golden goblet—the cup that had been Bryan's prize when he won the horse-swimming race. It swung from side to side as Anfa walked, flashing brightly in the soft grey light of the day.

Behind Anfa, one of the men led a bull by a rope halter, with another man walking behind to tap the animal with a rowan stick if he grew too reluctant. The bull had a beautiful gold plate tied around his neck with red linen, and also had long streamers of bright blue and red and green and yellow linen tied to his horns.

Third and last in the strange little parade was a fine brown ram being both pulled and pushed by three strong men. Like the bull, he also had bright linen streamers tied to his horns. A heavy gold brooch had been tied around his neck with yellow linen, and it flashed brightly against his dark brown wool.

Strangest of all, Niamh saw as they passed by first the cattle pen and then the horse enclosure and the sheepfold, were the multitude of glimmering, dancing lights that flashed up from within each enclosure. Every animal now wore a piece of fine gold or bronze around its neck, tied there with a piece of brightly dyed linen. It was as though every small object of gold and every fine piece of bronze to be found in the encampment had been placed on one of the animals.

Niamh continued to lead Anfa through the camp with the bull and the ram following along. As they walked, more and more people from the camp came out to the road to watch them pass. Some of the folk shook their heads and looked completely baffled, but most were grinning and even laughing and clapping their hands, quite amused by the whole odd spectacle.

They reached the foot of the mountain, where King Conaire and his chief druid stood waiting for them. In the open grass beside the king and queen's camp, three fine stone pens with cowhide shelters propped in one corner had quickly been constructed. Niamh stopped before the first one, and the handlers of the bull and the ram took their charges to stand before the barred gates of the other two pens.

The chief druid stepped forward and addressed the crowd. "Lately the peace of the Lughnasa Fair has been broken by a strange and violent creature like nothing we have ever seen before. Not even the best men were able to destroy this supernatural beast, and it continued to attack and plague us.

"Another way had to be found. One young woman, Niamh of the Forest, found the courage to call this creature to her and learn why it holds such anger toward men. Once a natural animal itself, this creature is obsessed with making certain that no horse or cow or sheep ever suffers mistreatment at the hands of man.

"So, that is why we have placed a fine piece of gold or bronze around the neck of every animal at the Fair—to turn the angry eye of the *puca* from this Fair and show it that our animals are so prized that we place our most treasured gold and bronze on them to wear. This, we hope, will convince it that we do not value shining metal more than we value the living creatures who serve us.

"To further persuade the *puca*, these three animals—this stallion, this bull, and this ram—shall be kept in a place of honor beside the High King's own encampment, for they will be treated as kings among animals for the duration of the Fair. This will demonstrate to all how such beasts should be treated while in the care of anyone from any of our five kingdoms."

The druid looked from left to right over the crowd, and then he raised both hands high. "Now, then! Place these three animals in their fine new enclosures, and spend the rest of this day in celebrating them and this Lughnasa Fair!"

The music began again as the people applauded the druid's words. Niamh led Anfa inside the large stone-walled enclosure, onto the thick bed of clean wheat straw beneath the shade offered by the partial cowhide roof. She slipped the rope halter off his head and left him to find the mound of good grass hay in the corner. Two of King Conaire's men came to slide the heavy beams across the opening, and Niamh turned to see Bryan waiting for her.

"Thank you," she said, placing her hand on his arm. "Thank you for helping me speak to the king."

Bryan smiled at her, and he took the rope halter and hung it over the end of one of the wooden bars. "You were the one he believed. Now all we have to do is wait to see whether the *puca* believes us, too."

The afternoon went on with more music and laughter and storytelling, with plenty of good food and beer to make everyone forget their fatigue. Niamh walked through the encampment with Bryan and looked closely at every animal they saw—horses, cows, sheep, and even dogs—and every one of them wore some bright piece of precious metal around its neck.

"I think we are ready," Niamh said as they walked together toward her family's camp. "I think the *puca* will see, now, that no animal ever needs to fear how it will be treated while it is at the Lughnasa Fair. I can do little once they are gone, but while they are here, they are safe."

"That is all anyone can do. We can only hope it will be enough for this creature."

Niamh nodded, and she placed her hand on Bryan's strong arm. "I am going to lie down and sleep for a while. I plan to stay awake tonight to watch for the *puca*'s return. It seems almost certain that it will return this night, either because it is pleased or because it is still angry."

"Or because it is just an evil trickster that enjoys making us dance to its drum."

"Not evil, Bryan. An *angry* spirit, determined to have justice."

"But a trickster nonetheless." He stopped and caught

both her hands. "I will come back for you as soon as the light has gone. We'll watch for this creature together."

She smiled. "Thank you. I would not mind your company for such a task." Niamh closed her eyes as he leaned down and kissed her, his mouth as soft and warm as sunshine. "At darkness, then."

Chapter Nineteen

When night fell the encampment fairly glittered, for not only were there torches everywhere but they reflected off of the shining gold and bronze ornaments worn by every animal. And it seemed to be working, for Niamh and Bryan had walked two full circuits around the perimeter without seeing any sign of the *puca*—and neither had any of the guards posted every few steps around the edge of the camp.

The celebrating, music and laughter that marked every night of the Lughnasa Fair went on as it had during the day, and it seemed to Niamh that everyone breathed a little easier.

She almost dared to do so herself.

At last, as the waning moon rose high above the trees and glowed down through thick and broken clouds, Niamh stood with Bryan in front of Anfa's stone enclosure and fed the horse bits of bread and honey.

"I have never seen him look better," Bryan said, as the horse ate greedily from Niamh's hand. "Not even when he was a horse of the Fianna. He still shows an uneven step—I fear he will never be completely sound—but he no longer seems to be in pain. And for that I am grateful."

Niamh turned and leaned back against the bars, allowing herself a sigh of relief. "I am so happy that he is feeling better. Some say that the water from Lugh's Well is healing to them. I am glad to know that it seems to help the animals, too." She smiled at Bryan. "I want to thank you for helping me. I think we did find the answer."

"It was something a queen might do, Niamh. It does not surprise me at all."

She tore off another piece of bread and honey and, still looking at Bryan, held it up for Anfa. "I am no queen. You heard how my people reacted when they realized the king was acting on my advice. I am only a woman who grew up close to the spirits of nature and so was able to converse with a most extraordinary one. If I had grown up within the walls of a fortress, I would never have had any idea of what to do," she continued, as the horse took the bread from her hand.

As she gazed at Bryan, his expression changed. His eyes were large and staring, and he could not look away from where Anfa licked the last of the honey from her fingers. He opened his mouth to speak, but could make no sound.

"What is it?" Niamh asked. She looked back at the horse—and saw not Anfa licking her fingers, but a heavy black pony with a huge head and fiery eyes.

Quickly she drew back. Bryan caught her arm and pulled her away from the stone enclosure. "*Puca*," she whispered. "What do you want? Speak to me. You know I will do what I can to help you."

But the *puca* only glared at them both as it stood beside Anfa. After touching noses with the horse, it stood tall on its hind legs, leaped over the barred gate from a stand-still, and took off through the camp with a shrill sound that sounded like its raucous laughter.

"Not again. Not again!" Niamh cried, running after it. "Do not do this!"

Bryan held her arm as she ran, keeping her close to him. "Look—there it is," he said, and pulled her to a stop. "Just watch. I don't think it means to harm anyone. It never did before, and it was laughing differently this time."

"Oh, Bryan—if I have failed, the king will think me just a foolish girl and regret the day he listened to me. And the people will still have to live in fear of the damage this creature might do. They would never trust me again—not as queen, not as servant, not as anything!"

He shook his head. "You did all you could do. No one could have done more, or would have been brave enough to try."

They watched as the fire-eyed pony galloped through the camp. Its appearance was as terrifying as ever as it raced about, snatching up any remnant of bread, dried apples, honey, or cream that it could find, and at first all that could be heard was the fear and frustration in the voices of the people.

"It's back! All that work was for nothing!"

"Such a silly ritual, and the creature is still plaguing us!"

"I want my bronze plates back!"

Then Niamh began to realize that all the *puca* was doing was stealing food—anything a horse might like—and then dashing off again. All other possessions were left untouched, and though it galloped past the animal pens it seemed to pay no attention to them.

Then the *puca* snorted and turned away and began to

run down the main path in the direction of the mountain. Bryan and Niamh raced after it, and just as they rounded the corner they saw the *puca* standing in the road glaring in their direction—but Niamh realized that it was not looking at them. It was facing down Ardal, who stood with his javelin raised to his shoulder. The torchlight gleamed on the weapon's leaf-shaped bronze tip.

"Time to make an end to you," Ardal growled. "You're no spirit. You're just an ugly piece of bone and hide that wants killing."

The *puca* lowered its monstrous head and charged. With a chill of fear, Niamh realized that Ardal was about to get the most terrifying ride of his life, a ride that could end in his death if he did not kill the beast first.

"If they destroy me," the *puca* had said, *"I will be gone for a time, but then I will only come back stronger and more determined than before."*

Bryan charged past her, straight to Ardal, grabbing him around the waist and throwing him hard to the ground just as the *puca* thundered past. Together they rolled off the path until stopped by a low bench in front of a tent. The bench fell forward onto them, depositing a bowl of bilberries and cream—hastily abandoned by its owner when the *puca* appeared—right onto Ardal's head.

The two men sat up just as Niamh ran up to them. "Bryan! Are you all right?" she cried, crouching down beside him. "Are you . . ." She caught sight of Ardal then, struggling to sit up and slowly wiping the mess of thick cream and squashed and broken berries from his face.

The tension of the evening, and her relief at seeing that both men were unhurt, finally caught up with her and she began to giggle.

A crowd gathered, and they too began to laugh. "The beast is gone. We saw it run off into the forest. It bothered no one this time, save for Ardal! Look at Ardal!" And soon everyone in sight was laughing, both with relief that the *puca* had been placated and at the sight of what it had done to the one man who had tried to harm it this night.

"You will pay for this, Bryan," Ardal swore, through gritted teeth and clots of cream. "I could have destroyed the beast that terrorizes our people, but you chose instead to make a fool of me." He got to his feet, wiping his face with his sleeve. "You will pay," he repeated, and walked away into the night, carrying his shining javelin with him.

Niamh began to feel as though she could breathe again, but then her eyes widened and she caught Bryan's arm. "Someone said they saw it leave, but no one ever sees the *puca* leave. It's still here. I'm sure of it!"

"There," Bryan said, looking in the direction of the mountain.

She followed his gaze, and there behind the last row of tents she saw the swish of a long black tail as it disappeared behind the shelters. "Look! It's turning back toward Anfa's pen. If it comes back inside, perhaps I can speak to it. Hurry. Hurry!"

Together they ran past the tents, past angry and shaken people who were relieved to find that only a few dried apples had been taken or a bowl of cream overturned, but when Niamh and Bryan turned the last corner and hurried to the stone enclosures, they found only Anfa inside. There were no glowing red eyes to be seen anywhere, and no eerie raspy laughter to be heard.

Niamh placed her hands on the bars, even as Anfa

walked over to greet her. "As I stand here, I do not know what else I could have done."

"I do not know, either. If there is something more the *puca* wants from us—and it seems there must be—it will have to tell us what that is."

Chapter Twenty

The rest of the night passed peacefully enough, as did the following day. Only a few of the most die-hard players chose to spend the morning playing hurley; most of the folk stayed close to their campsites and did only the most necessary of tasks, and spent the rest of the warm and cloudy day in the luxury of sleep.

Niamh, too, spent the afternoon beside Aine and her mother in the soft thick straw on the floor of their cowhide tent. Yet her rest was often broken by a sense of urgency, almost like intruding nightmares, and she would jerk awake with a little gasp as, one after another, a series of disturbing images rose into her mind:

A raging black monster tore through the encampment. A huge storm threw planks of wood at her head. Laughing, flirtatious young women elbowed her out of their way so they could win all the attention from the young men. A tall and handsome man with soft brown hair and shining eyes turned his back and walked away from her, for the Fair was over and she had rejected him at every turn,

217

and what choice did he have but to move on and find another partner?

She sat up. Her mother and sister still slept in the straw and did not notice her at all. Quietly Niamh got up and went outside, glad to see that the shadows were lengthening. She would wash up and get a little food, and then perhaps take a basket of wool and a spindle and find a peaceful spot where she could spin the wool into thread and try to think of nothing at all.

A short while later, as the first stars began to appear, Niamh found a comfortable place a short way up the mountain. She settled in just behind the king's camp, behind the three new stone enclosures where the ram, the bull, and Anfa now enjoyed the best of care.

Here she could see the whole encampment spread out before her, and could watch for any sign that the *puca* was about—though she did not feel there was much to fear from that strange and angry spirit. Except for its threat to Ardal, it had not harmed anyone or damaged anything the previous night. Yet it had still seemed to want something from her, and if she saw the creature again she would do all she could to find out what that was.

A few other couples walked past her, hand-in-hand on the way up to their secluded meeting places beneath the low trees on the mountainside, but they did not stop anywhere close to her. She would be left in peace to perform her simple, useful task of rolling tufts of dark brown wool between her fingers to form yarn, adding more bits of wool to the end of the yarn, and rolling it again to lengthen the strand until soon there was a length of yarn to wrap around her wooden spindle.

She did not require much light for such a simple task, one she had done since she was old enough to hold the spindle. The glow from the torches and the stars was enough. Before long, the waning moon would rise and add its light to the mountainside.

She knew that Bryan must be looking for her, but on this night she wanted some quiet time to herself.

A tall shadow near Anfa's stone pen caught her eye. Niamh recognized Bryan's broad-shouldered form and long new green-and-gold cloak. He greeted the horse and fed it a bit of something from his hand, and then looked directly across the stone pen toward the base of the mountain.

Directly toward Niamh.

She sat very still. There was no way he would see her, not out here in the deep shadows of the mountainside, but he walked away from the pen and started heading straight toward her.

Niamh pushed one end of her spindle down into the basket of wool. Again, she could not avoid him. Perhaps she could just greet him politely and then bid him good night, and stay far from him after that, for she found that she could not bear to say farewell forever.

She rose to her feet just as he walked up to her. "Good evening to you, Niamh. You are out here alone?"

"I am. How did you find me?"

He grinned. "I saw the glint of gold from your comb. I knew it could be no one else."

She reached up to touch her comb, and then looked away without a word.

His voice was full of curiosity. "I walked all over the camp looking for you." He peered closely at her and cocked his head. "I feared that perhaps you had grown tired of me, and that . . . and that you had gone away with someone else."

"Never." She drew a deep breath and folded her hands.

"I only came here to spend a quiet evening alone and get a little useful work done—and to watch for the *puca*, should it return."

"Many are watching for the *puca*. If it should return, the whole camp will know instantly." He took a step toward her. "Our time together grows short. I only wished to see you when I could, for the Fair ends—"

"I know this." She turned away from him. "The day after tomorrow, you will be gone and we will not see each other again."

"Why must it be so? You can tell me how to find your father's *rath*. I would like nothing better than to come and see you when I can."

"When you can." She tried to smile. "I do not believe you will have any reason to come and visit me."

He tried to take her hand, but she held it close to her bosom. "I do not understand why you would say such a thing. I have loved your company during these days of the Fair. We have done such things together as I never imagined doing with any woman. I was there to see you take part in the harvest ritual and hear the king call you a daughter of gold. You were there when I won the horse-swimming race. And with that creature called the *puca*, Niamh, I never thought to see anyone do the things that you—"

"We did that together," she whispered. "Neither one of us could have done it alone."

"That is exactly what I mean!" he said urgently. "We are good together. I do not want it to end just because the Fair is over."

She twisted her fingers and tried, without much success, to keep her breathing steady. "Yet I do not see how that is possible."

He caught her arm and turned her around to look at

him. "I asked you to be my Lughnasa Sister because I found you both beautiful and desirable."

"And I refused."

"You did. And I took no other, for I still wished to spend my time with you."

"You did. And I felt the same."

"Next I asked you to make the Fair Marriage with me, because I believed we could find great joy in each other over the coming year."

She nodded. "Again I refused. Not because I did not desire you, but because I did not want to risk being left after one year . . . not when I knew I would certainly grow to love you during that time." She looked away.

He placed gentle fingers beneath her chin and turned her face back to his. "I have already grown to love you," he whispered with his lips nearly touching hers—and then kissed her again.

For long moments the Fair and the noise and the starlight all faded away. Niamh was conscious only of Bryan's mouth on hers, as soft and warm as she had remembered it, and of her knees feeling weak and her body growing heavy and warm.

"We are good together," he whispered again, his lips still brushing against hers as he spoke. "Tell me where in the forest I may find your father's house, and I will—"

With the greatest effort, she pulled back from him. "I am still waiting," she said, catching her breath, "waiting for my third answer."

His fingers tensed on her arms. "Still waiting for an answer to a riddle? Is that truly all you want from me—or from any man? If Ardal managed to answer your riddle, would you have made the Fair Marriage with him?"

She raised her chin. "Of course I would not. Do you

think I would merely walk through this campsite and take the first man who could guess the answers to my question? I asked them of you because you were a man I respected and admired—quite possibly a man that I could grow to love."

"Have you . . . have you ever asked any other man to give you these answers?"

She stared directly into his eyes. "I have not. You are the first. And the only."

He stared off into the night, then looked back at her. "You asked me to tell you what three things a woman wants from the man in her life. I have given you two of your answers. I said that a woman wants to feel safe when she is with her man, and comfortable as well. If I can give you your third answer tonight, does that mean you will give yourself to me before this Fair is over?"

"Of course it does not. It only meant that I might—*might*—consider marrying a man who would go to the trouble of learning the answers for himself." She turned away from him, her hands beginning to shake. "I am surprised at hearing such cold words from you, Bryan. I had thought better of you than that."

He moved to stand behind her, placing his hands on either side of her shoulders. "I am sorry," he said quietly. "I never thought I would grow to care so much for any woman. I should be thinking about the horse race to come tomorrow, yet I find that all I can think of is the idea that the Fair will be over soon—and that I fear I will not see you again."

She turned to him. "Even if you gave me your answer, and you came to my father's house to visit me—the fact remains that tomorrow morning, the horse race will be run. You and Luath will possibly win, and then you will be named tanist of Cahir Cullen. After that, the day will come when you will be made king—and I cannot hope to believe a king will remember a simple farm girl he happened to meet one year for a few short days at the Lughnasa Fair."

"Niamh, none of that is certain. True, I have no intention of losing that race tomorrow, whether the kingship is at stake or no. There is no horse that can get close to Luath, now that Anfa cannot run, but I do not forget for a moment that Ardal will stop at nothing to keep me from winning. It is not over yet. Nothing is certain. And—"

"It is certain enough for me," she whispered. "It is certain that you will leave here and go back to your life, whether it is as a warrior or a king. I must go back to mine, which is as a simple daughter of forest and field."

"But you are wrong," he said, and reached up to touch the shining comb fastened in her hair. "You are a daughter of gold, as well as of forest and field, and you would make as fine a queen as any woman raised within the walls of a fortress—far better, in many ways."

"But would your people think so? I am no high-born lady, Bryan. Would they wonder why their tanist chose for their queen a woman who spends her days among cattle and manure and mud, and is content to do so? Would they wonder why their tanist refuses to honor them by giving them a noble, learned and high-born queen?

"I have seen the curious stares when I sit among the nobles at a feast. I have heard the whispers and grumbling when I dare to offer help to King Conaire. They do not accept me now, for they know what I am and they know that will never really change. Why should they ever accept me?"

"The people of Cahir Cullen will accept you when they see your beauty, and your wisdom, and your kindness—and when they come to know that I love you, Niamh. That I love you."

He kissed her again, and held her close with the side of her face pressed against his chest so that the pounding of his heart seemed to encompass the whole world. "I love you, Niamh," he said again.

"And I love you as well," she replied, raising her face to look into his eyes, to kiss him once more, to lean against his solid strength and know she could always find safety and comfort there . . . at least for two more nights.

"Come away with me tonight. Come away with me into the shelter of the mountainside or the quiet of the forest . . . let us both love one another while we can, while we are still together. We shall be married on the last day of the Fair and I will take you home with me to Cahir Cullen, whether I am named tanist or no. It is a beautiful place, set deep in a holly grove in one of the oldest forests in Eire. I know you will like it there—"

Niamh closed her eyes. "Find the last answer to my riddle, Bryan," she said. "And when you have done so, ask me then. Ask me when you have won the race and your entire kingdom is cheering you as their new tanist . . . or ask me when, by some mischance, you do not win, but realize that you are still free to return to your life with the Fianna and take any woman you choose as you travel the country. Ask me to marry you then, and tell me these same sweet things then, Bryan of Cahir Cullen, for I dare not believe them until that time."

She caught up her basket of wool and hurried away toward the campsite, toward her family's tent, for she knew Bryan would not follow her there and that she would have the rest of the night alone.

Chapter Twenty-one

Time passed. Niamh pushed aside the cowhide flap of the tent and saw the hazy light of the moon behind the clouds as it rose above the trees. The camp was peaceful, with the sounds of casual laughter and conversation floating through the night. Her family was away, visiting with other friends, and Niamh could have stayed and had the quiet tent all to herself.

But instead she picked up a waterskin, poured a little cold water into her hands and splashed it on her face. Then she found her wooden comb and made certain that her long dark-gold hair was smooth and free from knots. Feeling a little better, she walked out into the warm night and started across the path that encircled the campsite, until she was just within the shadows of the trees and heading toward the river.

She tried her best to put all thoughts of Bryan from her mind. It had been a wonderful twelve nights with him at the Fair, a Fair she would never forget—but he was a man destined to be a king. It was one thing to court and flatter a young woman at the Lughnasa Fair and say he did not care about her station in life, but Niamh was certain once Bryan wore the golden tanist's torque around his neck he would never consider taking a simple farm girl as his queen.

Best to forget him and go back to her peaceful home in the forest, and to go on as she always had before—though she knew in her heart that this would be far more difficult than she could ever imagine.

Yet there was one other to whom she wished to say farewell, one who had been of great help to her in dealing with the *puca*. As Niamh walked in the shadows along the river, she watched the horse pens, which, like the other animal enclosures, were surrounded by torches and by guards watching for the *puca*, but she did not see any sign of Bryan. Quietly she walked across the path toward the bars of the pen, nodded to the guard, and then slipped between the bars into the enclosure.

Most of the horses raised their heads and watched her with bright and curious eyes, and they either held themselves away or turned and walked off as she made her way through the pen. But there was one small dark mare who stood picking through the gravel at the foot of the stone wall, searching out any stray bits of hay or tiny blades of grass trying to push their way up through the rocks.

So calm was the mare that she did not even bother to raise her head as Niamh approached, but went on with her grazing even as her human companion reached out to stroke her shoulder and gently scratch the roots of her mane the way another friendly horse might do. Only when Niamh reached into her small leather bag and took out a strip of rolled flatbread with honey inside did she raise her head, then politely accepted the treat and went back to her searching among the rocks.

Niamh sighed and rested her arm on the little mare's

back. "Thank you," she said. "You helped me when I needed it most. I am glad that you will be going home with Bryan. I know you will always have the best of care so long as you are with him."

She stepped back from the mare and walked through the pen once again, carefully avoiding the milling herd. Just as she slipped out through the bars and walked into the shadows again, she froze—for walking the other way, heading toward the separate stallion pen with Leary behind him, was Bryan.

She could not help but smile. It seemed that he had had the same idea as she, which was to seek solace among the horses. No doubt he had put all thoughts of her out of his mind and could think of nothing but the race tomorrow and the kingship that was possibly to follow.

Leary sat down outside the stone wall as Bryan stepped through the wooden bars. Niamh paused, wanting with all her heart to go to him and share a moment with him and his magnificent stallion, and to wish him well at the race tomorrow—but that would only negate the farewell she had already said and force them both to go through it again. Far better to just leave well enough alone and return to her own campsite in peace . . . as much peace as she would ever have again.

Niamh stepped back into the shadows and began making her way along the river toward her campsite, when a sudden shout made her turn around.

"He's gone! Leary! He's gone! Go and get some men—we've got to find him!"

Bryan flung himself through the bars. But just as Leary got to his feet to take off, Bryan grabbed his brother by the shoulders. "Never mind that. We'll go right now! He's got to be here somewhere. Someone must have taken him! He would not leave the other horses on his own!"

Bryan turned to race down the path—and nearly collided with Ardal. "Looking for something, Bryan?"

Bryan stopped and stared hard at his cousin. "Where is Luath?"

Ardal smiled at him, his expression so cold it sent chills up Niamh's spine. And, as she watched, he caught up an edge of his cloak and used it to wipe a dark stain from the dagger in his hand. Then he took his time in carefully replacing the weapon in its sheath at his belt. "Luath," he said, as though he had never heard the name before. "Oh! I remember now. Your horse. The one you plan to ride in the race tomorrow."

"The same," Bryan said, his voice low and snarling.

A man stepped out of the shadows behind the stone wall of the pen. Ardal nodded to him. "Cole, did you see the stallion Luath this evening?"

"Why, now that I think of it, I believe I did," said Cole. "He was walking through the ford toward the forest."

"What do you mean, 'walking through the ford'?" Bryan cried. "He was loose?"

"Loose? Why, not at all. How would he get loose? Even he cannot leap a stone-and-gorse wall that is higher than any man's head. He was being led through the water, of course."

"By who?"

"By Leary, of course. I can only suppose it was to get some cold rushing water on the horse's legs, and then perhaps to let him have a bit of grass in the quiet of the forest."

Leary jumped to his own defense. "I did no such thing! I have not taken Luath out at all this day! I would never do that unless you asked me to!" Stepping forward, Leary looked first at Bryan and then fixed a hard glare on Ardal.

"You know perfectly well I did not take that horse out to-day! You could not possibly have seen me do that!"

Ardal glanced over his shoulder and gestured toward the horse pens. "Flannan, come and join us!" Another man stepped out from behind the stone wall and walked toward them, taking his time with an arrogant swagger, and swinging from his shoulders was a blue-and-yellow plaid cloak exactly like the one Leary wore.

"I am positive that I saw a man wearing Leary's cloak take Luath out of the stallion pen, walk him into the ford and then lead him into the forest. Ask any man or woman who was nearby. They will all tell you the same thing: that they saw Leary take your horse into the forest."

Bryan's fists clenched. He reached out and grabbed Flannan by his duplicate cloak. "Where is he? What have you done with my horse?"

Niamh pushed away from her place in the shadows and ran to Bryan. Taking hold of his rock-hard arm, she tried to draw him with her. "Forget them, Bryan. They are playing with you. They will drag this out all night. We must find Luath ourselves."

She took a step toward the river, and then another, gently pulling him along. "Come with me, Bryan. Come with me. Leary, go and tell the king was has happened. Bring his men here. Go!"

To her relief, Leary took off toward the king's encampment, and Bryan began to step away, though he still glared hard at Ardal and Cole and Flannan, until finally he turned away from them and took hold of her hand. In an instant he and Niamh were dashing through the cold ankle-deep water of the ford and heading straight for the blackness of the forest.

The moon vanished behind heavy clouds and the towering tops of the oaks. Never had the forest seemed so dark. Niamh could barely see her hand in front of her face. "We should have brought a light," she said, staying close to Bryan as he went striding through the woods with terrible determination.

"No time. We'll find him. He's probably tied out here somewhere. They left him to be terrorized by wolves." He made a snorting sound of disgust. "The worm-ridden bastards—they will pay for this. Luath! Luath!"

They stopped and held very still for a moment, listening for the answering cry of a lone and frightened horse who might have heard his master's voice. But there was nothing.

"Should we get another horse? How will we ever find him? They could have taken him anywhere."

Bryan gripped her hand even more tightly. "They made a great show of letting people think it was Leary who took him through the ford and into the woods. He must be tied here somewhere. No horse would stay alone in these woods by choice. He would have come back on his own if he were loose. They want me to find him, just to let me know they can take him whenever they please. I'll keep him inside my own tent tonight—I swear I will never let him out of my sight again! Luath! Luath!"

Again they waited . . . and this time, a faint whinny came floating through the forest.

"This way!" Bryan cried, and he took off through the blackness toward the sound. Niamh followed close, grateful for the faint light that began to filter through the trees, and strained to listen for any sound of the horse's plaintive call.

"Luath! I'm coming! Tell me where you are!"

The answering deep whinny came again, louder this

time, and after just a few more moments they caught sight of the dark form of a horse out among the black silhouettes of the trees.

Quickly Bryan pulled his knife from his belt. "What sort of man ties a lone horse to a tree in the dead of night, leaving him as bait for every wolf in Eire? The worst sort," he spat, "and I swear my cousin will not live to do such a thing again."

Niamh took a deep breath. "Think, Bryan, please. You are still at the Lughnasa Fair. If you break the king's peace in a fight with Ardal and wound him here, you will be exiled from your home forever. If you kill him . . . If you kill him, the law says you will soon join him in the Otherworld. Please think of these things before you challenge Ardal to a fight."

But Bryan only went on striding through the forest, staring intently in the direction of that one plaintive whinny.

They hurried up to the horse where he stood very still beside a tree. Luath raised his head at their approach, but Niamh was startled to see that there was no halter around his head—no rope around his neck or even around his leg. Nothing secured him to the tree.

"Where did they take him, that he only got this far in such a time?" He stroked the stallion's neck, and the horse sighed and lowered his head until he was all but leaning against Bryan's arm. Bryan took a handful of the stallion's mane with his right hand and placed his left on the horse's chin. "Come on, old fellow. We'll get you home. Niamh, perhaps you could have Leary bring me a rope and halter once we approach the camp."

"Of course," she said, and placed one hand on Luath's back so she could walk alongside him in the darkness of the forest.

Bryan started to walk away and urged the horse to follow close beside him. But Luath hesitated, and stood with his head very low, and finally took two short hitching steps before stopping again with his head low and his front legs braced.

"What's wrong with him?" In a near panic, Bryan turned to look at the horse, but Niamh was already crouched down beside the stallion, running her fingers over the joints and sinews of his hind legs.

When she drew back her hand, it was covered with dark wet blood. "Oh, Bryan . . . no wonder he did not come home this night."

He got down beside her to see for himself, and discovered the same thing Niamh had found—a deep gash cut into the back of both hind legs, just above the large joint.

For a moment he was very still. Then Niamh could feel the trembling rage building in him. "I *will* kill him for this," he hissed, through clenched teeth. "Ardal was not enough of a man to face me. He had to torment an animal instead. I swear, he will not live to see tomorrow—though if he does, he will *wish* he were dead. I will see to that."

"Let's just try to get Luath home," Niamh said.

In a silence born of the coldest anger, Bryan urged Luath forward again while Niamh walked behind the stallion with her hand up on his rump to encourage and steady him. Step after painful step, the little party hobbled through the forest, while the moon rose ever higher. Off in the distance, Niamh heard the chilling sound of a wolf-pack howl.

"He is lucky you found him when you did," she said. "A horse alone in these woods, unable to run or kick . . ."

"I do not know how he survived. The injury is bad

232

enough, and with the scent of blood to draw the wolves . . ."

Just then they heard the crack of a twig and the low snort of a horse—and then, echoing through the forest, hoofbeats. Luath managed to raise his head and nicker at the sound.

"Which way are they going?" Niamh asked. "I cannot tell—are they approaching us, or going another way?"

"Listen," Bryan said. He halted Luath and stood very still. Again they both heard something walking through the forest—but now it was clear that these were not hoofbeats, but the footsteps of men. And this time they were clearly headed straight for them.

"We are almost to the river. Who else would be out here?" asked Niamh.

"Who else, indeed?" Bryan growled. Pushing away from Luath, he pulled his sword and stood looking into the dark forest, watching as the shadows of three men emerged from behind the trees and into the faint moonlight.

Niamh stood close by Luath's shoulder, her heart beginning to pound as she recognized Ardal, Flannan and Cole.

"What are you doing here?" demanded Bryan. "Haven't you done enough for one night? Did you want to watch the wolves eat Luath, too?"

"Why, not at all," Ardal said, his voice dripping with innocence and concern. "When you did not come back, we worried for you. The wolves were close enough to hear in camp tonight."

"Why did you do this? Why did you take Luath and cut him so that he will never run again? Why were you not enough of a man to face me on the racecourse or on a fighting field?"

"Why, I do not know what you mean," Ardal said, glancing first at Cole and then at Flannan, who both shrugged. "We told you, your brother Leary took the horse into the forest. That's all anyone knows." He nodded toward Luath. "I see you found your horse. Cole, Flannan, go and see to him, will you? I'd like to know how he fares. Will he be able to run tomorrow?"

"Stay away from him!" shouted Bryan. With sword raised, he stepped in front of the two men and slashed it viciously through the air barely a hair's breadth away from both their faces. "Get back! Get away! Don't you even think of going near him—or Niamh!"

A third sword joined those Cole and Flannan drew, one directly across from Bryan, and Ardal pressed its blade down over Bryan's. "I told you," Ardal said, and his voice was cold and angry. "I told you that you would never be the king of Cahir Cullen, and that you would pay for keeping me from destroying that *puca*. Not to mention the humiliation you heaped upon my head when the creature ran through the camp last night. The contest between us ends here. Tonight."

"So it does!" agreed Bryan. He whipped his iron sword out from under Ardal's weapon and slashed down at his opponent, who managed to block just in time. "Nothing would make me happier than to kill you right here, right now!"

Chapter Twenty-two

The fight began, the two men dark shadows with flashing blades in the moonlight, slashing and shouting at each other as they moved around the trees. Niamh knew she could not stop them—even crying out Bryan's name might distract him enough to give Ardal the opening he wanted—but neither could she just stay back and watch while Bryan engaged in a battle to the death.

She slipped away from Luath and got behind the nearest tree, and began searching the damp ground for any large fallen branch she might be able to use as a club—all the while keeping watch for Ardal's two cronies. They had stepped back once the fight began and now she could not see them at all.

"Aren't you afraid of drawing blood at the Fair, Bryan?" taunted Ardal, as their swords clashed again. "You'll be exiled for that."

"You have already drawn Luath's blood. For that I intend that you suffer far worse than exile." Niamh felt a chill at the sound of Bryan's voice, for his shouted anger had now turned to cold and deadly rage.

"You are the one who will be exiled," warned Ardal. "Perhaps I will let you cut me just a little, so that your exile is assured."

"I will cut you far more than a little. You will lie dead and bleeding on the forest floor."

"Will I, now! Will you kill me, Bryan, when you know it will mean your own life to do so at the Fair?"

"If I kill you, then justice will be done! And it will be far better than you deserve!"

Heart pounding, breath rapid as she listened to what could be Bryan's final battle, Niamh felt quickly along the wet earth until she found what she was looking for—a thick and sturdy branch as long as her arm. She picked it up and peered cautiously around the tree.

Ardal's two cronies were creeping around behind the crippled Luath. The stallion flattened his ears and bared his teeth and lashed his tail at them. *Pity he cannot kick them into the next fortnight!* Niamh thought, though a sharp strike from his long tail did slash one of the men across the eyes. With a muttered curse he stopped to rub his stinging face—and the other man paused with him.

She would never have a better chance. Quickly, silently, Niamh took the club and moved through the trees to where the two cousins fought. She crept around behind the blond-haired Ardal, who was so busy taunting Bryan that he noticed nothing else.

When Bryan spotted her, he held his ground so that Ardal would not see her and then fell back, shouting at his enemy to keep his attention, and to draw him away even as Niamh got up behind him and swung the club hard at the back of his head. It connected with a thud.

Ardal staggered and dropped to one knee—and slowly turned his head around to look at Niamh. Then he got back to his feet, breathing hard but standing upright, and laughed out loud to Bryan.

"So, you get Niamh to fight for you! I am not surprised that the very bold Bryan would have to have his *woman* stand up for him. Will she ride the race for you tomorrow, too? If you are king, will she confer with your druids for you and lead your men into battle in your place?" He waved his sword at her, then moved to face Bryan directly, and Niamh ran to Bryan's side.

"Go from here before I do kill you," Bryan said, with one hand gripping Niamh's arm. "Before I forget again that this is the Lughnasa Fair. Your death is not worth my life, any more than the death of a vicious dog would be. We mean to take Luath back to camp and leave you to the king's justice. Do not force me to do otherwise."

"Not at all," Ardal said with a cold grin, and he took a quick step forward and raised his sword again. Instantly Bryan shoved Niamh behind him—straight into the waiting arms of Flannan and Cole.

"Bryan! Run! Go back! Get the king's men, get away from here!" she shouted, even as she struggled and kicked against the two men dragging her off into the woods. "Get King Conaire, bring his men here! Get away!"

Bryan turned and started to go to her, but was stopped by the sound of Ardal's voice. "Now I will prove to you once and for all that you are not fit to be a king—or anything else. I have both your horse and your woman and they will never be yours again. She will make a fine Lughnasa Sister for me, don't you think? Keep her there for me, Flannan, Cole," he called. "I will be there in just a—"

With a shout of rage Bryan flew at Ardal, raising his sword and knocking the other man hard to the ground with the force of his charge. Niamh saw the sword rise up

237

again, the iron blade gleaming in the moonlight. "Bryan!" she cried, throwing herself violently back and forth in the grip of her two captors. "Do not kill him! Do not!"

The sword came down. She heard a sickening sound of the heavy blade striking flesh and bone, and then Ardal lay motionless at Bryan's feet.

Niamh closed her eyes.

Breathing hard, his face a cold shadow of rage, Bryan came striding over to Niamh and stopped in front of Flannan with his sword at the ready. "Let her go or die. Now."

Flannan hesitated. He looked at Ardal, who lay like a man dead, but then the blond head moved just a little and Niamh heard a faint groan.

"Go now," Bryan told Flannan, his voice still thick with rage. "Take your man and go."

But Flannan and Cole only grinned, and they gripped Niamh's arms tighter and raised their swords. "This one stays with us and with Ardal. He'll get up in a moment," said Cole.

"We saw what you did to him—you and that monster you call the *puca*," said Flannan. "He will be king. And he swore to have both your horse and your woman, and we said we'd help him. You can't best both of—"

Bryan reached out and grabbed him by the throat and tore him away from Niamh. The man staggered, and Bryan threw him hard to the ground. Then, before he could get up, he struck Flannan hard across the head with the flat of his iron sword. The man dropped to the ground unmoving, just as Ardal had.

After a moment of shock, Cole grabbed Niamh by the roots of her long hair and put his sword to her throat.

"Just leave us and go, Bryan! If Ardal cannot have her, no one will! Just go!" He pulled Niamh close to him and began dragging her back into the woods.

He did not get far. Bryan moved forward like a flash of lightning. He immediately struck Cole down with both hands on his sword. Niamh gasped in horror, and she leaped out of the way of the dark fountain of blood that sprayed out, glinting in the moonlight as Cole dropped to the earth.

This man would never get up again.

The night closed in around them with a darkness and a silence that seemed even more frightening to Niamh than the cruel and threatening men had. While she stood at Luath's head, she and the horse drawing what comfort they could from one another, Bryan securely tied the hands of both Ardal and Flannan with their own belts and took all of their swords and daggers and slings away from them. Then he came back to Niamh and took her in his arms, and they stood together in silence for a long time.

"Do they yet survive?" she whispered, drawing back from him at last.

He gave a short nod. "Ardal and Flannan will live, though they will be silent for a while. Cole, though . . ." He shook his head. "Cole has gone to join his equally worthless ancestors in the Otherworld, if any of the gods can be persuaded to open the door for him."

As the shock of the violent standoff and the sickening injuries and death began to sink in, Niamh walked on trembling legs to sit down on a fallen oak a few steps from Luath. "You have broken the king's peace at the Lughnasa Fair. You will be subject to his justice. You know what the law says about killing at the Fair. Bryan, what will we do?"

He sat down beside her, careful to stay where he could see the outlines of his two captives lying on the forest floor, and took hold of her hand. "Niamh, do not be afraid. This was no drunken brawl after a hurley match, or some long-standing grudge that a family decided to settle while their enemy was conveniently nearby at the Fair. These men stole and crippled my horse, and worst of all, they grabbed you and held you at swordpoint and made the worst kind of threats against you. What else was I to do? Ardal and Flannan and Cole were not going to be persuaded by a polite request. They deserved what they got. They deserve far worse."

She began to feel cold, and it was from far more than the faint mist that rose from the ground into the night. "The law is the law, Bryan. It is up to the king. There has never been an exception made before. You killed a man at the Fair—and I am afraid for you."

He drew her close. She closed her eyes and rested her head on his shoulder. "I am sorry, Niamh," he said quietly. "I am a man of the Fianna. I should have found another way to handle these three. But when he put his sword against you and started to drag you away, I swear to you, I could not hit him hard enough or fast enough. He got exactly what he asked for. Did he really think I would just stand there and allow him to take you into the woods?"

He drew in a deep breath, and looked down for a moment. "I will tell you that I am afraid now," he whispered. "Not of anything that Ardal or any of his wretched cronies might do—but of having to leave you and never see you again, and of never having the chance to truly make you happy . . . for that was the third answer to your question, wasn't it? A woman wants to feel safe, comfortable, and, above all, happy when she is with the man she loves. For I do love you, Niamh, and I can only hope that you love me half as much. And I wanted to make you happy."

Her eyes filled with tears. "I do love you, Bryan. I will be here for you no matter what happens. You have kept me safe more than once, including on this terrible night, and oh, I have been ever so comfortable with you on these beautiful moonlit evenings on the mountaintop . . . but I too am very afraid that we will never have a chance to find happiness together."

Luath raised his head and neighed loudly in the direction of the campsite. The sound of hoofbeats began to fill the forest. Shouted cries floated through the air, and soon glowing spots of torchlight appeared among the silhouetted trees.

Bryan and Niamh stood up, holding each other close. He said, "Whatever happens, Niamh, I will be yours. I promise."

"I promise, too," she said in return, and together they watched as Leary and ten of the king's men rode up.

Time seemed to move slowly as the warriors got down from their horses, and it seemed to Niamh that events unfolded as in a dream. Leary and a few of the men went straight to Bryan and Niamh, while the others hurried to see what had happened to Ardal and Flannan and Cole.

Before long, Niamh found herself walking through the dark forest beside Bryan, with a line of horses both in front of them and behind. The glare of torches served to show their way this time, and allowed her to see that Ardal and Flannan walked in front of the horse ahead of them. Their hands were unbound and they seemed steady enough, though she could see them occasionally rubbing

241

their heads as they walked along. They would not soon forget their encounter with Bryan this night.

She was aware that Leary and another man had stayed behind on their horses—slowly, slowly leading Luath back to camp. She did not want to think of what a painful journey it would be, for the stallion to make his way home, but at least he was no longer alone and at the mercy of wolves.

And just then, as she saw a faint yellow gleam deep in the forest and heard the nickering of the horses that looked in that direction, she realized that the cruelly injured Luath had not been alone in the woods on this night, and that he would be most carefully watched until he reached the safety of the camp. The *puca* had been there . . . and still was.

Somehow they arrived at the encampment of King Conaire. Niamh blinked in the bright light of the surrounding torches, each of which had a guard standing nearby by to keep away the concerned and curious men and women who stood as close as they could to the king's camp . . . including her own parents and her sister, Aine.

Niamh found herself standing beside Bryan in the wide grassy circle with the light of the torches bright upon them. A few steps away stood Ardal and Flannan, and as all four of them watched, two men carried out the dead body of Cole and laid it down in the center of the brightly lit circle, just a few steps in front of Ardal.

Three druids walked in and stood facing the silent four, and then both King Conaire and King Nessan took their places in front of the druids. They stood and studied the three men and one woman who had been brought before them—as well as the dead man lying in the grass.

"What has happened here?" King Conaire said at last.

"How is it that a man is killed at the Lughnasa Fair, where the king's peace decrees that no one is to be harmed—that no hostilities be pursued—while the fair runs its course?"

"Bryan killed him," Ardal said. "He struck Cole down with his sword."

"Is this true, Bryan?" asked Conaire.

"It is true, my king. I have done this thing."

The king's voice grew very quiet. "Did you not know the penalty for killing a man during the Lughnasa Fair?"

"I did."

"Then explain this to me."

Bryan closed his eyes for a moment. "I went to the forest to search for my stallion. Two of Ardal's men—Flannan and Cole—led him there and crippled him with a knife."

Ardal quickly spoke up. "It was Leary who took the stallion. Several people saw him go."

"Of course I did not take the horse, my king!" Leary cried, turning to Nessan. "I would never do such a thing!"

King Nessan looked at Ardal and gave him a cold glare. "And I suppose Leary was the one who crippled his own brother's horse? Why should he do that?"

"He may well have done exactly that," Ardal said, gazing steadily at his king. "What better way to keep his brother from the humiliation of losing the race—and the future kingship of Cahir Cullen—to me? This way, he has an excuse, and he will not have to run the race at all."

King Nessan took a step toward him. "The rivalry between you and Bryan is well known. Perhaps your men mistakenly thought to help you by harming the one horse that had a chance of defeating you in the race tomorrow, and thus have him named tanist instead of you."

Ardal shook his head. "It was Leary, my king. He was clearly seen leading Luath across the ford and into the woods. He was trying to spare his brother."

Niamh drew a breath. She could barely force herself to stay silent as the solemnity of the king's court demanded, and she could feel the equally rigid control within Bryan as she held on to his arm—but this was too much even for him.

"That is not true!" he cried. "Niamh and I went to the forest to search for Luath. When we found him, we saw that he had been cruelly lamed by cutting the sinews of both hind legs and then left alone in the woods for the wolves. A crueler treatment of any horse I never hope to see."

Conaire turned. "So, you found Ardal and his men with your crippled horse, and that is when you killed Cole?"

Bryan drew a deep breath. "It was not. When we found Luath, he was entirely alone."

"Alone?"

"My king," Ardal said, "as I told you, my men and I went searching for Bryan and Niamh when they went into the woods and did not return. We only meant to help them, but Bryan blamed us for the harm done to his horse. He fought with Cole—and he killed him."

Niamh could contain herself no longer. "That is not true, King Conaire! I was there the entire time. Ardal and Flannan and Cole knew where we would be, for they knew where they had left the horse. Ardal gloated over what they had done and swore that he would never let Bryan become king—that he would take both his horse and his woman. Me." She raised her chin. "And that is exactly what they tried to do."

"I am a man of the Fianna!" Ardal cried. "And tomorrow I will be named tanist of Cahir Cullen! Are you going to believe this ignorant farm girl, or will you believe me?"

"Flannan and Cole tried to drag me into the forest while Bryan and Ardal fought. They fully intended that Ardal should kill Bryan and then all three of them could do what they liked with me."

The chief druid stepped forward to stand beside Conaire. "Ardal and Flannan say one thing. Niamh and Bryan say another."

"Bryan came to my defense. These men would have used me the way three dogs would use a bitch. He warned Cole he would kill him if he did not let me go, but Cole laughed in his face. Would you not expect Bryan to do whatever was necessary to save a woman from such treatment?"

The king studied her. "It is a difficult case. It is understandable that Bryan would leap a woman's defense—but there is supposed to be no exception to the rule of the king's peace at the Lughnasa Fair." He glanced back at his waiting druids. "I will speak with them." The king turned and walked away, and stood with his back to Niamh and Bryan. His druids gathered close around him and they all spoke together in low voices.

Every heartbeat seemed to take forever. Niamh looked up into Bryan's eyes, and she could see the deep apprehension there beneath the enforced calm on the surface. She reached for his hand and he clasped her fingers tightly, and together they stood and waited for the king to make his decision.

At long last, when Niamh was beginning to tremble from tension and fatigue, the king broke off his conference with the druids and came back to stand in front of Bryan, Niamh, and Ardal. The druids stood close behind him.

"It is a difficult decision," the king said. "Even the druids cannot agree on what should be done. But I will tell you what I have decided.

"We have already said that since the free men of Cahir Cullen could not choose between Ardal and Bryan, we would ask Lugh to decide. The next tanist would be whichever one of them scored the better at three of the contests—the horse-swimming race, the javelin throw, and the cross-country horse race. Bryan won the horse-swimming race. Ardal won the javelin throw. Tomorrow morning is the horse race, and whichever of these two men defeats the other during that race was to have been named the next tanist.

"Now, however, the situation has greatly changed. Bryan is accused of killing a man during the Lughnasa Fair, which means that his own life is forfeit. He will either be executed or he will be taken away and sold as a slave in some far corner of Eire, never to return to his own kingdom again.

"Ardal is accused of stealing and ruining a horse, and of causing other men to hold a woman against her will—as well as attacking a man with his sword during the Fair. These things, the druids agree, should carry a penalty of not only Niamh's honor price but of exile of at least five years.

"Yet because these are no ordinary men—because they have both been favored to be the next tanist, the next king of the people of Cahir Cullen, we have decided to let Lugh decide this question as well, as we intended him to do with the question of the tanist.

"If either man wins this race—not just defeats his opponent, but wins outright and beats all contestants—he shall be named tanist and return in triumph to his kingdom. That shall be Lugh's will. The loser—both men, if neither one wins outright—shall be immediately blind-folded and taken away to be sold as a slave, and will never see his kingdom again."

King Conaire looked first at Bryan and then at Ardal. "Is this understood?"

"It is, my king."

"It is."

Niamh glanced at Ardal as he answered the king, and saw the faint smirk behind his seemingly polite and re-spectful expression. He knew that with Luath unable to run, there was no other horse that could outrun his grey. The race belonged to him.

Guards came to take the two men away. King Conaire ordered, "Keep them each in their own separate camps, and do not let them leave until it is time for the race to be run tomorrow."

"Bryan!" she cried, as the guards took him and his hand pulled out of hers. "I will send Luath with my fam-ily! They will take him home and heal him."

He nodded, saying nothing, and she could only stand and watch him go as fear built up within her. If Bryan lost, and King Conaire's men took him away, Niamh knew that he would never return. He must win this race!

But how?

Chapter Twenty-three

Once again, Niamh found herself walking out alone in the dark forest. She had a linen sack filled with neatly rolled strips of bread smeared with honey in one hand, and a small waterskin dangled from her shoulder, but there was nothing else between her and the black, forbidding wood, where clouds obscured the moon and it was all but impossible to see.

Yet she went on through the forest, feeling her way through the trees and trusting her memory to get where she was going—and accepting the help offered by the hazy light of the moon and stars whenever the clouds thinned enough to allow it through.

She felt certain she was not far from the *puca's* cave. She could only hope that she could call it to her again, and that it might consider what she was about to ask.

Many times in her life she had turned to nature for help—to look for signs that might tell her and her people whether a winter might be early or late, or whether the crops might be generous or poor, or even where to look to find the best wild berries or apples or watercress. But now she was about to turn to an unnatural, unreliable creature, and it would have her at its mercy if she somehow offended it.

Yet the thoughts of Bryan's fate if he lost the race tomorrow pushed her onward through the heavy darkness. She would stop and listen from time to time, straining to hear either the howl of a wolf or the snort of a horse, but the only sound was that of the soft summer breeze blowing high in the trees.

Finally she reached the clearing in front of the shadowed mound. All was dark and quiet here, so dark that she could not see the cave entrance dug into the base of the mound. Niamh stood in the center of the clearing, shook out the bread and honey she had brought with her onto the clean green grass, and stepped back to wait.

"*Puca*," she called, "I know that you can hear me. I know that you know I am here. I did the best I could to help you, to give you what you wanted most—and now I ask you to help me in return."

There was a deep throaty laugh from somewhere above her. Gathering her courage, Niamh peered upward at the top of the mound, and caught a glimpse of a fiery red-yellow eye.

She did her best to steady her breathing and keep her heart from racing. "*Puca*," she said again. "I know you must be angry after the cruel way the stallion Luath was treated. I am angry, too. Bryan is enraged. I have come to ask you for your help. Please—show yourself to me."

She walked toward the side of the mound, gazing up at it and straining to catch another glimpse of a glowing eye. But then there was a sudden rush of hoofbeats off to one side in the surrounding forest. Quickly turning, Niamh saw the flash of an angry red-yellow glare.

"*I was far away. I watched the encampment of the men from the mountaintop. I did not see them take Luath. Why did no one stop them?*"

Niamh shook her head. "We did not know," she said, and began walking toward the spot where she had heard the *puca*'s voice. "Bryan killed one of them. He would have killed them all if he could have, for what they did to Luath. He loves Luath the way a father loves a son."

She reached the edge of the clearing and placed her hand on a tree trunk. Again she stared hard into the darkness, and again she saw nothing.

There were hoofbeats, and a deep snuffling snort came from some distance behind her. She turned, and there in the center of the clearing, right before her, were the deep black shadow and glowing eyes of the *puca*. It was greedily eating up the bread and honey that she had brought for it, and Niamh walked up to the creature with all the calmness she could summon.

"Bryan must ride in the horse race tomorrow," she began, as the beast continued to eat. "Because he killed the man who harmed Luath, he must win that race. If he does not, he will be sent away forever. He will not see his home—or any of us—ever again."

"*Another horse—,*" the *puca* began, licking the honey from its lips.

Niamh shook her head in the darkness. "There is no other horse that could beat Ardal's grey—no horse except one. That is why I have come. *Puca* . . . I am asking you to carry Bryan in the race tomorrow. Carry him to victory, and save his life."

The *puca* stopped chewing. It raised its heavy head and fixed its fierce red-yellow gaze on her. "*I am no longer a tame beast to be used and ridden by men.*"

"I understand that. And I am not asking you to behave as a tame beast. I ask only that you save Bryan's life."

Another snort. *"He must save himself. I will never serve men again. They will fear me—not use me."*

Niamh closed her eyes. "We kept our promises to you. Bryan kept you from harm, from death, at the hands of the other men. I helped bring about the ritual of the Animal Kings and the placing of beautiful shining objects on every animal to show that it is valued and cared for."

The clouds covered the moon once more, and the *puca's* black form and glowing eyes were swallowed up in the darkness. *"Men will fear me. They will never use me,"* it said again. *"I was not valued. I was not cared for. I was beaten and starved and ridden to my death."*

Niamh took a step forward. "I understand your fear and hatred of men," she said. "They treated you badly and used you in the worst possible way. But Bryan has shown you—and I have shown you—that all men are not this way. Please. I beg you. Come to me at the race tomorrow. Come to me at the edge of the field, in the forest. Please save the life of a worthy man who risked himself to help you. A man who has always loved and treated his animals well."

There was silence in the clearing, silence and the soft wind blowing in the trees. Niamh walked to the very center of the dark clearing and strained to see the dark outline of the *puca*, or its frightening glowing eyes, but there was nothing; he was gone.

The clouds broke and moved off into the night, leaving a clear black sky with the waning half-moon and bright stars shining down—and Niamh could see no trace of the *puca*, nor where it had gone, not in the clearing or on the mound or in the cave.

She looked up into the beautiful clear sky, and there, in the direction of the mountain, she saw a few bright silver streaks fly through the black sky and vanish as quickly as they had appeared. This was Lugh's Rain, only seen at this time of year. Some folk said that if Lugh's Rain could be seen during the Fair, it meant that Lugh himself was present.

The druids and the king had called upon the god to make these decisions for them: first the choice of tanist; and now whether Bryan or Ardal, or both, should be exiled for allowing their rivalry to end in violence and death at the Fair.

And Lugh *had* come to the Fair, it seemed, and he would make his decision known to them tomorrow, in spite of what anyone might do to change it.

The first traces of dawn were beginning to show in the eastern sky when Niamh returned to the camp. She could see Bryan's tent from the main path, and it was surrounded by guards. He would be going nowhere until it was time for the race.

She stopped at her own tent, where her family still slept, and crept inside just long enough to get a little food and refill her waterskin. Then she left the tent, walked across the camp and through the line of trees, and started across the great open field where the hurley games were held and where the horse race would begin in a very short time. She walked all the way across the field until she was at the edge of the forest, and there she sat down to wait, even as the sun rose above the horizon and the first of the eager spectators for the race came walking out to stake their best spots to watch.

Soon the field was lined with people on both sides,

laughing and talking and feasting from the baskets of good roast beef and hot buttered bread and dried apples in honey that they had brought with them. There were many wagers made and many discussions held, some heated, about the penalties Bryan and Ardal faced. Bryan seemed to have no chance to win, many said, for what horse besides Luath could possibly beat Ardal and his grey?

From a short way up the field, Niamh heard a familiar female voice. "If he wins today, he'll be the next king of Cahir Cullen! And I could be the next queen!"

She turned to see Urla standing with a few other young women, wearing a bright red-and-green-and-yellow gown with Ardal's gleaming gold belt wrapped around her waist. "Oh, look—there he is!"

A roar went up from the crowd, for the horses were being led to the starting line. Their riders walked beside them, sixteen in all, with their fine racing horses prancing and jogging alongside them as the servants struggled to hold the excited animals.

The very first man was Ardal, tall and slim and arrogantly confident as he walked beside his nervous, long-legged grey. Last of all was Bryan, with Leary leading a small bay gelding with four white legs.

Niamh had never seen this horse before. No doubt it belonged to some man of the Fianna whom Leary had managed to persuade to loan his horse to Bryan. But it was clear to Niamh that this animal, sturdy and honest as he appeared, could never be expected to outrun even half the field—much less defeat them all.

Quickly Niamh got to her feet and stepped into the dense shade of the forest, out of sight of the eager, shouting crowds. "Please," she begged, as the cool dimness of the forest closed over her. "Please, *puca*, come to us now.

Do not let Bryan be lost to me forever. Let him be the king he was meant to be, a fine king who has a love for horses more than he has for gold or power or fawning attention. Surely any man who would stand and fight to defend his horse deserves to be a king, a king who would come to the defense of both the greatest and the least of his people. Please, *puca*," she whispered, "please come to us now."

Deep in the forest, a twig snapped.

Niamh looked up. Her eyes searched the dimness. And there, beyond hope, moving toward her, was a small, heavily built black pony with a flax-rope halter on its heavy head and a lead line trailing on the ground—and a fierce yellow glow in its eyes.

She let out her breath. Her knees felt weak with relief. The creature had come. It was here. Now, if it would only agree to do this; if it would actually allow Bryan to ride it in the race—

"Thank you!" she said, taking a step toward it even as her heart pounded. "I am so glad to see you. Will you . . . will you carry Bryan in the race?"

It swung its great head to look at her, and then looked again in the direction of the playing fields and the excited crowds. Through the trees Niamh could see the racehorses being led on parade for the people. Each horse had a small and shining piece of gold or bronze tied into its mane with a brightly colored ribbon of linen.

The flashes glimmered in Niamh's eye—and, it seemed, in the eye of the *puca*. She stepped close to it, and then reached out to gently touch the beast's shoulder.

"You were not valued. You were not cared for. You were beaten and starved and ridden to your death. Yet I have come to tell you that from this day on you will be valued and you will be cared for, and no horse will ever again be beaten or starved or ridden to death so long as Bryan of Cahir Cullen is tanist or king."

She reached up for the gold comb she wore, pulled it out of her hair, and held it out for the *puca* to see. "This is the most valuable and most beautiful thing I own," she said. "It was a gift from my father. It could never be replaced. Yet I give it to you now, as a symbol of the esteem in which all horses should be held when they agree to carry men upon their backs."

She reached out and worked the gold comb securely into the *puca's* thick black mane, wrapping the coarse hairs around the pins. The graceful golden stalks of wheat shone out even in the soft light of the forest, a bright counterpoint to the *puca's* night-black form.

The creature cocked its head and regarded her, and flicked back an ear as though turning its attention to the beautiful gold charm it now wore. It took a deep breath and sighed heavily, and turned to Niamh with lowered head. *"I will carry Bryan in the race."*

Niamh reached down and picked up the trailing lead rope. "Thank you," she said, and rested her hand for just a moment on the creature's heavy arching neck. Together they walked out of the forest and into the light of the morning.

She led the *puca* through the crowd of people and onto the open grassy field. To her relief, it walked slowly with its head down, and—most important—its eyes looked the soft brown of any quiet pony.

The racehorses were lined up across the field with their heads toward the mountain, their riders still standing beside them, and as the animals caught sight of Niamh and her pony coming toward them they all raised their heads and watched closely. Many of them nickered softly and began to creep forward, though they were quickly jerked back by the servants holding their bridle reins. Niamh focused only on Bryan, who stood with his back to her talking intently to Leary, but who turned around when Leary elbowed him.

She would never forget the look on his face. His eyes widened, flicking from Niamh to the *puca* and back to Niamh again, and his mouth opened as if he meant to speak but could not find the words. Niamh brushed her long hair back from her face and as she did, the breeze caught it and draped the dark-gold length over the *puca's* back.

What a very strange sight they must be to the men lined up for the race!

"Niamh," Bryan said, as she brought the black pony to stand before him. "Niamh, what is this?"

"I have brought you a horse for the race," she said. "He is quite a willing creature, if you are willing to try him."

Bryan could only stare at the black pony. He raised his hand as if to touch Niamh's golden comb, which rested in its thick mane, but quickly drew back. "Is this . . . is this . . ."

"It's the *puca!*" hissed Leary. His eyes held a look of terror and his face was white as milk. He struggled to hold the white-stockinged bay as it crept forward and tried to touch noses with the black pony, and finally managed to force the gelding back. "Niamh, what are you thinking?"

She placed her hand on the terrified Leary's arm. "It's all right. Do not be afraid. This is the horse that will carry Bryan to victory."

There were footsteps on the grass behind Niamh. She turned to see Ardal walking up.

"Victory? On this? Bryan means to ride *this?* Oh, that is very funny, Niamh. A very good joke!" Ardal turned and looked out at the other riders, most of whom had begun to gather round. "Look at this! Niamh has gone and found an old black pony that resembles that *puca*-monster, and brought it out for Bryan to ride!" He reached out and grabbed the pony's mane, tugging on the lock that held the golden comb. Niamh saw Leary freeze, but the pony never moved.

"She's even put a shiny bit of jewelry on it, just like all the other horses have!" Everyone laughed, and none louder than Ardal. "Oh, Bryan," he went on, "I do think you should ride him. He is a far better mount than any-thing the Fianna could provide!"

Bryan raised his head and looked directly at Ardal. "I agree," he said. "I believe I will ride him in the race."

The crowd fell silent for a moment—and then all of them laughed again. "That's very funny, Bryan," Ardal said, "but it's time for the race to start. Unless you plan to still be trying to finish the race at the time of the next Lughnasa Fair, I suggest you get on the horse Leary has brought for you so that your defeat does not take quite so long." He turned to go back to his horse. The rest of the riders, some of them still laughing and shaking their heads, went back to their own mounts.

Niamh placed the lead rope over the pony's neck so that it draped like a single rein. "Here, Bryan. He has agreed to carry you in the race. And you know there is no horse that can defeat the *puca*." She smiled at him with love and hope.

"So, it truly is the *puca*," he whispered. "I will have to ask you later how you have arranged for this to happen." Bryan looked down at the sleepy-eyed pony before him, and hesitated. "But why would he agree to carry me? He is a trickster of the first order. He may only be fooling us. Racing is hard work for any horse. Surely it would not be pleased at having to strain itself to the utmost, as all horses do in any race!"

"It has said that it does not object to animals working. It only objects to cruel treatment of them at the hands of men."

But Bryan did not look convinced. "He may well be angry at me about Luath's treatment. He's looking for a way to get revenge."

The pony swished its tail, but did not look up.

"Luath was stolen and ruined by cruel and devious men," Niamh said. "The *puca* knows that you did not do him any harm."

Brian looked unconvinced. "That may not matter. Luath was still my horse. I should have protected him."

Niamh reached across the *puca*'s neck and placed her hand on Bryan's arm. "This is no trick. He will carry you."

Still, he did not move toward the beast. "I saw what it did to Leary. And to the man it threw in the sheepfold. It's strange," he said with a shake of his head. "Usually a rider fears falling. But with this creature, I fear being trapped on its back."

"Bryan," Niamh said, "this will take all the courage you or any man could have. But if you do not do this, all chances for your future—any kind of future—are lost. You will not be tanist or king. You will be banished. What of us?"

He nodded and drew a deep breath. "I will do this. I will ride the *puca*."

Chapter Twenty-four

The pony's back was only as high as Bryan's waist. He took hold of the halter rope where it lay on the creature's neck, grasped a fistful of the thick black mane, and easily vaulted onto its broad back.

Steeling himself, a determined look on his face, he calmly reined the creature around with the lead rope. It walked quietly, turning this way and that at his direction, and Bryan rode him back to Niamh with an increasing look of confidence in his eyes.

"He seems agreeable enough, as any quiet pony might be. Niamh, are you sure you have not brought me an old pony that simply resembles the *puca*—as Ardal said?"

She grinned back at him. "Go, Bryan. The others are lining up at the start. Go now, and know that I am with you every step of the way."

He caught her hand and pressed it hard as he passed by, and then he urged the pony into a shambling trot toward the lineup.

Niamh held her breath as Bryan guided his shaggy black mount into place beside the sleek, long-legged racehorses. The riders held their reins with one hand and kept a firm grip on the roots of their mounts' manes as they waited on the slick bare backs for the starter to throw down his white linen banner.

The racehorses all snorted and danced in anticipation. Even Bryan took hold of his pony's thick black mane and leaned forward, ready for the start, though his mount stood absolutely still with its head down low.

There was a moment of complete silence . . . and then the starter threw down the flag. "*Go!*"

The racehorses took off past the shouting crowd, but Bryan was not with them. He was not even sitting on the pony. At the moment the flag had dropped, the sleepy black creature had launched itself forward and sideways so quickly that Bryan found himself sitting on nothing but air, and dropped hard to the grass.

In an instant he rolled over and was on his feet, but his face was pale as he clutched Niamh's arm. "I thought I was a good rider," he said, as the rest of the field galloped away. "But I see that I am not enough of a rider to stay with a creature like this. There was no warning. None at all. One moment its neck was in front of me, and the next it was off to one side and I was sitting on nothing. How can I hope to ride such a creature?"

As he spoke, the black pony wandered back over to him, its long halter rope trailing in the green grass. "You must ride it!" she cried, catching up the rope and throwing it back over the pony's neck. "You must! You know you can catch them, but you must go now!"

He walked beside the beast and placed his hands on its neck, but again he hesitated. "I told you it would not want me to ride it. I cannot stay on its back if it makes such a move again—"

"Of course you cannot! But Bryan, don't you see?

Tricky though he may be, the *puca* has shown you that you will not be trapped on its back as the others were. Now, go and ride it, and win this race! Go!"

Bryan swallowed hard, then took up the rope and vaulted onto the *puca*'s back. Instantly the creature spun around and tore after the field of racehorses at supernatural speed. Bryan gripped its mane tight with both hands.

The horses ahead galloped up the wide grassy strip with shouting, cheering crowds on either side. But by the time they reached the stone-walled pasture beside the mountain, where the workhorses and oxen rested and grazed, the black pony had caught up to them and raced right alongside.

The gap in the pasture's stone wall, normally barred with heavy logs, stood open and waiting for the racers. But as Niamh dashed up the grassy field with the rest of the crowd, trying to keep the horses in sight, she realized that it was only wide enough for perhaps four of the horses to fit through at once. The rest would have to pull up and wait.

As Niamh started up the steep sides of the mountain as fast as she could go, all of the horses descended on the gate at nearly the same time. Ardal's grey managed to slip through first and was untouched, but hot on his heels were seven animals in a row all dashing headlong for the same narrow opening.

One of them was Bryan's black pony. But then, at the very last moment, the *puca* veered hard to one side and soared over the high, wide, jagged dry-stone wall. Bryan clung to its coarse black mane with both hands. That left six horses to jam and squeeze through an opening only wide enough for four, even as the other eight horses caught up to them and piled in on the heels of the six stuck in the gate.

For a moment all six were stopped and frantically trying to force their way through, their riders shouting and cursing and scraping their legs raw on the stone wall. Finally one horse and then another refused to battle his way through the pack any longer and threw himself backward out of the jam.

One horse spun around and ran back the other way, dodging the rest of the field and charging headlong back to the starting line no matter what his rider tried to do. Another threw himself all the way down on the ground, leaving his rider to fend for himself amid the hooves of the rest of the horses, then rolled to his feet and took off riderless after the first horse.

Halfway up the mountain, Niamh paused to catch her breath. The last man in the pack turned away from the crowded gate and tried to follow Bryan's lead. He circled around and sent his red-gold horse galloping straight at the jagged stone wall, but the animal slid to a jolting stop at the last moment. His rider ended up on top of the wall, and his horse, too, fled such madness for the comparative safety of the starting line.

Now the racers were down to thirteen, including the *puca*. The rest of the field finally managed to fight its way through the narrow gate and took off through the pasture, dodging the curious cattle and horses and straining to catch up with Ardal on his grey and Bryan on his heavy black pony.

Niamh struggled through the brush and hurried past the rest of the crowd. Most of them had taken their places on the mountain long before the race had started, since they would be able to see nearly all of it from up here. She reached the top of the mountain just in time to see Ardal and Bryan galloping side by side across the pasture and disappearing around the other side of the mountain. The rest of the contestants were strung out across the pasture and galloping as fast as they could to catch up.

Niamh ran a short way across the top of the mountain, watching for Ardal and the *puca* to appear on the wide dirt road that stretched alongside the encampment . . . but much to her surprise, Ardal's grey emerged alone.

A small stab of fear struck her heart. Had the creature played some trick on Bryan after all? Was it even now running back the other way, giving its rider a merry trip all the way back to the starting line and ensuring that he would be exiled for what had happened to Luath?

In a moment the first of the remaining horses swept past the curve of the mountain and galloped down the dirt road. And there was the *puca*—weaving in and out among them, reaching out to touch noses with the other horses and drawing them all around it in a tight knot that moved slower and slower down the road, despite their riders' frantic kicking and shouting in an effort to force them on.

Bryan could only hold on to the *puca*'s mane and to its halter rope. At one point he leaned down low over its neck and the creature's big ears flicked back as though he were speaking to it. In a moment, it began to pull away from the confusion it had caused in the ranks and galloped alone down the dirt road, heading for the sharp turn that led to the far boundary of the encampment along the river.

Niamh could see the line of guards at the turn into the camp, there both to keep the spectators back and to try to keep the riders on course. Still riding alone, Ardal made the sharp turn into the camp in front of the cattle pens, and just as quickly turned away toward the forest and the river. Niamh could just see him send the grey splashing through the knee-deep ford before he disappeared from sight among the tall oaks of the forest. She knew that just a short way into the forest there was a rowan tree tied with bright red ribbons and watched by several guards. The riders would have to gallop around it and then head back the way they had come.

Next to arrive at the river, well ahead of the rest of the pack, were Bryan and the *puca*. The small black creature splashed methodically through the ford, actually stopping briefly for a drink, and then moved on into the forest just as the rest of the horses reached the bend in the road and came tearing through the zigzag turn.

One animal's hooves went flying out from under him as he tried to make the treacherous turn, and he fell heavily on his side. His rider scrambled to his feet, and just barely managed to catch the mount before his horse could run off and join the galloping herd. The rest headed for the river.

Much to their surprise, a black streak shot out of the woods ahead—straight at them and through the ford so fast that the water hardly splashed at all. It flashed through the startled pack of racehorses, weaving in and out and around them, and darted through the two turns that led back to the road.

As with the gate to the pasture, the ford was not wide enough to hold twelve horses across and all of the riders knew it. Every one of them aimed squarely for the center, which caused them to go slamming into one another as they reached it. Two of the horses on the outside stumbled over the unseen edges of the ford and went down into the deep water, throwing their heads up and snorting the river out of their noses as they and their riders swam for the bank. But those who remained jostling for position on the ford soon found themselves facing a new obstacle.

Ardal came bursting out of the woods, driving his grey

at a dead gallop straight for the center of the ford. The other riders had no choice but to give way or be struck—and none of them was about to give way.

He forced his grey through the ranks of the first three riders, and when the way was blocked he kicked his horse's sides with all the strength he possessed and jerked on the reins so hard that the horse rose straight up on his hind legs. The outside rider had no choice but to pull his horse away, lest both of them be struck by the pawing hooves above their heads, and so they too leaped into the deep river with a tremendous splash.

Ardal pushed his way through the remaining riders and galloped back toward the starting line, swerving through the tight turns and then back out on the road—and almost ran headlong into the *puca*, with Bryan still sitting on its back. The creature had chosen to stop near the edge of the road and catch a few bites of the lush green grass that grew on the narrow strip of earth between the road and the stone wall of the cattle pen.

As Ardal lashed his horse to force it past the grazing animal, the black pony lifted its head, still grinding a mouthful of grass, and took off again stride for stride with Ardal's grey. Both animals galloped down the road, but the pony pulled ahead and then ran in a complete circle around Ardal and his mount, who lashed his horse in utter fury as Bryan's pony circled him a second and even a third time. Finally they swept around the corner of the mountain together just as the other seven horses reappeared out of the forest and fought and jostled their way back through the ford.

Niamh hurried a few steps to the very top of the mountain again, expecting to see the tall grey horse and the heavy black pony running side by side over the green grass. But instead, the two animals both slowed to a canter and then to a jog, their ears up and their heads close, and finally they both stopped and stood nickering to each other as though they were two long-lost brothers who had just been newly reacquainted.

Ardal shouted and cursed and lashed his grey horse, but except for a few quick sidesteps the animal ignored him. Bryan just sat very still and waited, his fingers locked in his pony's black mane. Sure enough, just as the rest of the racehorses came running past the mountain, the pony took off again. Ardal's grey did too, staying with him stride for stride.

But instead of heading for the gate and the finish line, the black pony circled back and began running the other way. It ran past the pack of trailing racers, then turned in a wide circle to run in their direction again.

Ardal's grey stayed right with the pony. Then, the moment it and the grey had caught back up to the rear of the pack, the black pony shot away with lightning speed. In an instant it was far in front, while Ardal and his grey were left far in the rear. Ardal could only watch as the rest of the horses made the final curve around the mountain and headed toward the open gate in the stone wall.

As before, the black pony soared over the obstacle and galloped on down the grassy stretch leading to the finish line—the same place where they had started. The remaining eight horses streamed one after another through the opening and ran toward the finish, following the black pony as it and Bryan crossed the line first.

"Bryan wins! Bryan wins!" cried Niamh, over the shouting and cheering of the crowd. "Bryan wins!" She ran to him just as the pony swung around and trotted back toward her with a lowered head, leaving the course just as the rest of the field thundered past.

Bryan grinned at Niamh as the creature stopped in

front of her. It shook its head, and the golden comb in its mane fell to the grass at her feet. She picked up the comb and placed it back in her own hair, her eyes edged with tears.

Carefully and deliberately, Bryan placed both hands on the *puca's* neck, leaned forward, and stepped down to the ground beside the beast. "Thank you," he said to it, gently straightening its coarse mane. "You have given me back my life." The black pony sighed and lowered its head to graze.

Bryan turned to Niamh, held her by her shoulder and leaned down to kiss her gently on the forehead. "You have given me my life as well. There can be no doubt in your mind any longer that you are surely meant to be a queen, for I would never have become the tanist of my people—one day to become their king—without the help I received from you."

Niamh smiled up at him. "I was not meant to be a queen. I was meant to be your wife and companion. And if that means being your queen as well—and that of your people—then I will find my courage and do the very best I can for you and for all who live at Cahir Cullen."

"That is all anyone can ask, Niamh, and all that anyone can do." He held her close and leaned his cheek against hers, even as Niamh closed her eyes and rested her head on his shoulder and the people all around them shouted out, "Bryan and Niamh! Bryan and Niamh! Bryan and Niamh!"

Chapter Twenty-five

One final set of galloping hoofbeats came toward them on the grassy field. Niamh and Bryan looked up to see Ardal lashing his exhausted grey horse with the ends of his long reins, leaving long red cuts on the animal's dark wet sides. As he crossed the line dead last, Ardal vaulted off and sent his horse trotting away with an angry shouted curse. Then he turned his rage and frustration on his rival.

"Bryan!" he shouted, stalking over to him with fists clenched. "You have cheated! That is no natural horse! You have used magic to win this race! It was meant to be a horse race, not a contest of enchantments! No one else used such methods in this race. You have cheated!"

"I did no such thing," Bryan said, walking away from Niamh and the black pony to face Ardal in the center of the open field. "You had no objection to my mount when the race began. You got a good look at him then, and said only that you thought he was so slow that I would still be running the race this time next year! It is too late to complain about him now."

"It is not too late to fight you and to take what should be mine!" Ardal shouted. He jerked his dagger from his belt and threw himself at Bryan. He grabbed him by the shoulders before Bryan could react and threw him to the ground.

Right away the crowd began to gather round, calling out to the fighters and making wagers on the outcome.

"Ardal will take him. Look how angry he is over losing the race!"

"It's Bryan for me. He's the better man!"

"The outcome will not matter. They will both be exiled for fighting yet again at the Fair!"

The two men struggled with each other on the grass. Bryan held Ardal's wrist with one hand, trying to force the dagger away from his throat, and gripped his opponent by the neck with the other.

"Give up! Give up! You are not king!" Ardal cried, though his words were choked by Bryan's grip. Then Bryan forced him to roll so that Ardal lay on his back.

"*You* will be the one to give up," he growled, and shoved his cousin down hard to the ground.

Niamh grabbed Leary by the arm. "Get the king. Get him now!" But before Leary could dash away, Niamh looked up to see King Conaire standing right in front of her. He held in his hand a large, heavy, gleaming gold brooch set with softly glowing amber—the horse race winner's prize, which he had come to present.

"Please, King Conaire," Niamh begged, standing before him and looking up into his eyes. "Please have your men put a stop to this!"

But the king only shook his head. "Not this time. These two will not rest until one of them is defeated. It obviously does not matter to them whether they are at the Fair or not."

"But Bryan won the race. Lugh has made his choice known to us—and he chose Bryan!"

"So he did," King Conaire said, "but it seems he has one more test that Bryan must pass before he can become tanist. I will not stop that test. This must end here and now. Only Lugh can decide the outcome, and he has chosen this way to show us who he wants."

Niamh could only set her teeth in frustration and watch the terrible battle unfold in front of her. She looked at the faces of the surrounding crowd, searching for any of Bryan's men who might be willing to break up the fight, but all she saw was a blur of shouting faces and tightly clenched fists as the mob urged the combatants on.

She glanced over her shoulder to see if anyone else might come. There were only a few servant boys leading away the tired and sweating racehorses. Ignored and forgotten, however, was Ardal's blood-streaked grey, who stood close by the black pony with their heads close together. She wondered what Ardal's cut and exhausted horse might be saying to the *puca*.

Niamh turned back to the fight just as a great shout went up from the crowd. Bryan had finally forced Ardal to drop his dagger, but then Ardal threw Bryan off of him and both men were on their feet—with Bryan standing right over Ardal's knife and then kicking it away into the crowd.

As the crowd's shouting and wagering rose to a fever pitch, Bryan drew his own dagger from his belt and faced the furious Ardal.

"Do not make me kill you," Bryan said to his cousin, his breath coming fast. "Give up the fight. You have already lost. End this now."

"Never!" roared Ardal, and began to charge.

Niamh held her breath. She could only hope that

273

Bryan could handle an opponent who was also a madman.

Then, from behind her, she heard the furious pounding of hoofbeats.

Before she could even turn around, she saw the monstrous black form of the *puca* sail over the heads of the crowd. Its eyes blazed an enraged yellow-red even in the light of day.

Still racing at full speed, the *puca* lowered its head and charged up behind Ardal. It got him on its neck and threw him onto its back, and then leaped high over the other side of the crowd.

For an instant, all were struck silent in astonishment. Then the crowd broke ranks and charged after the galloping black streak that was the *puca* with the terrified Ardal on its back.

The furious creature tore across the grass and headed straight for the stone wall—but then turned abruptly and raced back the way it had come, galloping down the field as the crowd scattered in front of it and dashed across the grass in a frantic effort to get out of its way.

Niamh clutched Bryan's arm as they watched the *puca* go tearing past. They could see Ardal trying to throw himself off its back, but his legs were clamped to the beast's sides with an iron grip and his fingers were locked deep in its thick black mane.

Niamh shivered as though she were cold. Never had she seen any beast so enraged. Its eyes burned a fierce and furious red, and its ears were tightly pinned against its head. As it galloped it swung its neck around and snapped again and again at Ardal's feet with its huge yellow teeth. Ardal's face was white with terror and he was too frightened even to cry out.

The *puca* turned around again and shot back up the field, still snapping at its rider and sometimes bucking violently, jerking Ardal's head back and forth but at no time coming close to dislodging him.

It was every rider's nightmare come true: the horse who attacks his rider and rejects every attempt at control or cooperation, responding instead with violence and ferocity. And Ardal now had no choice but to take the *puca*'s rage, for he could not get away and he had no control over what the *puca* might do.

The creature bolted through the gap in the stone wall and galloped straight up the side of the mountain, sending men and women scurrying out of its way. It raced along the spine of the mountaintop, sometimes stopping abruptly to spin in tight circles and then take off again, leaving its rider whipping back and forth in terror and disorientation.

At last the creature galloped to the top of the high conical peak at the far end of the mountain, where the *puca* stood so high on its hind legs that Niamh was certain it would go all the way over backwards and crash to the ground on top of Ardal. There was no situation more terrifying for any rider, but it did not fall. It leaped forward again from its standing position and galloped around and around the top of the mountain at top speed, sending up a cloud of thick grey ash from the remains of the Lughnasa bonfire.

Then it made a sudden sharp turn as if it were going to leap off the side of the mountain . . . but instead it stopped short with its forelegs braced and its head down low, a move that would have sent any other rider flying down the steep sides of the mountain. But Ardal could only stare in horror at the rough slope where the *puca* could have thrown him if it wished, and realize yet again that now he was entirely at the mercy of his mount instead of the other way around.

The *puca* whipped around and tore along the top of the mountain again, running so hard that Niamh could see the rocks and dirt thrown up by its hooves. It raced down the mountain, across the field and through the gap in the stone wall once more, cutting so close to the wall that one side of Ardal's heavy woolen trews was left scraped and torn by the rough stones.

The *puca* galloped back down the grassy field and kept going straight for the river. It reached the edge still racing at full speed . . . but then stopped in an instant and sent Ardal flying over its head, through the air and almost all the way across the water. He landed hard on his right shoulder on the rocks of the far bank, his legs splashing into the water. Then the *puca* spun sharply and trotted into the shadows of the trees along the bank, where it turned and stood watching.

Ardal tried to raise himself up on his hands, but he quickly collapsed. The creature threw its huge head up and down as it watched, and bared its teeth in a grimace that looked like a cruel smile.

Niamh was the first to run to the river. Bryan followed her closely and then the others began to make their way down. Many of them were torn between intense curiosity over what had happened to Ardal and fear of what the *puca* might do next.

But when Niamh reached the river, she saw no sign of the *puca*. The beast had vanished. There was nothing under the trees on either side of the water, save shadows and the wind.

"Ardal!" Niamh cried. "Are you hurt? Can you stand?"

Bryan started to step across the rocks of the bank as though prepared to swim across the deep water—it was the same place where the horse-swimming race had been held—but Niamh caught his arm and stopped him.

"Wait, Bryan. He is nearly on his feet. He may be able to walk, though I do not think he will be able to swim back with you."

Gritting his teeth with effort and pain, Ardal leaned heavily on his left arm and managed to push himself to his knees in the shallow water. Slowly, painfully, he got to his feet. He managed to take two steps up out of the water before staggering and nearly falling—but caught himself, again with only his left arm. He stood trembling on the bank, looking left and right and then behind him, clearly searching for any sign of the terrifying monster that had taken him for the ride of his life.

Several of Ardal's men rushed up to the bank beside Bryan. "Wait there! We'll bring a horse across the ford. Wait for us!"

But Ardal only stared at them with a look of pure horror on his face. "Do not! Do not bring a horse!" he cried. "I will walk!" And he began moving slowly down the bank of the river in the direction of the ford, cradling his useless right arm with his left and keeping a close watch for any sign of a shadow or a rustling in the trees.

"He will never ride a horse again," Niamh said quietly, watching him go. "The *puca* has seen to that."

"Nor will he ever be a king," added Bryan. "No man who is crippled or maimed can be a king. The *puca* has seen to that, too."

"He will be naught but a common footman for the rest of his life."

"And that is no more than he deserves."

Just then Urla and her friends came hurrying up to the riverbank. "Well!" sniffed Urla. "Not only did he lose, he is a cripple now!"

"Oh, never mind," said one of the other girls. "You did get a pretty belt out of it."

"Come on!" said another. "The other men are leading their horses back to camp. Let's go and see!" And all of the girls turned and hurried away toward the great encampment.

"Bryan!" He and Niamh turned to see Leary running toward them. "Bryan! King Conaire awaits you. Hurry!"

Niamh took hold of Bryan's hand and caught up her skirts, and together they ran across the grassy field to where the High King and his men stood waiting for them.

"You have won the race, Bryan of Cahir Cullen. We agreed to accept whatever decision the god Lugh chose to make, and it is clear to all of us that he has chosen you to be the tanist of your kingdom. I congratulate you on your victory—and I am happy to also give you the winner's prize."

He held out the shining gold-and-amber brooch in both hands, and smiled as Bryan took it from him. "I thank you, King Conaire," Bryan said, and turned directly to Niamh. "I wish only to give this beautiful prize to the Lady Niamh—and to ask her if she will honor me by becoming my wife, and later my queen, for now and forever, tomorrow morning on Scattering Day."

An expectant silence fell over the crowd. Niamh could feel all eyes upon her as the people waited for her response. Taking a deep breath, she reached out to accept the heavy, precious object from Bryan, and gazed down at it for a moment before looking up at him again.

"I hoped to someday find a man who I could love—a man with whom I would always feel safe, and comfortable, and happy. I have found all that, and far more, with you."

He took a step toward her, his eyes shining, and she smiled up at him. She continued, "I never thought that one such as I might ever be a queen—and I never thought

I would wish to be one, even if I should ever have the chance.

"Yet I have learned that a queen might find she can help other people, and even nature's creatures, in ways that an ordinary woman cannot. Though I know that King Nessan will not leave his people for the Otherworld for many years, when that time comes I hope to learn that it is a privilege to be a queen and not a burden—certainly when the king is a man like Bryan of Cahir Cullen."

She reached out to take hold of his hand. "I *will* marry you, Bryan, and I will be your wife and one day your queen . . . and I will tell that you I am honored by your asking."

His answer was a warm and gentle kiss, and the crowd cheered them. The king called out, "In the morning, then, before the Scattering! First thing in the morning, at Lugh's Well!"

Chapter Twenty-six

When the sun rose the next morning, on the fourteenth and final day of the Lughnasa Fair, it shone down on hundreds of folk taking apart their cowhide tents, packing up their belongings and piling them in their wagons.

The oxen and horses were led out of the pasture where they had stayed for the last fortnight, and yoked to the wagons, or loaded with bundles and bags or saddled for the long journey home, wherever home might be.

A few families started off as soon as they were ready, waving and calling out to their friends as the ox-carts lumbered out onto the road, but many others left servants and field workers to hold the horses and oxen while they walked to the foot of the mountain below the high peak where the bonfire had been held. They gathered at the falling spring and rock-lined pool that was known as Lugh's Well.

Already standing together before the well, in the presence of King Conaire, Queen Treise and five druids, were Niamh and Bryan. Bryan wore new leather breeches and boots of dark brown, a tunic dyed deep gold, and a fine new cloak of green-and-gold wool.

Niamh wore a simple pale linen gown, as she always did, but over it was a fine cloak made of the lightest and most delicate of wools and dyed in glowing shades of blue and green and gold, with the colors interwoven in a lively plaid. Fastening the beautiful cloak was the amber-set golden brooch that Bryan had won the day before.

Close at hand were Niamh's parents and her sister Aine, as well as all of the remaining men of Bryan's Fianna. All stood and listened carefully as the druids recited their contract of marriage, hastily agreed upon the night before.

"This shall be a union of a woman of the fields and a noble man of the kingdom of Cahir Cullen. She shall go to live in the fortress of her husband, and she shall be supported by him," the druid said. "She brings to the marriage five baskets of clean wool, three lengths of linen fabric, two wooden dowels and two bone needles for spinning and sewing, and one half-wagonload of newly cut wheat. Should the marriage end, she shall be entitled to the return of goods equal to these, for these are hers to keep."

He turned to face Bryan. "You have not yet offered Niamh her *coibche*—her bride-gift. Do you have it for her now?"

"I do," Bryan said. He looked out over the heads of the gathering and caught the eye of one of his companions from the Fianna. "Bring it now!" he called, and then smiled down at Niamh.

In a moment, the crowd parted ranks, allowing the man to lead a horse to the foot of the well—a small mare, dark golden-brown in color, with a golden mane and a silver tail and a few white hairs on her forehead. The mare wore a fine new bridle of dark brown leather with a shining bronze bit, and a new saddle made of crossed wooden frames in the front and in the back and thickly cushioned with sheepskins.

Most important, the mare Criostal wore long braided streamers of bright blue linen in her forelock and in her mane—a sign to the *puca*, now and always, that this horse was valued and respected and well-treated.

"She is yours, Niamh," Bryan said, "and she is indeed a mount suitable for a queen, if I may say so."

"She is, she is," Niamh answered, unable to take her eyes from the beautiful mare. "I can never thank you enough."

"You can thank me by being my wife, and my queen."

She smiled. "And I will be your queen, for I have learned that living in a fortress does not mean I will ever forget what I have learned from the forests and the fields. It only means that I will have a chance to help many more people than I ever could have otherwise."

"Yet the forests and fields will be open to you whenever you wish, for now you have the finest of horses to carry you there and back again, farther than you could ever go yourself on foot in a single day."

She smiled. "More than that, Bryan, queen or no, I will always have what I want most: simply to love you and be your wife—now and forever."

He kissed her gently on her forehead. "Know also that I listened to you. I have learned from your questions. I offer you not just marriage, but courtship—courtship that lasts for the rest of your life. For that is what you want from the man in your life, is it not? To feel safe, and comfortable, and happy when in his presence? For that is courtship. And you wish for a man to continue to do those things forever. To not take you for granted, but to continue to be the man who won your heart. I will do all this and more."

Niamh could only smile up at him, her eyes shining, and then kiss him with all the warmth she possessed. The crowd laughed and then applauded.

"I say to you that Bryan and Niamh are now husband and wife from this moment on!" cried King Conaire. "Wish them well and then follow us to the encampment one more time, because there is one more ritual to perform."

The men and women came around to greet the newly married pair and congratulate them, and the first ones to reach Niamh were her mother and father.

"You look so beautiful!" her mother exclaimed, laughing so that she would not cry. "Beautiful because you are in love with a good man."

Her father stepped up and kissed her on the cheek. "Do not forget us, dear Niamh, when you are living in your fine house in the fortress as the wife of a tanist. We will keep Luath for your husband, but we are doing it in part to make sure you will return!"

"Oh, I will return as often as I can!" Niamh embraced first her father and then her mother.

"And I thank you for taking and caring for Luath," Bryan said as Niamh's mother stepped back. "He will have a slow and gentle walk to your home, where he can rest and heal, instead of a long and painful trek all the way back to Cahir Cullen."

Then Niamh caught sight of Aine with Leary close beside her. She embraced her younger sister, who held her tightly in return.

"Oh, I am so happy for you!" Aine said, laughing a little through her tears. "You have found a wonderful man and made a wonderful match."

"He was worth waiting for," Niamh agreed, giving her dark-haired sister a kiss on the cheek. "Never forget that. And oh, wait—I have something for you!"

Niamh reached up and pulled the golden comb from her hair, and held it out to Aine. The curving stalks of wheat gleamed bright in the morning sun. "This is yours now. Remember its lessons, and always be proud to wear it."

"Oh . . . it *is* mine now, isn't it?" Aine took the comb from Niamh's hand, and carefully worked it into the front of her hair.

"It's beautiful. It's perfect," Niamh said, and with a final kiss for her sister she turned back to Bryan and began walking with him toward the edge of the crowd where their two horses waited. Just behind her, Niamh heard Aine talking to Leary. "Now, then," Aine said, in all seriousness, "there are three things that any woman wants from the man in her life. You must learn . . ."

Niamh and Bryan mounted their horses—Niamh on Criostal, and Bryan on the long-legged grey that had been Ardal's—and led the merry procession around to the front of the mountain, where they reached the three stone enclosures where the Animal Kings resided.

"All of us owe Niamh our thanks for teaching us the rituals that would allow us to make peace with the creature known as the *puca*," King Conaire said. "I say to you now that we will keep two of these rituals every year at the Lughnasa Fair.

"For the first, we will always chose a king from the cattle, a king from the sheep, and a king from the horses, and they shall rule over the Fair just as these three have done.

"And for the second," he went on, "I say to you now that from this day forward, all horses who carry riders or

285

work in harness shall wear shining symbols of bronze or gold on their leather, or bright-colored ribbons in their manes, as a sign to the *puca* that this is a horse that receives the best of treatment, and thus turn away the *puca*'s angry gaze.

"Now then! Those men who own the bull and the ram, come and take them home, and remember always to treat them as the kings that they are."

Everyone stepped back as the bars of the two pens were pulled back and the animals were led out of their large and comfortable enclosures. King Conaire then looked up at Niamh and Bryan. "We will follow your advice concerning this last, Niamh," he said, and the three moved to the third pen, where the bay stallion Anfa stood watching them with his head over the bars of his pen.

Leary picked up the flax-rope halter that hung on one end of the bars and slipped it over the eager Anfa's head. Two other men pulled back the bars and Anfa trotted out, head up and tail flagged high, happy to be free among the lively gathering. His lameness was nearly gone now, after days of drinking only the water from Lugh's Well, and he no longer suffered any pain.

King Conaire moved to stand before the horse. He said, "You have been the most noble of kings, and we thank you. You have served men long enough. Now it is time for you to go home."

He stepped back, and Bryan leaned down from his saddle to take Anfa's halter rope. Then everyone watched as Bryan, with Niamh riding beside him, left the king and the people behind and led Anfa down the road through the encampment. They had one last task to accomplish.

The great field below the mountain now held only groups of wagons and oxen and horses, and large scattered spots of dead, crushed yellow grass where the tents had stood. Soon Bryan and Niamh reached the river and took their three horses out to stand in the middle of the ford.

The forest lay dim and quiet across the river. "Are you sure he will be there?" Bryan asked.

"I am certain of it. He will come," she answered, gazing steadily into the forest. After a moment, a shadow appeared beneath the oaks across the river, a shadow with softly glowing eyes.

Anfa, Criostal and the grey all raised their heads and looked closely at the shadow. Anfa nickered softly and took a step forward, and then the *puca* stepped into the ford and walked toward them.

Bryan and Niamh allowed the horses to greet and touch noses with it, and then, when the *puca* lifted its head to look at her, Niamh spoke to it.

"We have kept our promise to you. No horse will ever again be ill-treated at the Lughnasa Fair. And all who believe in good treatment for their animals shall, at all times, give them bits of shining bronze or gold to wear and weave bright ribbons in their manes. That is how you will know the ones who value their horses as more than merely beasts of burden—and we hope that, in return, you will remain at peace with the world of men."

Bryan slipped the rope halter from Anfa's head. There was a pause, as the *puca* continued to nuzzle with the three other horses. Then it snorted, and spoke again in its strange rasping voice.

"*If you keep these rituals,*" it said, "*then from midsummer to Samhain I will not trouble you. You may have your great gathering in peace. But I will watch, and at all other times I will take my revenge on any who deserve it.*"

Then it touched Anfa again with its nose, turned around in the water, and trotted into the forest with Anfa right behind. Both disappeared into the deep woods, gone as though they had never been.

Niamh sighed in relief. She felt as if some great weight had been lifted from her shoulders. "So long as these traditions are upheld, the *puca* will not trouble us again."

"At least, not from midsummer to Samhain," Bryan said, reining his grey around toward the encampment.

"That does cover the time of the Lughnasa Fair. It has agreed to stay away from midsummer to the start of winter."

"Are you so sure it will keep its word?" Bryan asked, as their horses splashed through the ford side by side.

"I believe it will," Niamh said, and smiled up at him. "You certainly kept yours."

A surprised grin spread across his face, and then he reined his tall horse up onto the road. "Come home with me, Niamh! Come home!" he cried, and sent his mount cantering toward the main road.

"I will. Oh, I will!" Niamh answered, and together they galloped down the road after the others, into the glorious autumn day and their new life together.

Turn the page for
a special sneak preview
of SHANNON FARRELL'S

CALL HOME THE HEART

Coming in December 2004!

I pray thee leave, love me no more,
Call home the heart you gave me,
I but in vain the saint adore,
That can, but will, not save me.
      —Michael Drayton, "To His Coy Love," 1619

Chapter One

Dublin, January 1845

The gunshot echoed throughout the corridors of the hotel. Lochlainn dropped his water glass and dashed up the stairs two at a time.

"Mrs. Caldwell, Mrs. Caldwell, open the door! Muireann! Open up, please! It's Lochlainn Roche!" he shouted as he hammered at the oaken portal.

Lochlainn could hear nothing in the chamber apart from the sound of someone weeping. After jerking at the latch futilely for several seconds, he threw all of his weight against the solid bulk.

"Muireann! Open up, please!" he demanded urgently between blows.

At last the manager of Gresham's Hotel, stunned by the gunshot and the commotion Lochlainn was causing in the corridor, produced his master key. With a deft flick of his wrist, Lochlainn opened the lock quickly and stormed into his employer's bedchamber. There he saw Muireann, kneeling beside the body of her husband.

It was evident from the state of his head, or what was left of it, that Augustine was dead.

"God, no, please, this can't be happening to me!" the raven-haired woman whimpered as she rocked back and forth, tugging at the lapels of Augustine's coat frantically as though she would strangle him.

"How could you! Oh God, why? What am I going to do?" she wailed, growing more and more hysterical, repeating the words over and over again.

At last Lochlainn, unsure as to what else he could do, tugged Muireann away from the corpse, and gave her a firm tap on the chin with his fist.

She crumpled like a rag doll into Lochlainn's arms. He caught her up before she fell to the floor and demanded of the manager, "Give me another room for Mrs. Caldwell, now!"

The little man, gaping at the carnage before him, barely heard a word Lochlainn said.

"I'll see Mrs. Caldwell's things are moved myself. She's not to be disturbed, is that clear?"

"I suppose I'd better fetch a doctor," the manager said doubtfully, shaking his head.

"For the lady, yes, Mr. Burns," Lochlainn replied grimly. "Augustine certainly won't be needing one."

The hotelier stared at the handsome, ebony-haired estate manager with something akin to horror. How could he remain so calm in the face of such an appalling spectacle?

Lochlainn's steely-gray eyes warmed a little as he tried to soothe Mr. Burns's ruffled feathers. "I'm sorry to sound so cold. It's just that everything must be handled correctly. I imagine there must be certain formalities in these sorts of cases. I shall trust you to look after things."

Lifting Muireann high, he followed the little silver-haired man as he led him down the corridor to a room at the back of the hotel, far from the noise of all the carriages passing outside through the busy streets of Dublin.

"This chamber is smaller, but the bed is quite large, and there is a trundle bed underneath as well. The lady shouldn't be left alone," the hotelier said, staring regretfully at the unconscious, disheveled form Lochlainn had lifted into his arms as though she were as light as a feather.

"She won't be alone. I'll look after her, never fear," Lochlainn reassured the worried man as he laid Muireann down on the bed. "Just ask the doctor to look in on her whenever he's finished with Mr. Caldwell, if you please."

"Yes of course, sir. What a terrible tragedy. And to think it happened in my hotel," the little man complained, almost in tears.

"A terrible tragedy to have happened anywhere, when someone takes their own life," Lochlainn observed with a set jaw as he began to undo the top buttons of Muireann's gown, and then removed her boots.

"But surely, sir, it was an accident!" the dapper little man gasped. "He was cleaning his gun, and—"

Lochlainn looked at the man in sheer disbelief, his eyes glittering dangerously. "You want me to lie, Mr. Burns?"

"Not exactly lie, Mr. Roche, more, well, give another plausible version of events. After all, his poor young wife . . . It's bad enough for her to have lost her husband on her honeymoon, without exposing the girl to unnecessary gossip and, well, dare I say it, scandal."

Lochlainn sighed. "I hadn't thought about that. You're absolutely right, Mr. Burns. I doubt that anyone's interests would be served if the whole truth were to be revealed. Thank you for being so considerate of Mrs. Caldwell's position. I'm sure I can rely on your discretion."

The little man nodded, and stared sympathetically at the lovely dark-haired woman lying prone on the bed.

"Can you stay here for one moment while I go get Mrs. Caldwell's things from the other room?"

"Yes, of course."

Lochlainn was back in a few moments with several valises and an armful of gowns, and said, "I'll wait here while you send a maid up to look after Mrs. Caldwell for a moment. Then I'll finish clearing the room, and go fetch my things from the coach."

"Thank you, Mr. Roche. I'll go attend to your, er, problem, and will see you later," Mr. Burns said, before scurrying out of the room.

Once he was alone with her, Lochlainn stripped Muireann's blood-soaked gown off her limp body and hurled it into the fire, before throwing the spare blanket resting at the foot of the bed over her.

Then he brought the armchair standing by the window closer to the bed. He sat down heavily, and cradled his head in his hands.

Why had this happened, just when he had begun to hope there might be some light at the end of the tunnel for the Caldwell estate, Barnakilla? How had the Fates conspired to have everything he held most dear be taken away from him just when it all seemed to be falling into place for the first time in years?

Disappointed in love, he had fled the estate where he and his sister Ciara had grown up, longing to escape from the memories.

The old lord Douglas Caldwell had been alive then. Barnakilla had been a prosperous estate, elegant, well ordered, despite Augustine's extravagance, which his parents had indulged him in willingly since he had been an only child. But Douglas Caldwell had died, and then his wife, giving Augustine free rein to despoil the estate with his gambling and devil-may-care attitude.

Lochlainn had run away from the home that held such bittersweet memories for him, and had traveled the world, trying to seek his fame and fortune. He had done well enough for himself, certainly, but in his opinion Australia could never rival the beauties of Ireland, the glories of his home. Augustine Caldwell's summons for Lochlainn to return to Barnakilla after three interminably long years had been the answer to his most heartfelt prayers.

But what would the future hold for him now? And what was he to do with the delicate young beauty who lay unconscious? Poor girl. How had she come to be mixed up in all of this?

But then, she had loved Augustine, hadn't she? he wondered, as he recalled her hysteria in the bedroom a few moments before. *I always did have the damnedest luck,* Lochlainn thought gloomily, as he reached out to stroke her fair, petal-soft skin, and fingered her silky raven-black hair, admiring her beauty while she slept. Her complexion was so pale, she looked as though she were a visitor from another realm. Her high cheekbones, long, moderately thin nose which turned up slightly at the tip, and ruby red, full lips, might not be to every man's taste, being so ethereal, but for Lochlainn she was lovelier than words could ever hope to describe.

He had never believed in love at first sight until he had seen this tiny nymph staring at him with her incredible amethyst eyes the day before, when he had greeted his employer and his new bride off of the boat from Liverpool straight from their honeymoon in Scotland and England.

Quite tall for a woman, though tiny in comparison

with himself, Muireann Graham Caldwell had moved down the gangplank like a queen, her head held high, her limpid eyes moving neither to the right nor the left, until they had lighted on his face. They had seemed to look into the very depths of his soul. She had taken his hand in greeting, and shock tremors had seemed to pass up his arm, until Lochlainn had berated himself for being so fanciful.

Now here she was, a widow, no doubt heir to the Caldwell estate, but probably completely unaware of the dire financial straits her husband Augustine had been in before he died.

But surely Muireann must have married him for love? After all, how could she not have known about all of his faults? Perhaps she was just as vain, frivolous, and addicted to gambling as Augustine had been. If so, the Lord help them all, Lochlainn thought with a shake of his head, looking at the lovely face resting on the pillow with a certain degree of resentment.

If Muireann was fool enough to have loved Augustine, she deserved whatever happened to her. He felt a twinge of guilt at the uncharitable thought as soon as it came to him. He was not normally so spiteful, but experience had been a bitter teacher.

He leapt from the chair impatiently and began to pace up and down in front of the window, until at last he stilled to watch the sun set over the rooftops of Dublin.

Damn it, how could a woman like Muireann, so lovely, so gracious, have married an idle, worthless, drunken lout like Augustine Caldwell?

And *what would she do with his beloved Barnakilla now?*

Chapter Two

Muireann awoke several hours later and rubbed her sore jaw tenderly. Clutching the blanket around her shivering form, she looked out the window at the snowflakes swirling, fairy-like, in the dim lamplight which glowed from the street below.

Moving her eyes slowly around the unfamiliar room so as not to jolt her throbbing head, she saw Lochlainn sitting in a low armchair by her bedside, a small case of documents open on the night table beside him. The expression in his unusual steel-gray eyes was forbidding as he toted up columns of figures, the scratch of his pen echoing in the high-ceilinged room.

The room was smaller than her other suite had been, but it seemed far more appealing to her, with a magnificently carved four-poster bed hung with flowered brocade curtains in blue and crimson. There were small tables on either side of the bed, and another low one with two chairs placed by the fire. In the corner by the large sash window was a screened-off area for one's toilette.

The most interesting and cheering aspect of the chamber was the magnificent fireplace, with a beautifully carved oak surround. A fire was roaring in the grate, and for the first time since she had left her family home at Fintry in Scotland, Muireann felt warm and secure. It was all over, she thought with relief, then quashed the guilty thought with a pang.

Attempting to distract herself from her horrifying thoughts, she turned her attention to her companion sitting beside her.

Muireann studied him unnoticed, and not for the first time admired his arresting masculine beauty. Hard as she tried, she could find no flaw in the enigmatic Lochlainn Roche except his arrogant demeanor. His raven-black hair, which glinted with mysterious dark auburn highlights, was thick and wavy, and just brushed the edge of his collar. He was also unfashionably close-shaven. Side-whiskers would simply have detracted from his high cheekbones and firm jaw, which showed only the barest trace of a shadow. His nose was straight and narrow, with delicately arched nostrils which enhanced his haughty appearance. But the deep cleft in his chin, and the single small dimple which peeped out whenever he moved his mouth, were intriguing.

Muireann found herself wondering what he would look like if he smiled. Certainly he would look a bit more human, a bit less like a prowling tiger about to devour its prey. Lochlainn seemed to perpetually glower, his dark eyebrows lowering threateningly over his thick-lashed gray eyes whenever she had come into contact with him since her arrival in Dublin the morning before. For a man so handsome, he seemed utterly joyless.

But perhaps he has good reason to be upset, she reflected tolerantly as she saw him tote up endless columns of figures over and over again, running his fingers through his ebony

Call Home the Heart

hair in frustration. She could remember her own father doing that many times over the years, or her brother-in-law Neil Buchanan, whenever she visited her sister Alice, now three months pregnant, at her new home in Dunoon.

Adding up had never been her father's strong point. Muireann had always helped him with his bookkeeping, though her efforts had never been taken seriously by anyone in the family, being considered "unfeminine." At least that's what her mother and sister had reminded her of often enough over the years, applying that adjective to every pursuit she had ever enjoyed which had met with their disapproval.

As Muireann recalled her family's criticism of her with a faint smile, Lochlainn reached the end of his tether. He threw the pen down, and rose to stretch his aching back. He stalked over to the fireplace and poked the coals vigorously, and then marched over to the window to gaze out at the blizzard wrapping the city in a freezing blanket of ivory.

Muireann admired his tall physique, watching with interest as his muscles rippled through the thin fabric of his shirt. He was certainly the tallest, broadest man she had ever seen. His hard, callused hand had been large enough to take both of her own as he had greeted her and assisted her off the boat at the quay at Dun Laoghaire the previous morning. She had noticed their roughness, but had certainly not been repelled by the contact. Here was a man who had never been spoilt or pampered, who had never been afraid of hard work. Yet at the same time, he had a certain dignity in his bearing which proclaimed him no ordinary farm laborer.

Well, Lochlainn was of course the estate manager. That had to signify he was intelligent and good with figures,

299

didn't it? But if his hands and clothes and his brown face, which testified to many years out in the elements, were anything to go by, he was not a man to leave all the hard work to others. She certainly admired that quality. Her own father and brother-in-law possessed the same traits. She herself was not averse to hard work, though her mother had always tried to keep her as a spoilt, pampered princess, the youngest of two daughters born to her very late in life.

Lochlainn heaved a huge sigh, and then moved over to the bed, where he was relieved to see that Muireann was at last conscious.

"Have you been awake long?" Lochlainn asked softly.

"Not very long," Muireann lied. "I've been trying to get my bearings. Where am I?"

"You're still at the Gresham, only in a different room. The snowstorm I feared has started. I'm afraid we'll have to stay at least another night," he said, being careful not to mention anything about the events of the afternoon.

"That's good. My head is pounding. I doubt I could travel all the way to Enniskillen after the terrible sea journey we had," she admitted, rubbing her temples.

Lochlainn reached down to test her forehead, and noted she had a slight fever.

"You're definitely warm, Muireann. Here, why don't I help get you get under the covers properly, and then we can see if they have any broth or soup downstairs?

"And I'll give you a headache powder as well," he offered, crossing over to where he had placed their bags on a low luggage holder to search his small bag.

She tried to raise herself off the pillow, only to slump back against it weakly.

"Lie still, my dear!"

"I, er, I have to use the chamberpot, but I don't think I can stand," she said sheepishly, blushing.

"Here, put your arms around my neck, and I'll carry you over to the screen." He tugged the blanket down over her bare shoulders.

Muireann was painfully aware that she was clad only in her flannel chemise and petticoats, but her companion didn't seem to take any notice. She knew she simply had to accept this stranger's help. She was all alone in Ireland now. What she would do next she had no idea.

But the thought of running back to Fintry to play the part of the grieving young widow was more than she could bear. She disliked being so critical of her own parents, but hadn't she married Augustine to escape from their stifling over-protectiveness and continual disappointment that she never seemed to fit into their world or do what was expected of her?

Her one chance of satisfying them had been to marry well. They had been delighted with Augustine Caldwell when he had turned up at a ball, and taken such an interest in her. Rumors had flown around Glasgow of his great wealth, his magnificent estate in Ireland. Her mother and father had actively encouraged Augustine's suit.

Muireann, tired of letting them down, and longing for adventure, had at last agreed to Augustine's impetuous marriage proposal. She had met him at Hallow Eve, and been wed on Hogmanay before she could even get to know Augustine more intimately.

"What's wrong?" Lochlainn asked, his concern evident in his tone.

"What? Oh nothing, I was just . . ."

"You're not going to be ill, are you? You made such a grimace."

"No, I'm not ill, just aching." She blushed, looking down at her bare arms, which she then looped around Lochlainn's neck.

His eyes followed her gaze. But far from looking at her leeringly, his eyes widened in alarm. "My goodness, where did all those bruises come from? I didn't hurt you carrying you in here, did I?"

"No, no, I fell on the boat a few times. It was a very rough crossing, you know, and I bruise easily," she replied hastily, trying to quell the shiver which rippled through her.

"There you are, Muireann."

He placed her gently on the floor by the screen, and held onto one of her hands until he saw she could manage a few steps on her own.

"I'll go bank up the fire. You must be freezing."

Muireann marveled at his kindness and delicacy in going out of the room to talk to the serving girl in order to get more coal, and tapping on the door to see whether it were safe for him to return.

Lochlainn tugged down the covers on the bed, and fluffed the pillows up against the carved headboard, and then went back to the small wash area to fetch Muireann again.

He laid her gently on the bed, and pulled all the covers right up to her chin.

"Shall I get you something warmer to wear? I'm sorry about your gown, but it was ruined, and . . ." Lochlainn trailed off with an awkward shrug.

Muireann paled slightly, but made no reference to the frock. "I should have a heavy flannel nightdress, lilac-colored, in that small black bag there," she indicated.

He brought the valise over to her, and helped her locate the nightdress and tug it over her head. She managed to pull it down over her ankles with a bit of wiggling and some help from Lochlainn, who seemed most assiduous in his attentions considering he seemed so manly and grim.

He tucked her in again, and after fluffing the pillows once more, stroked her tousled ebony hair back from her face softly, and said with a small smile, "There now, better?"

"Much better, thank you," she said, lifting her amethyst eyes up to his trustingly.

Though Lochlainn Roche was a complete stranger whom fate had thrown in her path, somehow she felt at peace with him. He might be somber and arrogant-looking, but he had treated her with every degree of consideration. At some point she had to start trusting someone. She was all alone here. She needed an ally desperately. Who better than her dead husband's estate manager?

"Here, now, take this draught," he said, offering her a glass of water, in which he mixed the powder from a small packet. "Your head will feel better in no time."

Their fingers touched as he handed her the glass. He retained his grip on it to make sure she didn't drop it as she drank the potion down. He put the empty tumbler down on the bedside table, and poured out a plain glass of water for her in case she was still thirsty.

"I'll just go see what's taking that girl," he said as he rose from the edge of the bed, where he had had been sitting gazing at Muireann admiringly for several seconds before he had caught himself staring.

He brought in the tray himself a few moments later. A second tap at the door several seconds after that signaled the arrival of the maid with some hot water bottles. She put three into Muireann's bed first and then, since it was getting late, she pulled out the trundle bed from under the large four-poster, and inserted the remaining two bottles between the sheets.

He waited until the maid had gone before answering Muireann's silent inquiry as she looked at the spare bed and then at Lochlainn. He put the tray on her lap, and handed her a napkin to drape over her nightgown in case of any spills.

"Because of the storm, they're short of rooms here, and I didn't like the idea of leaving you on your own tonight. Not when you're obviously unwell. I hope you don't mind, Mrs. Caldwell," he said stiffly.

"Not, not at all, Mr. Roche," she said with a shake of her head, before taking a spoonful of the tasty broth.

"Have you eaten yourself?" she asked after a moment, meeting his eyes once more.

"Yes, ages ago," he lied smoothly, managing to mask his surprise at her concern. In truth, he hadn't wanted to spend the money, but he was too disturbed by the day's events to feel hungry anyway.

He continued to stare at her, puzzled by her behavior. She seemed so unaffected, unworried by what had happened. Yet she had been absolutely hysterical only a few hours before. Was this normal? Or was she simply hiding all of her tumultuous emotions, too embarrassed to let anyone see her grief?

Looking at her delicate yet well-shaped chin and nose, her candid eyes, and noting her sure movements and carriage, which he had first noticed at the quay at Dun Laoghaire, he suspected she was a spoilt, pampered society woman, but one with a mind of her own. It was probably pride more than anything else which would prevent her from revealing to anyone just how she felt.

While Lochlainn could not pretend to feel any grief for Augustine, at the same time he knew how harmful it would be to try to bottle up all of one's misery inside oneself. He decided to broach the subject of Augustine's death as delicately as possible in order to test her reaction.

He waited until she had finished the soup and he had put the tray outside their room.

"Mrs. Caldwell, I know it's late and you're obviously upset and tired, but some decisions are going to have to be made about Augustine and the funeral," he remarked quietly.

Muireann's chin had begun to quiver then, and her voice cracked in several places as she said, "I've never had to deal with any of these sorts of affairs before. What would you suggest?"

He took her tiny hand in his own as he replied, "I think you have to do the whole thing quickly and quietly. There is of course no question of a wake under the circumstances. We might have some difficulty in even persuading a priest to bury Augustine in a churchyard."

Her hand trembled as she heard his words, but she looked at him frankly and nodded her agreement. "Ought we to bring him back to Enniskillen with us?"

He shook his head. "No, no, it would be worse there."

Lochlainn didn't want to tell her that they had barely enough money to pay for their hotel room and food, let alone the cost of transporting the coffin back to Barnakilla.

"If you'll allow me, I shall speak to one of the priests up here, Father Brennan, an old family friend who now has a town parish, and see if he would be so kind as to take care of the matter. If you're not up to it, you don't have to attend."

"It would seem so disrespectful somehow. But at the moment I feel as though I'm falling apart," she confessed frankly, starting to shudder again with cold and dread.

He felt her hand quiver in his. Though he knew he would have to tell her the truth sooner or later, for now the only thing the poor girl needed was comfort and a few kind words. So he sat down on the edge of the bed with his back resting against the headboard, and put one arm around her. As the tears began to fall, he held her close, feeling the heart-rending sobs wrack her slender body. He thought once more how lucky Augustine had been, and how foolish.

As she wept, Muireann wondered to herself how she could ever live with the immense guilt which threatened to engulf her. *I'm an evil person*, she reflected sadly. *How can I possibly feel so relieved that he is dead? How can I possibly think of myself at a time like this? But I have no idea how to cope! What on earth will become of me? What shall I do?*

These questions echoed in her mind over and over again. The past two weeks had been like her worst nightmare transformed into a hideous reality which she had no idea how to confront.

She wept as though her heart would break.

He damned Augustine for having left his lovely young bride in such a state, abandoned in Ireland with no friends, no family, no estate, and no money to support her.

"It will be all right, Muireann, you'll see," he heard himself reassuring her as her arms looped around his neck.

He allowed himself to relax and even take comfort from the warmth and affection of another human being, despite her being so grief-stricken she couldn't possibly know what she was doing.

"I'll look after you. Trust me. It will all be fine, you'll see."

Eventually her sobs began to die down, and she moved lower in the bed, further under the covers.

"Cold?" Lochlainn asked quietly, his lips pressed against her raven hair.

"A little."

"I'll go bank up the fire."

"No, stay with me, please. I'm warm enough like this, really," she said in a small voice.

He didn't need a second invitation to stay put. He was so weary himself, he felt as though he could lie down and sleep forever. He moved down lower in the bed himself and tucked the top of her head under his chin.

"There, is that better?"

"Mmm," Muireann murmured drowsily, drifting off blissfully.

"The doctor left you some medicine. Would you like some?"

"No, really, I just need to sleep, Lochlainn. The boat crossing was so awful, and there wasn't a cabin to be had."

No wonder the poor child was beside herself, Lochlainn reflected angrily. She had been pitched and tossed for three nights on the steamer from Scotland.

He tugged the spare blanket up over himself to keep off the chill as he lay there in his shirtsleeves. But despite his best efforts to keep awake to make sure Muireann was all right, he soon drifted off into a sound slumber, his arms wrapped around her as though he would never let her go.

SPIRIT OF THE MIST
JANEEN O'KERRY

An early summer storm rages off the coast of western Ireland, and Muriel watches. From inside the protective walls of Dun Farraige, she can see nothing, yet her water mirror shows all. The moonlight reveals the face of a man—one struggling to overcome the sea.

He is an exile, of course. By clan law, exiles are to be made slaves. Yet something ennobles this man. The stranger's face makes Muriel yearn for both his safety and his freedom. She, who was raised as the daughter of a nobleman, has a terrible secret. And she can't help but believe that this handsome visitor—swaddled in mist and delivered to the rain-swept shores beneath her Dun—will be her salvation.

CARNAL GIFT

PAMELA CLARE

Her body and her virginity are to be offered up to a stranger in exchange for her brother's life. Possessing nothing but her innocence and her fierce Irish pride, Bríghid has no choice but to comply.

But the handsome man she faces in the darkened bedchamber is not at all the monster she expected. His tender touch calms her fears while he swears he will protect her by merely pretending to claim her. And as the long hours of the night pass by, as her senses ignite at the heat of their naked flesh, Bríghid makes a startling discovery: Sometimes the line between hate and love can be dangerously thin.
